PRAISE FOR M. L. BUCHMAN

Top 10 Romance of 2012, 2015, and 2016.

— BOOKLIST: THE NIGHT IS MINE, HOT POINT,
HEART STRIKE

One of our favorite authors.

— RT BOOK REVIEWS

Buchman has catapulted his way to the top tier of my favorite authors.

— FRESH FICTION

A favorite author of mine. I'll read anything that carries his name, no questions asked. Meet your new favorite author!

— THE SASSY BOOKSTER, FLASH OF FIRE

M.L. Buchman is guaranteed to get me lost in a good story.

— THE READING CAFE, WAY OF THE WARRIOR:
NSDQ

I love Buchman's writing. His vivid descriptions bring everything to life in an unforgettable way.

— PURE JONEL, HOT POINT

WILD JUSTICE

M. L. BUCHMAN

Buchman Bookworks

Other works by M. L. Buchman:

CHAPTER 1

$\mathcal{T}$he low hill, shadowed by banana and mango trees in the twilight of the late afternoon sun above the Venezuelan jungle, overlooked the heavily guarded camp a half mile away. But that wasn't his immediate problem.

Right now, it took everything Duane Jenkins could do to ignore the stinging sweat dripping into his eyes. Any unwarranted motion or sound might attract his target's attention before he was in position.

From two meters away, he whispered harshly.

"Who the hell are you, sister? And how did you get here?"

"Holy crap!"

He couldn't help but smile. What kind of woman said *crap* when unexpectedly facing a sniper rifle at point-blank range?

"Not your sister," she gained points for a quick recovery. "Now get that rifle out of my face, Jarhead."

Ouch! That was low. He wasn't some damned, swamp-tromping Marine. Not even ex-Marine. He was ex-75th Rangers of the US Army, now two years in Delta Force. And as an operator for The Unit—as Delta called themselves—that made him far superior to any other soldier no matter what the dudes in SEAL

Team 6 thought about it. That also didn't explain who he'd just found here in *the* perfect sniper position overlooking General Raul Estevan Aguado's encampment.

It had taken him over fifteen hours to scout out this one perfect gap between the too-damn-tall trees that made up this sweaty place and, with just twenty meters to go, he'd spotted her heavily camouflaged form lying among the leaves. It had taken him another half hour to cover that distance without drawing her attention.

Where was a cold can of Coke when a guy needed one? This place was worse than Atlanta in the summer. The red earth had been driven so deep into his pores from crawling over the ground that he wondered if his skin color was permanently changed to rust red.

Why did evil bastards like Aguado have to come from such places?

More immediate problem, dude. Stay focused.

The woman's American English was accentless, sounding flat to his Southern ear. Probably from the Pacific Northwest or some other strange part of the country. But there was a thin overlay that matched her Latinate features—full-lipped with dark eyebrows and darker eyes, which was about all he could tell through her camo paint. The slight Spanish lilt shifted her to intriguingly exotic.

But she wasn't supposed to be here. No one was.

"Keeping you in my sights until I get some answers, ma'am," Duane kept his HK MSG90 A2 rifle aimed right at the bridge of her nose—a straight-through spine cutter if he had to take her down. It would be serious overkill, as the weapon was rated to lethal past eight hundred meters and they were whispering at each other from less than two meters apart. With the silencer, his weapon would be even quieter than their whispers, but he hadn't spent the last sixteen hours crawling into position to have her death cry give him away. If she so much as squawked as she went down, every goddamn bird in the jungle would light off, giving away his presence.

She sighed and nodded toward her own rifle that rested on the ground in front of her.

He shifted his focus—though not his aim—then let out a very low whistle of appreciation. A G28. Even his team hadn't gotten their hands on the latest entry into the US Army's sniper arsenal yet. Not quite the same accuracy as his own weapon but six inches shorter, several pounds lighter, and far more flexible to configure. A whole generational leap forward. Richie, his team's tech, would be geeking out right about now. The fact that he wasn't here to see it almost made Duane smile.

"A Heckler & Koch G28. What's your point, sister?" He drawled it out for Richie's sake, who'd be listening in on Duane's radio. Then the implications sank in. If his Delta Force team couldn't get these yet, then who could? Whatever else this woman was, she would be tied to one of the three US Special Mission Units: Delta, SEAL Team 6, or the combat controllers of the Air Force's 24th STS.

Or The Activity.

That fit.

The Intelligence Support Activity served the other three Special Mission Units. If she was with The Activity...that was seriously hot. It meant she was both one of the top intel specialists anywhere *and* a lethal fighter. And that meant that *she'd* been the one to put out the call that had brought him here and was sticking to see the job through. That at least answered why she was in his spot. It also said a lot that she hadn't taken any of several easier-to-reach locations that were almost as good.

"It is about time you caught a clue. Welcome to the conversation." She picked up her rifle as if his wasn't still aimed at her. Very chill. "You are being a little dense there, soldier." At least she got the *branch* of the military right this time.

"Hey, they don't call me 'The Rock' for nothing, darlin'," Duane lowered his barrel until it was pointed into the dirt. "They actually call me that becau—"

The moment his weapon was down, he suddenly was staring down the dark hole of the G28's silencer.

"Uh…"

"The Rock certainly isn't because you are a towering black movie star. It must be for your thick head."

Duane swallowed carefully, unable to shift his focus away from the barrel of her weapon to see if the safety was on or not.

"He spells his name differently. He's Dwayne 'The Rock' with a w and a y. I'm more normal, D-u-a-n-e T-h-e R-o-c-k." He made it sing-song just like the theme song from *The All-New Mickey Mouse Club* that he'd been hooked on as a little kid.

"M-o-u-s-e," she gave the appropriate response.

He couldn't help laughing, quietly, despite their positions—him still staring down the barrel of her weapon—because discovering Mickey Mouse in common in the heart of the Venezuelan jungle was just too funny.

"Normal is not what I need here," the woman sighed and there was the distinct click of her reengaging the safety on her rifle.

"Only thing normal about me is my name, ma'am." Always good to "ma'am" a woman with a sniper rifle pointed at your face.

"Prove it," she turned her weapon once more toward the camp half a kilometer away through the trees. Her motions were appropriately slow to not draw attention. However, it was too even a motion. A sniper learned to never break the pulses of nature's rhythm. She might be some hotshot intel agent—because The Activity absolutely rocked almost everything they did—but she still wasn't Delta, who rocked it all.

Duane breathed out slowly and spent the next couple minutes easing the last two meters toward her. Having the camp in view meant that one of their spotters could see them as well, if the bad guys were damned lucky. He and the woman both wore ghillie suits—that's why he'd gotten so close before he spotted her. The

4

suits were made of open-weave cloth liberally decorated with leaves and twigs so that the two of them looked like little more than a patch of the jungle floor. He'd dragged his on backcountry jungle roads for twenty miles to make sure he smelled like the jungle as well. Having a jaguar trounce his ass wouldn't exactly brighten up his day.

Even their rifles were well camouflaged except for either end of the spotting scopes and the very tips of the barrels. If he hadn't recently been lusting over the new specs, he wouldn't have recognized her HK G28 at all in its disguise.

Getting into position as a sniper took a patience that only the most highly trained could achieve. A female sniper? That was a rare find indeed. The two women on his Delta team were damned fine shooters, but he and Chad were the snipers of the crew. A female sniper from The Activity? This just kept getting better and better. He'd pay a fair wage to know what she really looked like beneath the ghillie and all that face paint.

"Maybe you and I should go to the party as a couple." At long last he lay beside her, close enough that he would have felt her body heat if not for the smothering sauna of his ghillie suit.

"What party? And we're never going to be a couple."

"Halloween. It's only a couple weeks off. We could sneak in and nobody would see us in our ghillies. People would wonder why the punch bowls were mysteriously draining."

"And why the apples were bobbing on their own," she sounded disgusted. "What I want is—"

"Let's see what y'all are up to down there," he cut her off, just for the fun of it, and focused his rifle scope on the camp below. He was a little disappointed when there was no immediate comeback, though there was a low muttering in Spanish that he couldn't quite catch but it cheered his soul.

The general's camp was a simple affair in several ways. The enclosure was a few hundred meters across. An old-school fence of wooden stakes driven into the ground, each a small tree trunk three meters high with sharpened points upward. Not that the points mattered, because razor wire was looped along the top. Guard shacks every hundred meters—four total. The towers straddled the fence. Not a good idea. The structure should have been entirely behind the wall to protect it from attack. Unless...

"You got a name, darling?" Lying beside her, Duane could tell that she was shorter than he was. Her hands were fine, but her body was hidden by the ghillie so he couldn't read anything more about her looks.

"Yes, I have a name."

"That's nice. Always good to have yourself one of those," Duane could play that game just as well as the next person. He turned his attention to the camp. "Our friendly general isn't worried about attack from the outside or he'd have built his towers differently. He's worried about keeping people inside."

∾

SOFIA FORTEZA HAD ALREADY KNOWN that from her research, but she wondered how Duane—spelled the "normal" way—did.

She'd spent months tracking General Aguado. Cripes, she'd spent months finding him in the first place. He was a slippery *bastardo* who did most of his work through intermediaries and only rarely surfaced himself. Tracing him to this corner of the Guatopo National Park—so close to Caracas, the capital of Venezuela, that she'd dismissed it at first—had taken a month more.

Duane had taken one look at the place and seen...what?

He'd have built his towers differently.

She leaned back to her own scope and inspected them again. It took a moment to bring the towers into focus because her nerves were still zinging as if she'd been electrocuted. Somehow, in all her training, she'd never looked down the barrel of a rifle or even a handgun at point blank range—perhaps the scariest thing she'd ever seen.

Scariest other than Duane's cold blue eyes. He was the most dangerous-looking man she'd ever met, which is why his jokes and his smooth Southern accent were throwing her so badly. He sounded half badass, macho-bastard Unit operator and half southern gentleman. It was the strangest combination she'd ever heard. One moment he was wooing her with warm tones, obviously without a clue of how to woo a woman, and the next he was being pure Army grunt with a vocabulary to match. She simply couldn't figure him out.

Finally she shrugged her emotions aside enough to focus her scope properly. *Stay in the jungle, not in your head.* She rebuilt it in layers. The strange silence of the wind—not a single breath of air reached the jungle floor, instead it stagnated, adding to the oppressiveness of the heat. Macaw calls alternated between chatter and screech. Monkeys screamed and shouted in the upper branches. Buzzing flies had learned to leave her alone and the silent ants were no longer creeping her out. All that was left after she canceled each of those out was the man breathing beside her and the compound of that bastard Aguado that she'd been staring at for the last twenty-four hours.

The guard towers were supported by four long, tree-trunk legs, two inside the fence and two outside. Outside! Where they were vulnerable to attack. General Aguado hadn't built a fort in the depths of a national park—he'd built a prison.

All of her research had only uncovered his location, not his purpose here. Because she hadn't cared. Cutting the head off the snake one target at a time worked for her.

She looked again at the camp. Wooden shacks for the most part—workers' cabins. What else had she missed?

"Locks on the doors," Duane answered the question she hadn't asked in a whisper that was surprisingly soft for such a deep voice. He ignored a fer-de-lance pit viper as it slid up and over the ghillie covering his rifle barrel, slowing to inspect them with a flick of its tongue before continuing on its way in search of mice. If he could ignore the snake, so could she. Mostly. A little. She watched long after it had slithered out of sight.

Sofia looked at the shacks' doors again. Locks on the *outside*. She'd been watching the camp for twenty-four hours and had missed that. The dozens of armed guards weren't being lazy on patrol as she'd thought. They didn't care about the outside world —they were worried about the inside one. And because they were the only armed personnel in the camp, and everyone knew it, they could afford to be nonchalant.

Back to the towers. The guards were leaning on the inside rails looking down, not the outside ones looking out. All of her work to slip into this position was probably meaningless. If Duane was right, she could walk right up and knock on the front gate before anyone would pay her the least attention. A band of red howler monkeys working their way noisily through the jungle canopy above the camp didn't even attract a glance from the guards.

Still, Aguado was here. She'd seen him arrive with his entourage. And he was never going to leave. Not alive.

"Not a nice place," Duane observed quietly.

"Not a nice man."

"Sure I am. You just don't know me yet, sugar."

Sofia brought her knee up sharply. Lying side by side, she was able to bullseye the Charlie-horse nerve cluster on his outer thigh. Her nana hadn't raised her to be a target.

"Shit!" He didn't sound so almighty pleased with himself any longer, though he did manage to keep it to a whisper as he continued swearing.

Why did guys always think they were so charming? With her looks, she should be used to it by now. Except her looks were hidden by the ghillie suit. What had kicked Duane-spelled-the-normal-way into such a guy mode? Just that she was female? When did Delta start recruiting cavemen as their standard? Actually, that one she knew the answer to—since Day One if past experience meant anything.

She hadn't ever deployed with Delta before, but she'd met enough of them to know the type. They were the rebel super-warriors of the US military. Everyone thought that their team was the baddest, but Delta Force, more commonly called "The Unit," completely owned that title. Somehow they drew the people that didn't fit anywhere else in the military. But where they'd been troublemakers in their old units, 1st Special Forces Operational Detachment-Delta collected them and honed their skills. They were like a barely controlled reaction just bubbling along, waiting for an excuse to explode.

"So, what's the general's story?" Duane, once he was done nursing his thigh, went for a subject change proving he wasn't stupid.

"Deep in the drug trade. Known to have called for at least three high profile murders, including a Supreme Tribunal of Justice judge (that's their version of the Supreme Court) even if he didn't pull the trigger himself."

"Oh, so *he's* the one that's not nice," as if Duane only now was figuring that out.

She was not going to be charmed by him. His every tone said that just because she was female, he'd switched into some weird-ass flirt mode. She'd had enough of that coming up through the ranks to last a lifetime.

"This isn't slave labor, so you'd better add human trafficking to your list." With the speed of a light switch, all the charm was gone from Duane's voice.

As if to prove his point, at that moment a couple of guards exited a small building, readjusting their pants and laughing. They kicked the door shut behind them and snapped the lock closed. No question what they'd just been doing to some poor women— one of the perks of their job.

Numerous guards. Locks on the outside of the cabin doors.

No large central building that might be an illicit drug lab or slave labor textile sweatshop. This was a holding pen, hidden deep in the jungle of a national park. The few people who were circulating around, aside from the guards, were almost all women. Women who were keeping their heads down and trudging about their tasks. The sickness that twisted in her stomach had nothing to do with lying still for the last twenty-four hours.

Sofia wasn't even aware of raising her rifle until Duane reached over and casually pushed it back down.

"Not yet." It was all he said, but she could hear the anger beneath the soft words.

Well that wasn't shit compared to what *she* was feeling at the moment. This place needed to be erased from the map. Scorched to the ground, removed permanently from existence!

"Why are you here? I sent for a goddamn team, not some Southern Rock."

He flashed a smile at her, "If you've got me, you don't need a team." All of his macho bravado was back. As if she'd misheard his momentary anger. He sounded too much like her useless brother and the rest of her useless family. She couldn't be rid of him fast enough.

As the last of the sunlight faded from the sky and the bird calls tapered toward silence, Sofia wondered who she was going to want to shoot more by sunrise: General Raul Estevan Aguado or Duane The Rock?

∿

DUANE HAD LEFT the video feed from his spotting scope open to Chad.

"Can't get a match on her face with all of that camouflage on," Chad whispered over the open frequency to his earpiece.

Duane did not need to be hearing this. "Were your plans just for the general or the camp as well?" he asked the nameless ISA woman, hoping Chad would get back on track.

"My job is to find the bad guys," she said softly.

"Found her!" Richie, the team's geek, jumped in, shouting loudly enough that Richie's distance from the microphone was all that spared Duane's eardrum from being caved in. "Once I eliminated any Deltas being in there and checked the cross-team mission coordination database for possible conflicts and still found nothing I—"

Duane sighed.

Chad cut off Richie with a low whistle of appreciation. "Sofia Forteza. Hot, bro. Very hot."

"JSOC. Listed as unassigned," Richie was back and only a little calmer. "Has a place near Fort Belvoir." Joint Special Operations Command had only one asset at Fort Belvoir, Virginia: the Intelligence Support Activity.

Duane already knew she was ISA, but it was nice to have it confirmed.

"Wow!" Richie again. "She is awfully pretty."

Duane could feel that he was sharing an eye roll with Chad over the radio. Delta Force veteran of dozens of missions all across Central and South America, happily married to a Delta shooter, and *still* Richie sounded like a high school geek.

"Your job," Sofia, the no-longer-nameless, continued her side of the conversation, "is to figure out what to do with them."

Easy. Smack both Chad and Richie upside the head next time he saw them.

"Code Black on her file. Eyes only," Chad continued. "Yada yada, but Richie says he doesn't want to try and crack that without more cause, which means he's a wussy-pants who's afraid of the little old Activity."

"Go on. You try to crack their firewall and see what happens to your life. I've heard that the last NSA hacker who took a run at them is serving a five-year deployment to Poughkeepsie, New

York. And that was after they formatted his hard drive, his computers at home, and his phone without ever going near him. Those guys are good."

"I think he's actually just pouting that you got to see a G28 sniper rifle before he did. Wuss-pants," Chad chided Richie one more time.

"Where's the general?" Duane asked, forcing his tone. One of these days he was going to murder Chad in his sleep. It was a nasty thing to do to his best friend—and he'd regret it—but it was fast becoming a necessity. He considered offing Richie while he was at it, but Melissa wouldn't take kindly to losing her man. Pissing off a Delta woman was never a good call.

"Third building to the right from the front gate," Sofia guided him toward the general's location with a tipping of her rifle.

Duane eased his aim over until he could spot it in his scope. A heavy concrete building, windows small and high—not a cozy villa in the jungle. It was the bunker fit for a paranoid bastard.

The sun had finally set but the camp was well lit, no need for night vision here. It was well shielded from observation above; the superstory trees had not been cut down, rather the prison had been built up around their gargantuan trunks. No helo, not even a drone was going to get eyes on this place. This would have to be strictly a ground op.

"So, the fort has a bunker," Chad was finally on the same mission he was.

"Underground escape?" Duane asked Sofia.

"Possible, but none identified." Her voice was a combination of lush and highly educated. She kept getting more interesting with every moment rather than less.

"Thought you Activity types knew some shit?"

"We know plenty," no reaction that he'd identified her role here. Very chill lady.

"Uh-huh."

"*Mierda!* I know that if we miss this guy here, it could take another six months to find him again."

"So you *do* know how to swear. Can you swear in English as well?"

Sofia buried her face against the stock of her rifle. This was going better than he'd expected. He debated attempting to elicit a whimper of frustration, but she was Activity and who knew what they could do to you if you really ticked them off—his desire to look down the wrong end of a G28 again was very low.

It *was* the sworn duty of every Delta operator to put down all other units as not up to their own standards, especially SEAL Team 6. But there were a few exceptions. The guys from the 24th STS Air Force combat controllers were too damned pleasant to really hold a grudge against them.

And The Activity? Way too sneaky to risk messing with.

The fast tropical twilight was shifting the sounds of the jungle, though the day wasn't done yet. There was the faint buzz of the camp's inward-facing floodlights starting up, but they were too far away to hear any of their voices.

"So, you're thinking it's a bad idea to back off and drop a MOAB on this place?" Chad was back. The Mother of All Bombs was the biggest bomb there was, short of a nuke, and had only recently been used for the first time. It would level at least three square miles of the national park and probably make the window-glass merchants in Caracas wealthy even though the city was over twenty kilometers away. Because they were so rare, Chad was always looking for an excuse to drop one.

"Are you calling in your team or not?" Sofia looked at him again. Her dark eyes were hypnotic in the lingering twilight. Was hypnosis another trick up The Activity's sleeve?

"My team?" Duane laid on his best Mr. Innocent, careful not to overdo it.

Sofia lifted an edge of her rifle's ghillie revealing a small device lying on the dirt. "I can see your signal."

"No one's supposed to be able to see—" Duane shut his mouth. He was using the most sophisticated piece of communications gear Delta had. Burst-mode transmissions, rotating frequencies so that he never showed up on scanners for more than a moment, deep encryption, low power to the repeater he'd stashed a hundred meters away so that a signal-strength meter would find the wrong target. They'd been told it couldn't be traced by any... Oh! The whole setup was probably *invented* by The Activity.

"Voice and video outbound," Sofia continued in that snake charmer voice of hers. Her accent might be flat American, but the richness of the Spanish undertones and rhythms was slaying him.

His first serious girlfriend had been Mexican, which had pissed off his too-white family to no end—even if they were too well-cultured to show it in public. Or maybe she just hadn't come from a rich enough family; someone from their own social status. He'd learned far more Spanish from her between the sheets than in the classroom, including the ability to tell that Sofia's language origin was Spain Spanish just by the rhythm of it, even if the absence from her accent said it was probably a couple generations back.

"It is difficult to tell with the encryption," she continued her chilly analysis. "But I think you have two different voices inbound."

At least she couldn't break the encryption, he hoped, or he really would have to kill Chad.

CHAPTER 2

Something had shifted.

Between one moment and the next, "normal-Duane" the overly-garrulous macho Unit operator was gone. A very precise man took his place.

He handed her an earpiece as he announced to his team, "Two on."

Sofia wondered just what comments had been occurring before that made him feel that it was necessary to announce her addition to the circuit, then decided that she'd rather not know.

"Hey there, Sofia."

So, they knew who she was. That in itself was interesting information about the abilities of Duane's team.

"I'm Chad. Ignore the other voice, Richie was born a dweeb and still hasn't recovered. I mean his nickname is Q, like the geek in James Bond. How sad is that. He's even more of a dweeb than the dude you're all cozied up with at the moment."

"Main gate," Duane declared, shutting Chad down quickly. He shifted to a rapidly whispered monologue, breaking down the encampment for his team. "Designate A. Fence ranging three to five meters high, topped with single-coil razor wire," tracking his rifle scope over each item he described. He broke down the fortification in minute detail—weak spots, close proximity of large trees, and so on—working his way around clockwise. "B," he began describing the left side of the compound.

Not only was he describing details she hadn't noticed, he was describing things he couldn't possibly see. When she figured out that he'd scouted all of the way around the camp before coming up to her—and that she hadn't caught a hint of him—it said that in addition to acting like a macho jerk, he also had incredible skills.

Then he did the same narration for the camp itself, layer by layer.

It felt like a painfully slow process, but the twenty minutes by her watch flew past. Half of it was practically in code, giving her trouble keeping up, but Duane sent a surprisingly detailed description to go with the images he was transmitting as he tracked his scope around the camp.

"That's full sweep."

"Roger that," and the radio circuit went silent.

Now there'd be some long drawn-out plan that was probably being discussed in Washington who would then... That part of it might be out of her control, but if the general showed his face, she'd take him down herself and worry about other details later. The more she learned about General Aguado, the creepier he became. Worse than her Uncle Maximiliano, the pederast who had mysteriously died during a family hunting expedition. Eaten by a bear or fed to a bear? Her grandmother—who'd been the only other one along that day—never said.

"Let's go for a walk."

Sofia could only look over at Duane in alarm...then realized that she couldn't see him. While they'd been concentrating through their scopes, observing the well-lit camp, night had fallen over the jungle. The bird calls, which had been a constant throughout the day (sometimes so loud she thought she'd go mad with it), had faded away. A jaguar roared in the distance and the fast flap of wings above said that the bats were emerging for their nightly feed.

The sweltering heat hadn't shifted a single degree down here on the jungle floor. The temperature might only be in the high eighties, but in tropical jungles, the humidity climbed at night and was now nearing a hundred percent.

No, *exactly* a hundred percent—it began to rain. A loud pattering began high in the trees. Within minutes, massive raindrops bigger than the end of her pinkie were plummeting down out of the sky. The water gathered on leaves in the canopy far above until a sudden release would scatter the oversized rain to the jungle floor far below—each drop almost big enough to hurt. In moments she wondered if a person could drown lying atop a hill in this godforsaken place.

She wanted to protest, but Duane had already moved out of sight of the camp behind a tree and was shedding his ghillie suit. Unsure what he was up to, she finally followed and unsuited herself.

With a quick flick, she had her night-vision goggles clipped to her helmet and swung down into place. The jungle turned from black to shades of green and pink. The image intensifier made her view as bright as day, and the blended infrared mode lit up everything with heat. Even in the rain, every guard, now huddled beneath the roofs of their open-sided green towers, was painted in shades of hot red.

It was her first time in the field with Delta. She'd been out with DEVGRU, better known by their thirty-year-gone name of SEAL Team 6. They moved in packs with the aggressiveness of Marines.

Duane moved alone as if he was dancing. He wasn't a particularly big guy, just a few inches taller than she was, but his movements were light and smooth. He wore a large pack that didn't seem to slow him down at all. It wasn't a major survival pack, but it was still hard to believe he'd been wearing it the whole time under the ghillie.

He moved so smoothly that, if not for her night vision, she'd have lost him within a dozen steps as merely being an element of the landscape.

It had taken her seven hours to infiltrate to within half a kilometer of the encampment.

It took less than two hours to cover that final distance.

At the speed Duane was moving, it should have taken ten minutes, but he was following a crazily weaving path, cutting sharply east, then back west. His movements were a study in smooth confidence or she'd have begun to worry that he was stoned.

He finally leaned back against a gigantic Ceiba tree within fifty meters of the tree-trunk fence. The Ceiba's roots rose like vertical walls, rising out of the soil in great triangles a foot thick and climbing to twice her height before joining the huge trunk. They leaned side by side against an expanse of smooth bark that was as wide as her apartment's living room wall and rose for fifty meters into the darkness.

"Eat. Drink," he grunted at her.

"Drink? I'm drowning!" The rain hadn't eased but once or twice in the last hour. Still, he was right. She knocked back half a water bottle and began chewing on an energy bar.

Duane kept chewing in silence.

"Why are you doing the drunkard's walk?"

"Searching for bobby traps, trip wires, anything to warn them that we're coming. Haven't seen squat. You sure this guy is as bad as you think?"

"Worse."

"Okay, sister. Guess we should do something about him then."

"Not your sister."

"Whatever you say, sugar."

Well, she'd walked into that one.

"You remind me of my brothers." She used her rifle butt to

push herself back to standing, planting it firmly in the middle of Duane's gut. His grunt sounded sincere.

"They that good?" He'd recovered too fast—next time she'd ram his gut.

"That awful." She hated even thinking about Emilio and Humberto.

He offered no answer to that, which actually felt like unexpected sympathy—if she was to credit a man with having an actual emotion unrelated to sex, food, or power.

Her nerves must have topped out at some point, because she was perfectly calm as they walked close around the perimeter wall. Duane barely broke stride at the towers, leaving her to watch cautiously upward at the base of the guard cabin directly above them for less than thirty seconds each time. Nothing, not even a spy cam of any sort. The general was an incautious man and she was going to make sure it cost him.

The rain streamed off her night-vision and over her cheeks like warm tears.

It was the dead of night when they rested again, this time behind a huge vertical liana vine close beside the main gate, so thick it made the tree it covered unidentifiable.

"Twenty meters to the gate. Two guards outside. Rain's easing," Duane spoke for the first time since they'd started circumnavigating the fence line.

"In ten," a woman's voice broke the radio silence that had lasted more than two hours.

"What's in ten minutes?" Sofia asked Duane.

"Go ahead and slip your weapon around the tree. Aim for the left guard."

She shrugged and did so. Just the barrel and the scope, nothing else showing. The scope fed the image into her night-vision goggles. As she aimed her rifle squarely at the man's nose, she herself remained safely tree-protected. It was an odd position, but she'd been trained in it.

Sofia glanced at her watch. Just past twenty-two hundred hours. Ten-oh-seven at night. "How long—"

"Three. Two. Fire...now!"

Not ten minutes.

Ten seconds.

She fired. Twice. And then a heart shot.

Exactly like training.

Except this was a live person. She'd—

"Duck!" Duane grabbed her around the waist and hauled her against him with a hard power that knocked the wind out of her in more ways than one. Part of it was his whip-strong forearm wrapped across her gut and slamming her back against his chest, but part of it was simply the effortless strength with which he'd moved her.

Then he held his other hand in front of her face, allowing her just enough time to see that he held a remote trigger.

His thumb went down.

The response was immediate. A blast of light washed the jungle beyond their hideaway as if daylight had suddenly been reborn.

A cascading heavy *Thump!* of powerful explosions followed a moment later.

"What the—" Though Sofia still lay in Duane's arms, she had to shout to be heard. The jungle went insane: screaming bird calls, grunts of wild hogs, and the monkeys. Jesus, Mary, and Joseph, the monkeys were beyond loud. It was like a secondary explosion of pure sound had been lit off by his trigger.

But Duane was up and on the move.

"Stay close behind me," he shouted.

She raced to keep up.

"Check for shoulder badges before you shoot." He tore aside the covers on his shoulders revealing small squares that were brilliantly bright reflectors in her infrared imaging. She pulled her own shoulder tabs open to identify herself as a friendly to any other shooters wearing night vision as she raced after him.

Straight into hell.

~

THE FOUR TOWERS WERE GONE. Cut off at the legs, they'd fallen outward exactly as Duane had planned. During their "walk" around the encampment, he'd placed cutting charges of C-4 plastique explosive on each leg outside the wall. He'd also placed a contact explosive where he'd expected the tower cabs to hit. Sure enough, all four towers hit their charges and the secondary explosives shredded them, along with any armed guards who might have otherwise caused trouble.

All of the camp lights had conveniently been attached to the towers, so the camp was plunged into darkness. Stupid design—perfect for his purpose though.

He'd also placed a larger charge against the midpoint of each tree-trunk wall. Those charges had punched massive holes that could be used three abreast.

"Better overkill than underkill," his explosives instructor had always been clear about that and Duane had thanked him for the lesson any number of times. There was an art to precision, but if the wall didn't come down, it could screw the whole operation.

He slapped a quick set of charges on the main gate and once more pulled Sofia against him before hitting the trigger. This time he merely blew off the hinges so there wasn't much to hide from, but she felt so damn good against him the first time that he couldn't resist even the briefest excuse to hold her again.

She felt even better this time.

Women never really worked out for Duane, they were always too mild. Sofia Forteza felt like she was ripped steel—inside and out.

After the explosion, he let her go and turned back to the gate.

"It's still standing, Mr. Rock," Sofia even *looked* amazing. Her face covered by goggles and camo paint. Her body hidden by an armored vest adorned with more electronics and less ammunition than he'd ever carry, but still pure soldier. And a G28 in her hands.

"You just keep giving me that sass, sister."

"I said I'm not—"

He kicked the gate. With the hinges gone, it tipped slowly inward, finally crashing to the ground.

"Okay," she said just a little louder than the quieting jungle. "That was nice."

"Uh-oh, a compliment. Hold on to that thought." Then he moved in. "Follow behind me with security shots. Only shoot people that I shoot."

Exactly as planned, the guards were still moving about in bewilderment at the shock-and-awe with which he'd just slammed into the compound.

He fired two rounds in the face of the first one he spotted.

No third round came from behind him.

He glanced over his shoulder.

Sofia was standing there like a statue. Staring.

"In the heart, like this." He fired a round into the falling guard's heart. He was already dead, but it was an absolute guarantee that he wasn't getting up anytime soon.

He took out the next.

He only waited a heartbeat before adding the third shot himself. It arrived at the same moment as Sofia's.

Good, she was back from whatever had thrown her.

Duane spotted the rest of his team rushing in through the other three holes he'd breached in the perimeter fence.

Three other holes in the wall, five other members on the team. Didn't matter which was which, not at a Unit operator level of training.

"Come on!"

Less than twenty seconds from breaching the main gate, they were up against the general's bunker. It was the only concrete building in the camp. The door was heavy steel. Really heavy steel, like a bank vault.

∿

DUANE'S SMILE suddenly turned evil.

"What?" Sofia wondered what he was going to do now after the spectacular job of taking out the towers and breaching every wall of the encampment simultaneously.

If she was overwhelmed, then the guards must be in cardiac arrest. The Delta shooters who came in through the walls moved so fast they were little more than blurs in her memory.

No radio traffic.

No elaborate planning. Definitely no achingly long conferences in some remote Washington office as she'd expected. Delta simply got it done.

They'd blown into the camp, as hard and fast as their explosive charges, and were fast taking down anyone holding a weapon.

"I'm just a Southern boy havin' a heyday, sugar," Duane was practically chortling. "Watch my back."

Not that there was much to watch. Armed guards were falling faster than mayflies, far too busy to worry about two soldiers blended into the night.

He dropped his pack and pulled out a large rope, coiled tightly. He began unrolling it and smashing it into the wall, several meters from the door. The rope stuck to the wall.

"But the door…"

"Belongs in a bank," he finished slapping on the rope in a rough circle four feet in diameter, which must be more C-4 explosive. "Besides, going in through the door is what's expected, darling. Where's the fun in doing the expected?"

He stabbed in a pair of detonators, then signaled her to lie flat against the wall well to one side of the circle of C-4. He flattened himself against the wall on the far side, then slung his rifle over his shoulder and pulled out a handgun.

Again, he showed her the trigger as he pressed it so she was ready for the explosion. Without Duane's arm around her, she wasn't ready for the shock wave—it almost knocked her down. *Note to self: lean into the explosion next time.*

Before she was steady on her feet and the cloud of concrete dust cleared, Duane dove fast and low into the new doorway he'd blown right through the wall.

There were four loud reports from his weapon. Then two more before she nerved up enough to go through the doorway herself.

Two corpses lay on the floor. Duane was kneeling on a third person, face down and struggling even as Duane zip-tied his wrists together behind his back.

"Is this your boy?" Duane flipped the man over. The lights in the bunker were still working.

Sofia flipped up her goggles and looked. Six months she'd been chasing that face, she'd know it anywhere: graying hair, pinched nose, worm-crawl style goatee around thin lips. "That's him."

"Alpha target in captivity. Building A-4. Two friendlies inside."

"Roger, west clear," someone called over the radio.

"South clear," a deep voice that she was fairly sure belonged to Chad.

"Hang on," the geek's voice, Richie. So he might have been born a dweeb, but he was still an operator for The Unit no matter what Chad said about him.

She didn't breathe for the next ten seconds. There were several loud rattles of gunfire outside, but all of Delta weapons had silencers—so what she was hearing was panicked fire from the last of the guards. Finally the audible gunfire stopped.

"Okay, east clear as well."

"C'mon, Richie. Get it in gear," the deep voice needled him.

"Eat shit, Chad. The guards' main bunkhouse is over here. What did I hear from you, three lousy takedowns?"

"Five."

"Liar. You never—"

"Full sweep. Assemble on A-4. Three minutes," a no-nonsense woman cut them off. She must be the mission controller, back in some remote aircraft.

"Let's check the room while we're waiting," Duane suggested.

No ledgers. No handy safe. No records of any kind. Not his main base of operations. But there was a large bin stacked solid with cell phones, probably taken from the women as they'd been kidnapped and imprisoned here before being trafficked off to the highest bidder.

Hadn't anyone thought to trace the phones' chips?

They were powered off, which didn't necessarily make a trace impossible. Then Sofia tapped the bin they'd been stashed in. Metal—blocking any ping from the chip.

She began booting them up. They all had some degree of charge on them. Most of the login screens were unique, meaning the women in captivity here should be able to pick out which phone was theirs.

"Find the general's phone," she called out to Duane.

He handed it to her a moment later.

Locked.

"Password?" Sofia asked nicely once.

The general barked out a laugh.

She nodded to Duane, expecting him to deliver a kick to the general's kidneys.

Instead, Duane slammed Aguado into a desk chair, cut his hands free and pinned them both to the desk with one big hand around the general's two wrists. The general struggled, but it was useless against a man of Duane's strength.

Duane snarled something into the general's ear and one of his hands twitched.

Duane rammed the muzzle of his sidearm down on the back of the general's hand.

"Five. Four. Three..."

General Aguado gave up his code at Two.

She opened his phone and discovered exactly what she'd expected. A Bitcoin account—a very well-funded one.

Sofia flashed what she'd found at Duane.

His brilliant blue eyes were still hard as steel, but she could get to like his smile.

CHAPTER 3

"*I* still don't understand."

"You playing dense or were you born that way?" Duane couldn't resist teasing Chad as they watched the women piling into the trucks—each clutching the cell phone that had been confiscated from them upon their kidnapping.

Chad opened his mouth, but Richie cut him off with a professorial, "Well!"

By Richie's tone, Duane knew that the team's geek was clearly in his element and couldn't wait to explain.

Better him than me, he thought as Richie started in.

Like everyone else, Duane kept an eye out for some stray guard. But his attention was mostly riveted on the woman standing quietly off to the side.

Kyle, the team's leader, stood over General Aguado, who was kneeling in the dirt along the line of the rescued prisoners. Some women spat on him as they passed by to clamber onto a truck. A few kicked him, but most of the women simply scurried by as if he still retained the power to steal their freedom again.

General Aguado's next stop wouldn't be before some corrupt Venezuelan court of injustice. He was going straight into the

27

gentle hands of the CIA who would continue the work of learning about and destroying at least the international arm of his trafficking enterprises.

Richie started explaining the Venezuelan economy to Chad. It was fun to watch.

All Chad typically cared about in any country, other than the bad guys, was the women. And he was such a goddamn charmer that the women always seemed to appreciate his attention. But that wasn't going to stop Richie once he got into his cool-factoids-lecture mode.

"You know that Venezuela has the worst hyperinflation in the world, right? It now takes shopping bags full of hundred-bolívar bills to buy a day's food. Since US dollars are as illegal as it gets, though they're still very common, Bitcoin has become the black market currency of choice." He continued rambling on about the interacting factors of dictatorship, an enormous bounty of crude oil that was such a heavy-weight grade that Venezuelans couldn't process it themselves—even before their infrastructure descended into shambles from neglect—and everything else that no one cared about except economists and Richie Goldman.

Once Duane and Sofia had unlocked the general's phone, it had simply been a matter of counting up how many women they freed from the various huts and dividing up his massive Bitcoin account evenly. The few women who didn't already have a phone, or couldn't find theirs in the pile, Richie had provided with burner phones from the general's stash—probably from women long gone. Load the app, transfer the Bitcoins to them, load the women in the general's trucks, and start them on their travels home. Before they left, the team handed out guns confiscated from the bodies of Aguado's soldiers to the women who claimed some skill. Others were driving the trucks. Anyone who messed with these women was in for a rude surprise.

They weren't wealthy—even by current Venezuelan standards

—but they were definitely well-to-do now. The women had wept their thanks on anyone they could get to, then hurried away fast.

Sofia looked dazed.

"You a'right?" Duane sidled up to her.

Her nod was far from certain.

They only had a few minutes, but he gave her what space and time he could.

"How…" she waved a hand vaguely at the camp, though he suspected that wasn't the real problem.

"We ran a similar training scenario about six months ago. That one we spent hours talking out, before and after. I saw this layout and we already knew what to do with it. Must be why we train so much," he made the last sound like a joke, but apparently she wasn't in a laughing mood.

Sofia cleared her throat several times before she could speak again. "What did you say to the general to get him to unlock his phone?" Which sounded like another evasion to him, but he answered anyway.

"I asked which hand he masturbated with, then offered to blow off each finger until he told us the code. I may have suggested that the sixth finger I'd blow off was his dick." He'd have to remember that one, it had worked really well.

Sofia nodded, then shrugged, then nodded again, but she wasn't looking at anything. *Oh, shit.* Duane had seen this before, but not since his early days in the Rangers, first tour in Afghanistan, so it took him until now to recognize what was going on.

A glance at the team and he saw he was no longer needed. He led Sofia around the side of one of the huts.

"Take a breath, Sofia. Just take a breath."

"I…can't."

Duane prayed that she didn't start crying.

He definitely wasn't up for that.

"If you've never shot someone before, why were you out here alone?" Get her talking; it was the best bet.

"I've done field work. A lot of intel...gathering," her voice was hitching in strange gulps that were almost more scary than tears. "Part of ISA training...first solo mission. It was just recon...in Caracas...spotted the general. Had a radio. If trouble. But this was supposed to be...observe-only assignment. Followed A-gu-ado here." The name was too much and she had to choke it out on multiple breaths.

"Then you called in my team."

"Then I called in your team," she collapsed back against the rough wood and closed her eyes. "You just assumed...I would follow you. You made it easy to. So I did."

"Shit. I'm sorry, Sofia," Duane didn't know what else to say. First kill was a brutal shock no matter how much you trained.

Talking to women was Chad's gift, not his. Women all melted around Chad's corn-fed Iowa-boy charm...even if he was really from the wrong side of inner-city Detroit lethal.

But Duane didn't want her melting around Chad. "Wish I'd known, I'd—"

Kyle's sharp whistle cut the air.

Duane was glad for the interruption, because he wasn't sure what else to say or what he'd have done differently. Leave her to sit on her ass alone out in the jungle? Not likely. He squeezed her arm and she nodded once, twice, then opened those lovely dark eyes and looked right at him.

"Thanks." She pushed off the wall, without ramming her rifle butt into his solar plexus this time, and they headed back around the building.

～

THE CAMP WAS NOW empty except for the Delta team and the general, who lay prone in the reddish mud. Alive but groaning. Apparently the last few women to depart had aimed their final kicks specifically. He was curled up in fetal position.

Now that the camp was empty, she could see the bodies remaining on the ground. Bodies that... She turned.

"No. Don't look away," Duane whispered close beside her. "Your imagination will always be worse than the reality. They're dead. They earned it. It's okay to look at them."

So she forced herself to do so. At these men who had kidnapped and imprisoned women for a living. That they were dead was on her shoulders. And, if she was being honest about it, that was a good thing as well as a bad one.

Last of all she looked at the one man by the gate that she had killed herself. She knew his face from looking through the scope earlier. He was one of the two laughing men, enjoying a bit of rape before going on duty. His companion also lay dead by the gate.

Duane was right. She'd probably have nightmares, but she was going to be okay with this. She returned to the team and nodded her thanks to him. She was a long way from steady, but at least her head was clearer now.

It was the first time Sofia had actually looked at the team. Three men and—two women! She had heard a rumor that Delta had women, but she'd never heard it confirmed. Now she was facing two of them. One was shorter than Sofia's five-seven, with long dark hair and features that were at least partly Native American. The other was a tall, slender, white-blonde. They couldn't be more different.

There were three other men besides Duane. A handsome dark-haired guy in charge. Richie, who'd been glad to geek out over Bitcoins (thankfully sparing her the task while she'd been busy fighting to not puke up her energy bar). And the blond guy, who looked even more broad-shouldered and dangerous than Duane, must be Chad.

31

"Let's go," the short brunette woman called out and began heading up the road on foot.

The dangerous blond guy dragged the general to his feet and followed along.

Sofia hung back at the rear guard position with Duane, "I thought that the dark-haired guy was in charge."

"Depends who you talk to. All of *us* think Kyle Reeves is the team leader. But his wife, her name's Carla, is a freakin' force of nature. She just assumes she's in charge and no one but Kyle has ever dared to tell her otherwise."

"They're married? Serving on the same team?"

"I know. It's weird, but Richie and Melissa just tied the knot too," he pointed to the geek and the tall blonde, "as if that isn't the oddest couple on the planet. We were sure the Army was going to bust them all into separate teams, but my guess is that Colonel Gibson didn't dare. After all, he might run Delta Force now, but pissing off Carla Anderson would be seriously bad news."

Colonel Michael Gibson's reputation said that he wasn't scared of anything. He was the most decorated Delta operator in the history of The Unit. But Carla was something else again.

Sofia didn't need anyone to explain the blond guy to her. Delta Force operators were badasses by trade, even the women apparently. But the guy manhandling the general up the trail was a whole different level of nasty.

She checked her watch and almost did a faceplant in a mud puddle. She'd gotten into position yesterday at sunrise. By sunset, General Aguado had arrived and she'd put out a call to see if there was an available action team in the area. Her deskbound counterpart at The Activity had mobilized this squad.

Duane had arrived at five p.m. today, just an hour before sunset.

Two hours to scout the camp, another to circle it and set explosives—the ten-second "go" had been given at 22:07.

It was now 22:37.

That couldn't be right. She checked her watch again and almost stumbled into another puddle. The rain was still drenching down, something she hadn't even noticed since the first explosion.

In thirty minutes Duane and his team—Sofia had no illusions about her marginal usefulness in the firefight—had razed the camp, taken down the guards, freed and enriched the imprisoned women, and they were now leaving.

She tried to account for the time. The attack had lasted... minutes. Less than five. Maybe less than three. It had felt like hours. The—

"You're late," a voice announced over her earpiece.

Late? They'd achieved the mission and so much more in thirty minutes and they were being called late? Who were these people?

Sofia had been the most competent person in her family—except for her grandmother. Nana was still the fierce fist behind the prosperity of the family's winery. Sofia had made a point of always striving to be the best: college, Army Intelligence, Defense Intelligence Agency, and now The Activity. This Delta squad had just proven that they were the same way.

Walking beside Duane suddenly felt very different. Out of all of the options, they'd sent *him* in as their point man. A sniper and demolitions expert. It was no surprise that he looked so dangerous—he really was.

"We're less than two minutes late, Patty," Carla called back over the radio. "Give me a goddamn break!"

"Dream on, Wild Woman."

Sofia would bet that Carla had earned that nickname fair and square.

Duane offered a big smile, looking surprisingly genuine despite the heavy camo paint he wore. *Yes,* it said, *Carla is Wild Woman. Absolutely.* And Richie was definitely Q.

"What are the other's nicknames?" Sofia kept her voice low as they trotted along.

"Kyle is simply Mister Kyle—like Mister Steed from *The Avengers*. Melissa The Cat moves with all the grace and silence of one. Chad The Reaper is our best shooter."

Then maybe Duane really was The Rock—strong and stable. It certainly felt that way to be jogging beside him along the dark jungle trail.

It was only then that Sofia became aware of the sound of helicopters close overhead. There was something odd about it—they sounded both louder *and* as if they were moving away.

Carla upped the pace as she shouted back over her shoulder, "Come on, you lazy sods." Though they were all within ten paces of her.

"That's our cue. She calls and we must bow," Duane whispered beside her again. She liked his quick humor. It was...unexpected to find a Delta operator with one. The view from her desk at The Activity was that Delta were all rough rebels—the military's outsiders who found the one place they could to serve. The former Delta operators who'd been recruited into The Activity were very hardcore guys—all about the mission.

It made Duane twice as unexpected.

They stepped into a small clearing at the same moment two MH-6M Little Bird helicopters descended out of the rain and darkness. Except there was something strange about them. Their shapes were bizarrely angular and the sound still wasn't right.

"Stealth," Duane nudged her forward.

She wasn't even aware of stopping.

"We aren't supposed to be in Venezuela anyway, so it's better if no one knows we've been here all week."

Part of ISA's purpose was to know everything and share everything. The Intelligence Support Activity was founded to gather and synthesize all those little bits and pieces of information from a hundred sources—CIA, Interpol, Mossad, whoever—and turn it into actionable intelligence for the nation's top-tier Special Operations Forces.

Stealth helos? Other than the one that had gone down in bin Laden's compound—she hadn't heard of even one.

A Delta team embedded into Venezuela all week? Not that either. Something was broken here. She could sort of understand about hiding the stealth helicopters, but Central and South America were her specialties. She should have known this team was nearby for a full week. Instead, Delta had retasked them from some other unknown assignment when she'd submitted an asset requisition.

Inside, there was only room for the pilot and copilot. Extended bench seats ran along the outside of the Little Bird helicopters—either side capable of carrying three soldiers with their feet dangling in the air. She and Duane ended up together on one of them.

Facing sideways, they snapped on belts; Duane double-checking hers, which she completely didn't need. She knew how to ride on a Little Bird, even if it was a stealth one.

"Hey, Patty, could you circle us once over the compound?" Duane looked toward the cockpit so the pilot must be female as well.

"Taking your lady out for a spin? Now that's a fine, fine thing to do on a dark summer's night." The pilot's accent was thickly Gloucester, Massachusetts. Sofia's sophomore roommate at Yale had the same, and the tone made her smile.

"Not his lady," Sofia wished she could take the words back even as she said them.

All she got back from the pilot was a rough snort of laughter. She sounded like one of the big, fat, bar-mamas. "Good luck with that. Duane's a cutie. Good thing I'm already married to a hunky pilot."

"Damn straight!" The low voice of the other pilot agreed.

They circled back over the camp, still being pelted by the last of the rain. There wasn't really anything to see through the leafy canopy. A building here. Another there.

"Oops!" Duane sounded upset as something tumbled out of his hands toward the ground. "Oh, my word!" Another. "Oh, I'm such a clod," two more objects followed. "We can go now, Patty. I simply don't know what came over me." In another moment he'd be holding his wrist to his forehead like a fainting Scarlett O'Hara.

The Little Bird helicopter circled around to the northeast, but stayed low over the trees creating a wild rollercoaster ride that had the bench seat and Sofia's butt losing contact with each other with far more frequency than she'd like. Maybe she was glad that Duane had double-checked her seatbelt.

Sofia managed to look back before the camp was out of sight.

A fire had bloomed in the distance. The camp would soon be scorched earth, nothing remaining. No signs of forced entry. Nothing but a few bodies that probably wouldn't be missed and that Mother Nature's scavengers would clear away soon enough.

"What about forest fire?"

"Calculated risk but, with the heavy rain, it shouldn't get far. The buildings, being deadwood, will burn easily enough though. Hopefully it will catch the towers as well so there won't be any sign of the explosions used to take them down."

"Damn, Duane," Patty cut in. "Full sentences there. Clear explanations. What the hell's up with you? You must have it bad."

~

DUANE TAPPED a frequency on his radio, along with an encryption key, and showed it to Sofia. He watched as she set the same one on hers; he really didn't need shit from Patty. The helo flashed past the beach and settled down to race mere meters above the waves. The rain that had been inundating the jungle was now just dispersing clouds over the Caribbean.

But now that he was on a private frequency with Sofia, he wasn't sure what to say.

"You okay?"

There was a long silence before she responded. "Getting there. But thank you for asking." Her voice still sounded tight and thin compared to the richness of when they'd first met beneath the trees. It also sounded like a conversational closer.

He knew they were punching for international waters, so it would be at least an hour before they met their ship. That was going to be a long, awkward time to sit in silence beside her.

"Full sentences, huh?" It was the first lighter tone he'd heard from her. Until that moment she'd been one serious chick.

"I'm trying to cut down. They've threatened me with detox programs if I use them too much."

He began counting waves flashing by below their dangling feet. Cruising at a hundred and thirty knots, roughly two and a half miles a minute, he lost count pretty quickly. They blurred into mere ripples in the moonlight that was just cracking over the ocean's horizon and punching through a hole in the clouds.

"I've seen the tapes of Delta team attacks before," Sofia restarted the conversation.

"The Unit. If you're gonna hang with us, we call ourselves The Unit. The 1st Special Forces Operational Detachment—Delta is for Pentagon geeks."

"I know. I know. Combat Applications Group."

"Army Compartmented Elements," Duane made it sing-song.

"And a partridge in a pear tree," Sofia finished on a near-laugh that tickled Duane. The women of Delta weren't exactly laughing types—Melissa more quiet and thoughtful, and Carla so damn serious about everything that he couldn't recall her ever laughing.

"Almost as bad as you guys." He knew that The Activity wasn't actually The Activity. Their name had been changed so many times—Centra Spike, Torn Victor, Gray Fox, Task Force Orange —that no one except the bureaucrats in The Pentagon could keep up with it, so the Intelligence Support Activity or just The Activity had been what stuck, out in the field.

"It works for us."

The helicopter began swaying gently back and forth. Not like trouble, more like…dance music? "What the—"

"You," Patty cut in, humming a dance tune that fit the timing of the helo's sway, "really need to learn how to use a two-channel radio."

He double-checked, it was set right. He'd muted their transmissions from the second channel.

"Or to unplug your intercom cable," Patty sounded utterly delighted.

He'd plugged in the connection to the helo without even thinking about it. He was in the command position at the head of the outside bench on the pilot's side, close beside Patty's right elbow. It had been an automatic gesture to make sure he was patched in.

He hoped that whoever was on the bench seat on the other side of the helo wasn't plugged—

"I think it's sweet," Melissa chimed in for her and Richie.

Across the water, on the other helo racing above the waves, Duane could see Chad sitting beside General Aguado—Kyle and Carla must be on the far side of the second bird.

Aguado was looking everywhere he could except at his seatmate, whereas Chad appeared to be in full predator mode. Chad reached over as if he was going to release the general's safety harness and dump him in the ocean at a hundred and fifty miles an hour. The general became very focused and started talking fast. It was a safe bet that Chad was recording everything and saving the CIA a lot of debriefing time.

At least Chad wasn't paying any attention to him and Sofia. He hoped.

Patty started humming a waltz.

Duane yanked the intercom cable.

CHAPTER 4

*a*fter only a three-hour debrief (six times the length of the actual operation from attack to bug out), they'd finally let her shower and sleep. Clean, in borrowed Navy camos and t-shirt, and well fed, she felt only slightly more human than crawling off the helicopter after nearly forty-eight hours awake.

Fred Smith—the CIA guy who insisted that was his real name so many times that Sofia would have believed him if he wasn't CIA—sat at the head of the steel conference table dressed in khakis and a plain white dress shirt.

"We've already done all of the Agent Smith-*The Matrix* jokes," Duane had told her right in front of Smith. "You think up any new ones, bring them on."

"I've heard them all," though Smith looked cheerfully resigned to it despite his complaint.

"Doesn't mean we aren't going to keep trying," Richie the geek chirped in like a young knight-errant on an exciting quest. Just so damn glad to be here and admiring the crap out of the other guys. Except he was also Delta and a top warrior. It made him constantly surprising.

Typical of shipboard spaces, the cramped room painted in

battleship gray was overwhelmed by her, the six-person Delta team, and the CIA guy. The only decorations were a poster on procedures in case of a fire and a whiteboard with nothing written on it.

"General Aguado," Fred Smith was rhapsodizing, "has been highly cooperative."

Chad, the nasty-looking blond Delta, just grinned. Sofia fought back an actual shiver. She was awfully glad not to have been in the general's position last night, flying for an hour beside Chad the Reaper.

"Rumors are spreading rapidly through Caracas about an attack on Guatopo by a team of fifty SAS agents last night."

Six mistaken for fifty. With the force this team had blown into camp, literally, she wasn't surprised.

"Nice guys, the SAS," Chad acknowledged.

"The best," Duane added.

The two of them sat side by side across the small table from her. She'd ended up between Fred and Richie. She'd gotten on Richie's good side last night by letting him handle the G28 rifle. Within minutes he'd been off to the stern of the ship to fire off a clip into the darkness. "It's good," he'd reported back, "but I need to trial it against the HK416 and the MSG90 before I can decide about its cross-adaptability between a combat rifle and a sniper rifle. I suspect that it's good at both, *but* is it better than one or the other at their specific roles?" He had appeared ready to carry on the conversation with himself even as she took her rifle and headed for the bunk they'd assigned her.

Chad was still being delighted with his misdirection, "Can't imagine how all those women got the idea that it was the Brits who freed them."

"Isn't that weird?" Duane was grinning. "I thought it was us, but I must have been wrong."

"Personally, I wish it *was* the SAS rather than you guys," she couldn't resist breaking up their tag-team thing. "If it had been, I wouldn't be sitting here hearing about it."

They both turned to her in surprise, but she ignored them. Wild Woman Carla, the woman who acted like the leader, smiled briefly at Sofia's sharp riposte but didn't look her way.

Of course The Unit would never admit to actually being somewhere. The best way to avoid that? Hint that they were someone else.

It was also her first good look at the team, especially Duane. He was almost a shock out of his camo paint and fighting gear. He still had broad shoulders, but he was a smaller man than she'd thought. Between his vest and the large pack filled with explosives, he'd looked superhero strong. Now he merely appeared... larger-than-life. Unlike most Delta, whose hair was typically well past Army regulation-length, his brown-black hair was close shaved, shorter than a soldier's buzz cut.

Chad didn't look any less dangerous than he had before. His eyes traveled to her, stopped at her breasts, then up to her face. He must have thought his smile was charming, and she supposed it would be if she didn't recognize the type so well.

Duane's eyes followed where Chad's had gone and his expression darkened, glaring at the side of Chad's head. Interesting.

They both had blue eyes. Chad's were the inviting blue of a summer sky, which was a total lie. Duane's had all the warmth of ice crystals, so blue they looked fake. Perhaps the chill in his eyes was a lie as well.

Sofia went back to listening to Fred Smith. He was a nondescript guy, pale with slightly reddish hair and an unlikely happy smile that showed no signs of abating. She'd done what she came to do. Now it was just a question of when she could catch a flight back home to Fort—

"This team has a training opportunity coming up," Smith called the meeting back to order. "There's a disabled cruise ship under tow into a Colón, Panama, maintenance yard with no passengers aboard. They lost an engine and got everyone off. We've dropped a team of 'hostiles' aboard. You have been authorized to 'remove' those hostiles."

"No rest for the wicked," Chad commented.

"Speaking of yourself," Duane tone was sharper than it had been before.

"He definitely is," Sofia added, earning her a snort of laughter from farther up the table. She could get to enjoy this. Too bad they were leaving so fast.

"The Activity has assigned Ms. Forteza here as your liaison for this op."

"Oh, like that's gonna be a good thing," Chad sounded disgusted.

"Excellent," Duane brightened.

"Only if—" Sofia practically choked on her own words. "Wait. Could you wind that tape back for a second?"

She ignored Chad and Duane and focused on the CIA guy. He might look mild mannered. But if he was handing out assignments—to her—then he was... She squinted her eyes and somehow he came into sharper focus.

"You're not merely some Spec Ops debrief liaison for the CIA."

Smith grimaced and she now had the whole team's attention. They were looking between her and Smith in surprise.

He finally sighed, "Takes one to know one, I suppose. I really need to remember to be more careful around you Activity types."

"How long have you been hoodwinking them?" Sofia wanted to know.

"Still is," Chad grumbled. "What's going down, Smith?" Of course he didn't ask *her*, misogynistic jerk.

The first one to figure it out at the table was Duane.

"Holy shit!" His whisper carried in the silent room.

Sofia could have thumped some of these folks on the head as they all appeared to be giving Duane the credit for figuring it out.

He at least was looking at her, then offered a careful nod. Maybe there was a decent guy behind those pretty ice-blue eyes.

~

"S-A-D. SPECIAL ACTIVITIES DIVISION," Duane whispered in surprise and the shock rippled around the table. Took a lot to shock a Unit operator, but this snagged their attention.

SAD was the CIA's own military arm—and they were bad news.

They'd been working with him for over a year and Smith didn't look like a total scumbag.

Because the rest of the team were all still looking at him in surprise, Duane was the only one who saw that Smith's look said...something else. Until Sofia's comment, he'd been as accepting of "CIA Agent" Fred Smith as the rest of the team.

By Smith's expression at the moment, Duane could see that he was hiding something more.

Duane had been trained by two masters of a different life—one he'd almost ended up living. If ever there were two people who knew how to tell when someone was hiding something, it was his parents: Dad, a high-level executive at Coca-Cola, one of the world's Top Hundred Companies ("Number Eighty-three and climbing"), and Mama, a leading women's rights lawyer. He hadn't gotten away with shit as a kid.

"Special Operations Group," he got out before Fred could cut him off.

He might as well have dropped that freaking jungle viper—the one that had crawled over him and almost made him shit his pants in front of Sofia—right on the table. Everybody whipped around to inspect Fred except Sofia, who raised one of those strong eyebrows at him in question. Not asking if he was right, but rather asking who he really was that he'd known. It was all rooted in a skill set he'd rather forget, if his parents would ever let him. They'd raised him to be an inveterate bastard in the games-manship of the corporate landscape and it was hard to shed at times.

Thankfully the mayhem in the room allowed him to simply shrug at Sofia's unvoiced question and turn to watch the fun.

"SOG?" Richie sounded totally excited. "I've never met one of you guys before. I've got so many questions."

"None of which he'd answer," Chad snarled.

"Not likely," Duane had to agree.

"Only because he doesn't exist," Sofia finished.

Duane traded quick smiles with her. He was really getting to like this woman. She'd recovered fast in the field, her training keeping her going even when Delta-level chaos was going on around her. There were a lot of seasoned soldiers who couldn't do that. Teasing Chad made him like her too. And the fact that she was one of the most beautiful women he'd ever seen wasn't hurting matters either.

Out of her camo paint and ghillie suit, Sofia Forteza was softly Latinate in perfect curves. In her Spain-Spanish he could pick out exposure to both Mexico and South America in her speech—along with that dose of accentless American. Pacific Northwest maybe. She was strong, but with a slender waist that had tucked into his arm like a dream. He hadn't danced since he'd walked out of college one semester shy of his MBA and joined the Army, but she made him want to take it back up just so he'd have an excuse to hold her again.

"SOG?" Carla sounded as if Fred Smith might not make it out of the room alive for deceiving them.

If the Special Activities Division was the CIA's own personal army, the Special Operations Group was its black ops arm—as if a black ops army needed a black ops specialty team. The CIA assassin teams were all part of SOG. They tended to recruit the roughest and toughest of SEAL Team 6 and Delta. Those guys got in deep and their moral code sounded pretty dicey. Worst of all, when SOG shit rolled downhill, it always seemed to be up to Delta to squat in the ditch and clean it up.

Fred Smith's popularity had just gone straight down the toilet.

Chad's glance back to Duane said it all, "Oh, fuck!"

He nodded.

Yeah, Fred wasn't the real problem, though he certainly represented it. The problem was that somewhere up the chain of command—without bothering to tell them—their team had become the SOG's go-to squad in South America.

That didn't sound any kind of good.

Duane knew one thing: whatever was coming next, they, too, were in it deep now.

CHAPTER 5

*F*our and a half hours later, and no wiser despite all the talking, Sofia sat in the back of a massive, blacked-out Chinook helicopter, inside a rubber Zodiac boat, as the helo slammed through the tail end of a hurricane. The boat filled the cargo bay with only inches to spare. The dual, roof-mounted turbines turned the cargo bay of the Chinook into a roaring steel box eight feet wide, six high, and about thirty long—and that was if you didn't count the rain lashing against the hull and the storm trying to plant them on the ceiling of the helo as often as the deck. They'd been in it for four hours flying from the ship off Venezuela to the Panama Canal, and it felt as if she had been living her life inside an eggbeater and would never escape.

Like most Spec Ops teams, The Unit's operators could sleep in any environment. Most of them were sacked out, stretched out on the boat's pontoons or atop a couple of lined-up packs filled with lumpy gear as if they were lying in a rocking cradle.

She hadn't slept a wink.

Duane might have been asleep, but she had the impression that he was watching both her and the cabin. It was too dark to tell—

the cargo area was lit with only dim red nightlights—but occasional hints of ice-blue gave him away. Or was it her imagination? Out of his camouflage paint, he looked far less dangerous except for those unreadable blue eyes. Of course a Delta operator wasn't supposed to *look* dangerous; he was supposed to *be* dangerous.

Sofia's gift was intel analysis, sorting the critical from the mundane. There were small motions, little tells, that informed her each of these people were Special Ops soldiers. Even Carla and Melissa had an attitude of invincibility. For Kyle, the team leader, it was the extreme degree of his calm, complacent attitude—they could announce a nuclear war and he might say, "Huh, really?" before heading out to personally stop it. Richie was somehow the definition of excitable geek stuffed inside a Delta soldier body. For Chad it was a constant unspoken statement of "Don't fuck with me or you're dead."

Duane, despite his close-shorn hair, could be a college professor napping who just happened to be napping inside a roaring helicopter on a rubber raft but was ready to discuss Chaucer or global geopolitical dynamics at a moment's notice. There was nothing odd about him, quirky or bragging. Duane simply...was. Until she caught another glimpse of those chilly blue eyes. No hint of summer sky soft or warm winter's smoke about them.

Sofia had learned long ago to confront what she didn't understand. She didn't believe in fear, so she didn't have to confront *that* —not too often anyway—but she almost thought Duane could teach her what fear meant. An uncomfortable shiver slid up her spine.

Maybe it wasn't just her.

Oddly enough the helicopter's crew was singing a song. They had started with a cheery country song from the Top 40 about beer for their horses and whiskey for the men (with the one woman on their crew altering the gender of the last line particularly emphatically each time). But with the Delta team aboard, they had now shifted into some minor key, all about the ghosts sailing round Cape Horn, which was at the opposite end of South America from their current target—a cruise ship in Panama.

"The song's relevance to this moment eludes me," she swung her microphone out of the way—which she had double-checked was muted anyway—and leaned over so that she could talk to Duane without shouting, much. The two turbine engines of the Chinook were dauntingly loud, even inside the helo.

Either he went from asleep to awake instantly, or he'd been shamming. Either way, he answered her right away.

"Would you rather hear these guys singing 'La Bamba'?"

"Well, as long as they don't start dancing the Macarena while we're flying, I guess we're okay." The lead pilot was a tall Texan with a white cowboy hat hanging from the back of his seat, and a good baritone. The lone female crew chief had a pretty alto. "So what's the plan?"

Duane shrugged. "Cruise ships are pretty standard to take down. Quiet arrival by rubber boat," he thumped his elbow against the pontoon he'd been slouched on. "Though two or three Zodiacs arriving from different directions would be better. Scale the ship. We have a fairly standard plan on how to work it forward and up the levels. Don't know why they're running us through it again as we did a pirated oil tanker just a couple months back. Practice never hurts, I guess."

"And the OPFOR don't expect that?" Besides, taking a small rubber boat out into the storm-lashed night wasn't her idea of a good time.

Duane's shrug said that they were The Unit and what the Opposing Forces—the OPFOR—expected or not wasn't going to be a problem. His eyes slid shut again as if sleep had reclaimed him.

Being in The Activity, Sofia had honed a very finely calibrated sense of not only what fit, but what didn't. And something here definitely didn't.

She stared around the helicopter again. Two pilots forward. Three crew chiefs chatting in the seating close behind the pilots. The singing portion of the flight was apparently done, or on temporary hold until they found a new theme.

Of the Delta team, only Chad was awake, cleaning his weapon. The other four were out.

Fred Smith was still back on the Navy ship she'd seen so little of. Arriving in the dark of one night and departing in the dark of the next, she'd only seen enough to identify it as the USS *Peleliu*—a ship she was fairly sure had been decommissioned and scrapped. Yet there it had been, eight hundred feet of helicopter carrier ship with a skeleton Navy crew and a team of stealth helicopters from the 160th Night Stalkers.

Fred Smith. *There* was the piece that didn't fit.

She lightly nudged a boot against the nerve cluster on Duane's thigh that she'd kneed in the Venezuelan jungle. Duane opened one eye.

"Fred Smith. He's ringing my Itch-o-meter."

"Your what?"

"Itch-o-meter. Right between the shoulder blades."

"Need me to scratch it?"

She booted the nerve cluster hard enough to make him twitch.

"Easy, sugar. Easy," he sat upright. Rather than scratching at his head in thought, he rubbed his palm over his short hair.

She wondered what it would feel like to do that, then she wanted to smack herself to drive that question back to wherever it had come from.

"What's the itch?"

"Fred Smith."

Duane began nodding.

"If he's really SOG..."

"Yep," Duane agreed. "Those boys waiting for us aren't some standard crew. They're probably using us to test their own."

"Any bets on how many they put aboard?"

That earned her a thoughtful grunt.

"No takers?"

"I only bet on a sure thing."

"And you aren't sure of winning this?"

That brought one of his smiles. "Okay, Sofia. There are seven of us, so more than ten but less than fifteen."

"No, over twenty," she guessed. The entire SOG was rumored to have less than sixty field personnel, but she'd bet they were going to commit hard on this exercise to show up The Unit. Which meant the stakes were sky high.

"Twenty?" Duane squinted at her.

"The CIA is always trying to get the ugly tasks for themselves. Glory is all for them. They threw a major hissy fit trying to get the bin Laden mission. They were some kind of upset when it went to the SEALs." She'd been the assistant to the director of the Defense Intelligence Agency at the time and thankfully only watched the by-blow without being caught in it as her boss had. It would have made the actual storm they were now in—bouncing them up and down until sitting on the boat's seat felt like being in some kids' party bouncy house—seem mild by comparison.

"So you're thinking that they're going to use this as an excuse to take Delta down a notch because there's some operation coming up that they want?"

She cocked one eyebrow and shrugged. It fit.

～

Duane liked her honesty as if to say, "Just what I'm seeing." And her well-defined Spanish eyebrows had a whole expressive language of their own.

Out of the heavy combat gear and ghillie suit aboard the ship,

Sofia Forteza was indeed very hot as Chad had said. Only she was nowhere near that simple. Her strong Spanish features were backed up with a warmly-amber skin and the darkest-brown eyes he'd ever seen. With a gaze that missed nothing, her looks said this was a woman who kicked ass and didn't bother coming back to take names later.

He'd watched her fussing while the others slept. She watched everything. Assessed everything—all at once. He'd wager that Sofia's thoughts were always busy about something, which made sense for someone working for The Activity.

This time her eyes said that the CIA's guys were going to be playing this scenario dirty. She didn't need to declare it. It was simple fact and he could ignore it at his own peril.

With his own Itch-o-meter—damn she was cute—now stoked to life, he broke down the standard training plan for her on how The Unit took back a cruise ship held by terrorists or pirates. Come in fast and low from slightly to the left of straight behind— straight behind, the bad guys had probably come from there themselves. To the left because most people were right-handed and would tend to scan over their right shoulders more than their left for attacks from behind. Everyone lying low in the boat for minimum radar signature. The near-silent, battery-driven, electric engine wrapped in a carbon-fiber cowling for minimum radar signature. Jet rather than prop-driven because the sound signature was also smaller.

"After that, it's pretty standard. Grappling hooks and suction gear. Team goes up both sides. One side hits the top first to draw all of the attention their way. The other team cleans up from behind."

Then he waited for questions.

"That's the best plan?"

"It's how we train for it."

Again the nuanced shrug, one shoulder and a slight tip of the head making her long dark hair shimmer in the red night-light as it shifted. "How do the CIA's Special Operations Group train for it?"

Now it was his turn to shrug. "Who the hell knows with those guys."

"Guess."

Duane thought about how he'd defend a cruise ship if he knew that a team from The Unit was going to board. It would be easy to anticipate. Duane knew that it would be a hard-won battle, but the more he thought about it, the less he liked it.

"Well?"

"Huh," was the best he could come up with. There was no love lost between the teams—and the SOG would run it hard. Even the damned SEALs would play it nicer.

"So now what's the new plan?"

Like he was supposed to outthink the best that The Unit's trainers had ever come up with. He checked his watch—and do it in the next twenty-eight minutes.

The female crew chief was walking by, barely bothering to reach for handholds despite how hard the Chinook helicopter was bucking through the winds. He called her over, "Hey, Carmen."

"Oh. My. God!" Carmen slapped a hand to her chest and put her wrist to her forehead. "I'm gonna faint. It only took four hours for one of the silent warriors to acknowledge that they weren't the only people on this flight." And she collapsed onto one of the Zodiac's pontoons, fell upside down into the bottom of the boat, and sprawled at his feet like she was out cold.

Several of the Delta startled awake, inspected them both strangely for a moment, then went back to sleep. Chad hardly bothered to look up from where he continued to work over his already immaculate rifle.

"Got a question for you, once you're done playing the lead role from a Bizet opera."

"What are you talking about?" She continued lying upside down, but raised her head to inspect him.

"The opera *Carmen*? The dazzling man-killer?"

"There's an opera named after me?"

How could she not know? Then he saw the flamenco dancer painted on the side of her helmet—maybe she wasn't so surprised. She switched herself around to sit beside him on the floor of the boat.

"How cool is that? Dazzling man-killer—perfect fit. Are you my next victim? This should be fun."

Duane checked his watch. Contact was in twenty-six minutes. As amusing as she might be to banter with, it was time to get down to business.

"How would you take down a cruise ship?"

"Couple'a Hellfire missiles at the waterline? We don't carry heavy arms, but we got an escort bird—Lola LaRue in a DAP Hawk—that most certainly does. She be more than glad to kick some cruise-ship ass."

"I'm looking for an attack plan that doesn't destroy the boat."

"Sometimes it's the best way. I remember this one time we were in a place I can't mention and we had to shoot down a forty-million-dollar Chinook. Four Hellfires didn't leave anything as big as a name badge." She flicked the one on her chest, which was how he'd remembered her name was Carmen.

"Israel in the Negev Desert," Sofia said softly. "I didn't realize that was you."

Duane had heard about the Chinook lost on a training exercise there, a bad one that had cost the Israelis a couple of jets. Unusually, as helicopter losses were never pretty, no crew members had been killed—or at least none were reported.

"Us," Carmen nodded forward toward the rest of the crew. "All of us. How do you know about that shit?"

"I'm sorry. I can't say."

But Duane could see that she knew every detail. Too bad, a good story he'd probably never get to hear.

"Crap! Another Activity spook? You guys were all over that one. Figures. Could have used help a little sooner than it came. Might still have our first helo if it had." Carmen turned a cold shoulder toward Sofia, but offered a saucy grin to show she was just teasing. Then she turned to him, "How about just destroying the cruise ship's bridge?"

"Not very subtle."

"Picky. Picky. Picky." Carmen shrugged and climbed to her feet. "Unless you want us to land you directly on the ship in the middle of a firefight—even if it would only be a simulated one— can't help you much." She wandered off whistling an old Bee Gees song. Soon the entire helicopter crew was working their way through "Sinking Ships." He supposed it was better than the *Mission Impossible* theme.

He looked at Sofia sitting on one of the Zodiac's low seats, leaning forward to look at him. The zipper at her throat was down just enough to expose her collarbone. No more, but it had been giving him trouble throughout the flight. Every time she spoke it took everything he had to not stare at her throat or lips as they moved. He'd been around plenty of pretty women—Carla and Melissa were knockouts in their own way—but Sofia was action-flick wet-dream stunning.

At least she was for him.

Was there a "look" for each guy? On the first day of intake testing, he'd seen Kyle go nuts for Carla. Duane hadn't known who Kyle was yet, but Carla as the only woman in a testing group of over a hundred had stood out big time. From the first moment, Kyle had been front and center to greet her.

Richie had done the same thing the moment Melissa showed up. Richie, who only got hot and bothered by the latest piece of tech gear, had turned...well, nasty wasn't in him but, much to everyone's surprise, ultra-protective was.

Chad's normally successful play for any pretty woman had fizzled on Sofia even worse than it had on Melissa. Maybe Chad was losing his touch since he'd briefly landed Tanya Zimmer from Mossad—she'd certainly spun his head around but good.

Duane couldn't force himself to look away from Sofia. He hadn't slept longer than a minute at a time of the last four hours, not with Sofia sitting so close by. And no Spec Ops soldier wanted to be awake for the entire duration of a storm flight, but he had been. Women didn't give him those kinds of problems. Yet she did…

For a moment he flashed on how she'd look in a bathing suit, all wet and—

He laughed.

She raised just one of those dark, strong eyebrows at him in question.

Duane called Carmen back as he thumped a hand twice on the hard rubber of the Zodiac boat. Chad looked up from his spotless rifle, then snapped it back together with a fast series of sharp clicks. The other four who'd been asleep but leaning against different parts of the boat jolted awake, automatically resting their hands on their pistols as they blinked to life and made sure of where they were.

Duane made a circle motion with his hand, calling them together.

"Bet you look great in a bikini," he whispered to Sofia alone.

That sent her other eyebrow arching up, saying not a chance.

He could still hope.

CHAPTER 6

*S*ofia had considered kicking Duane's thigh again, but missed her chance before everyone had gathered around and he'd begun laying out his plan.

Now she was standing at the back of the Chinook helicopter's rear ramp, gaping open above the night-dark ocean. It was her second time in twenty-four hours and only her second time in over two years to be in such a position. Was the night-ocean-helicopter paradigm a Delta Force thing or was this somehow her doing?

They'd flown out of the storm twenty miles back. They were now in the wind shadow of the fifteen-hundred-meter peaks of Panama's Serranía de Tabasará sheltering the Mosquito Gulf and the waves were at least manageable. Still, she was glad not to be in the tiny Zodiac.

They'd dropped the Zodiac and the other five team members several miles back, then raced to the ship with only her and Duane still aboard. She wore heavy gloves and had her rifle—loaded with Simunitions so that she didn't kill anybody on this training mission—strapped over her shoulder.

Outside the helicopter was nothing but black ocean. She

wanted to turn, look up the length of the helicopter and out the front windshield to see the approaching cruise ship, but that wasn't her worry right now.

She'd been uneasy enough with her first solo recon trip into the jungle. Sometimes ISA agents came back with "there I was, suddenly in the center of the action" stories, but they weren't common. ISA typically slipped in smooth and quiet, gathered their intel, and then slipped out just as quietly to brief the action teams.

Not this time. She was in it and, at least for the moment, appeared to be stuck in it. She and Duane were poised and ready —too late to be nervous.

The female loadmaster with the alto singing voice was pure business now. Every ten seconds like clockwork she said, "Hold... Hold... Hold" barely breaking the rhythm of the current rendition of "The Sound of Music" that the crew had picked up for some inexplicable reason.

Sofia could feel the adrenaline surging through her. If not for Duane standing close beside her, she might shake apart from the power of it.

A careful coil of thick rope lay at the loadmaster's feet. The top of the FAST rope was attached to the overhead. She and Duane wore thick gloves that would allow them to slide down the ropes quickly without burning their hands.

Beyond the steel lip of the cargo ramp lay nothing but the night. The helicopter was racing so close over the surface of the ocean that it felt as if they were no higher above it than the edge of a swimming pool. Even without the stealth modifications, the pilot was flying to keep the big helicopter below the cruise ship's radar.

"Hold... Hold..."

The helicopter jolted upward. The sudden force almost took her knees out from under her to sit on the steel deck. They were now climbing upward hard to clear the towering wall that was the side of a cruise ship.

"Five," the loadmaster started her countdown. And the crew's singing fell silent, though Sofia bet it would restart as soon as they were gone.

Sofia hadn't had a moment to explain or even apologize for what had happened in the past that had gotten an entire Chinook crew kidnapped in the heart of Israel's Negev Desert. The fault had been The Activity's. It had freaked out everyone and they'd initiated a full-team study. Every member of ISA, almost two hundred people, had spent three days analyzing every nuance of the event to make sure it never occurred again.

"Four," Carmen continued—still climbing fast.

Sofia could only remember two other events of similar scale. It was before her time, but she'd been told that they'd broken down and analyzed the 9/11 attacks in half that time—of course, every intelligence agency in the world had been working on that one.

Now there wasn't time.

Sofia grabbed hold of the thick FAST rope at the same moment the loadmaster kicked the coil off the back of the helicopter ramp.

"Three," there was a tug on her belt as the loadmaster unclipped her safety harness and the umbilical cord for the intercom. The climb eased and the helo slowed.

"Two," Sofia counted silently in her head. "One."

Carmen's slap on her shoulder came at the same moment Sofia stepped off the end of the ramp and out into dark space.

Everything happened at once.

The helicopter had slowed, but it hadn't stopped. It was hoped that no one would notice her and Duane's arrival, thinking the helicopter had simply been doing a side-to-side overflight to see what they could see of the "captive" ship.

As she slid down the rope, the black ocean was replaced by the brightly lit uppermost deck of the cruise ship. They had climbed over a dozen stories in the last few seconds and were now crossing side to side over the center, just high enough to not tangle with any of the safety rails or rigging.

Using her gloved hands and boots wrapped around the FAST rope to control her speed, Sofia descended on faith that their target would be there when she reached the bottom. Otherwise she was going to have a long fall over the side and into the ocean.

Sofia slid down the rope and—at the exact centerline of the cruise ship, with a timing she'd never understand but thankfully the loadmaster had—she plunged into the ship's top-deck swimming pool.

"Let go," Duane shouted from just five feet away where he'd been sliding down a second rope just like hers. It reminded her to release her grip before the helo dragged her into the sidewall of the pool.

She was a moment slower at remembering to unwrap her feet. The delay flipped her facedown into the pool as the helo dragged the rope a moment longer before the loadmaster let it fall free. One of the ropes fell onto the deck, the other slammed down into the pool on top of them like a very heavy snake driving her back under the water before she could get a breath.

When she surfaced, coughing and sputtering, Duane was already on his feet. The water was chest high. His rifle was up and on his shoulder as water streamed off him and he swept a quick circle to make sure they were clear.

"Wet look is good on you, sugar," his back was to her as he spoke.

"Still never getting me in a bikini, Delta."

"Can't blame a guy for trying."

The thing was, the wet look was good on him too. Rising out of the water and armed to the teeth, water sheeting off him and leaving a sparkle in his short hair... That was her kind of man, if she had a kind.

Men are way more trouble than they're worth, she had to remind herself as they slogged to the side of the pool. *At least so far,* some naive, uninformed part of her answered. She still had hopes of finding a decent guy, no matter how unlikely that hope might be. Of course, if she did, it wouldn't be some hardcore Unit operator type.

They left the ropes floating in the pool, wading together to the steps and clambering out among the empty beach chairs. The loudest sounds in the night were the deep grind of the tugboat towing the cruise ship toward port and the splatter of the two of them dripping on the polished wood deck.

Duane sliced a hand left, then forward; then he'd right and forward himself.

The ship itself was a good fit for the model that she'd built and briefed the team on.

Of course some intel was easier to gather than others.

The helicopter carrier USS *Peleliu* that they'd spent the last eighteen hours aboard, for example. She hadn't been able to verify the existence of it, even though she'd been sitting aboard, using a satellite uplink through its comm system. Every site she could find agreed: the *Peleliu* had been decommissioned and towed away for scrap. Too bad there hadn't been time to figure out how they hid an eight-hundred-foot ship in plain view.

Determining which cruise ship they were going to be boarding from a news item about the breakdown was easy. Then the layout: Oceanwide cruise line's website had detailed deck plans, at least for the public areas. She'd had to log into ISA's databases to get the lower deck configuration as well.

At the time, Duane hanging over her shoulder had bothered her. Now she understood that he hadn't been trying to look down the front of her t-shirt, or at least he hadn't *only* been doing that. He'd also reviewed and memorized the deck layouts even as she transferred them to a tablet. She'd enjoyed keeping from him that it wasn't really necessary to memorize anything past the general layout anymore.

Sofia had stacked the deck plans in 3D and fed the wireframe model to everyone's on-person computer. All they had to do was tap in their starting point and the exact direction to the bow of the ship. That would give the GPS a reference point to calibrate the model to its current heading. After that they could refer to the ship's layout while on the run, following the projection inside their shooting glasses. Virtual reality mapped over what they could see through the lenses, just like the helicopter pilots had, but reduced and ruggedized enough for on-person systems.

The Activity had spent three years developing the system. Since this was just a training mission, the Delta team had agreed to be the first to guinea pig it. They'd spent three hours running around the *Peleliu*—which also had required a surprising amount of work to get the plans for. Their consensus? The system "kicked ass"...then they'd given her thirty-seven mods they'd like added to the system ASAP. Turns out that Richie had implemented nine others while they were testing—which shouldn't have been possible.

On the cruise ship's projected wireframe model, she could see that the pool deck had an outer running track that split to either side of the exhaust stacks. With a tap, she was able to see a deck overview in the background that showed Duane racing down the other side. She cleared it with another tap so that she could see what lay beyond the lens more clearly.

From the top deck, Sofia had a real-world view down on the slightly wider deck below them.

Every time she saw someone standing at the rail and searching outward, she shot them.

Simunitions were simulated ammunition that were accurate to a hundred meters, left a tiny paint dot, and stung when you were shot with them. She left four hostiles cursing behind her. Remembering her experience with Duane, she made sure to shoot each one three times—twice in the helmet and once in the chest when they spun around to figure out who was shooting them from above.

One was angry enough to shoot back at her even though he was technically dead, but she was protected by the high railing designed to make sure that tourists didn't fall overboard.

～

DUANE DIDN'T HAVE to wait long for her at the front of the top deck.

"How many, sister?"

"Four. You...*brother?*"

"Crap! Three." And now he was starting to *sound* like her too. Definitely time to drop the "sister" thing. He'd initially done it to keep things easy between them. But his thoughts about the armed woman who had raced down the deck toward him were anything but brotherly.

He reached into his pack and pulled out a length of 9mm tactical line.

Flipping a knot around the forward rail, he looked over and double-checked the line that she'd set up. The knot looked good. Who knew competent women were so goddamn hot?

"See you at the bottom," she offered a cocky smile, then climbed over the rail and slid out of sight.

He just watched her go. He'd almost eaten the side of the pool by doing that. He'd been watching her slide down and had to yell "Let go!" to remind himself what he was supposed to be paying attention to.

And still he was standing here.

Duane grabbed the line and jumped over the rail. He slid down to land on the starboard side wing bridge, the tiny platform three stories down that stuck out the side of the ship's control bridge so that the commander could look at exactly what was happening over the edge of his ship.

No one there.

Door to the bridge...locked. Bastards. It would never be locked in real life.

He could see the bridge crew inside through the glass. A couple of SOG types with handguns still holstered and rifles slung over shoulders were looking forward, toward the helicopter that was now hovering a half mile ahead of the ship as a distraction.

Well, he was about to piss off the cruise company.

He yanked a small breaching charge out of his right thigh pocket, a detonator out of the left. Slapping the C-4 on the door and ramming in the detonator, he flicked the tip of it and moved as far away as he could. Not much space on the wing bridge.

The blast hit him with a body blow about equal to being tossed to the dirt during hand-to-hand combat training. A sharp kick and the door was out of his way.

He shot the first two hostiles.

Then there was a hard bang from the far side of the bridge. Sofia had found the guts to use the breaching charge he'd given her while they were gearing up for the jump from the helo.

Everyone turned from him to facing the other direction. He shot two more and watched two others come to a stop and look down at their chests in surprise.

Sofia had shot them.

"Seven," he shouted to her as she came into view.

"*Mierda! Seis.*" So he was finally one "hostile" casualty ahead of her.

The bridge crew were staring at him in shock.

"Captain," Duane picked out a tall blond guy. "Hit your security lockdown, please."

When the man didn't respond, Sofia walked up and nudged him in the ribs with the barrel of her rifle. "He *did* say please."

Shaking off his shock, the captain flipped up a cover and pushed down on a red button before turning back to them. "You blew up our doors."

"Blame them. They shouldn't have locked the doors in the first place. Would you have locked them?"

He ignored the captain as he grudgingly confirmed that the wing bridge doors would never be locked during standard operations. With his rifle, Duane waved all of the "dead" SOG agents toward an open spot between the navigation console and the helmsman's station.

"Have a seat, boys." They might be technically dead, but they looked some kind of pissed and he wasn't going to trust them for a second. Once they were on the floor, he stripped them of their weapons.

"Do it, Sofia."

A bunch of the guys twisted in surprise to inspect her. Though how they could miss her gender despite the combat vest and helmet was beyond him—Sofia *radiated* woman like a bomb's heat wave. Macho assholes being taken down by a "mere" woman...*very* not happy.

The SOGs began muttering among themselves about what they'd like to do to Sofia.

Duane was less than gentle as he disarmed them, slammed them facedown onto the deck, and zip-tied them hard. They shut up fast enough.

In the meantime, she'd been studying the control console with an intensity that drew her brows together. She reached for a control.

One of the ship's crew protested.

Casually, almost as an afterthought, she pulled out her handgun and aimed it at the center of the officer's chest without turning to face him.

"You sure that you're a desk agent?" Duane could only grin. It was a move worthy of a Unit operator.

Sofia ignored him and hit the control she'd sought out.

An alarm ripped through the bridge.

"Wait," the officer protested despite her unwavering weapon. "We're at sea, you can't open that door."

Sofia ignored him and pressed it again.

The alarm silenced. The sea-level, cargo-loading door began to open a dozen stories below them. Sofia found a camera feed and moved it to the main display screen. Moments later, the Zodiac with the rest of the Delta team shot up to the door. The door was wider than the boat, so the team did a classic fast-boarding maneuver.

Everyone shifted to the rear.

A last-second burst of power.

The nose of the Zodiac lifted and cleared the threshold, pushing a wave of water aboard ahead of it—which the Zodiac rode partway across the threshold.

As the boat slammed to a stop, four of the crew let the momentum throw them forward, while Richie raised the engine. Jumping out the front of the Zodiac, they had it hauled the rest of the way aboard the cruise ship in seconds. They were Unit operators on a mission and didn't even slow down for a high-five or a fist bump.

Sofia closed the cargo door behind them—it had been open less than ten seconds.

Much faster than trying to scale the sides of a moving ship.

After that, it was a game of cat and mouse. Sofia had control of the cameras and the security doors. Duane transmitted the location of each bad guy they spotted to the action team coming unexpectedly up the inside of the ship rather than the outside.

The last three "terrorists" barricaded themselves into one of the master suites directly below the bridge.

Duane was going to go after them, but Sofia was out on the wing bridge before he could say a word.

She slid down the one deck to land on their outer verandah. Duane could only watch the security camera feed in admiration. She yanked her Glock from its holster. He could feel the hesita-

WILD JUSTICE

tion as she stared at it in perplexity—Simunitions wouldn't do anything to the locked glass door except leave a blotch of paint. Then she tossed the gun upward, caught it by the barrel in midair, and slammed the butt down against the glass, which shattered in a spray of safety glass. Flipping the gun back, she had it in her hand in time to shoot the first hostile to turn around.

As they spun to watch Kyle kicking in the front door to the suite, she shot another one of them in the back. Carla shot the third past Kyle's hip before the hostile knew what was going on.

Total time to clear the ship from first contact was under fifteen minutes.

Damn but Sofia was a stunner.

He didn't even mind that she was once again ahead of him in takedowns.

Not much anyway.

CHAPTER 7

*A*gain, the whole operation, which could have taken hours, was measured in minutes—seventeen of them to be precise. Getting the hostiles all squared away had taken longer than beating them in the first place.

Chad had wanted to throw the SOG team into the ship's brig.

Sofia had liked that idea, especially after one of the "dead" men shot her when she wasn't looking—which still stung—and another had tried to grab her ass—which Duane had stopped with a blow that broke the guy's wrist. Sadly, she was used to such treatment, but apparently Duane wasn't.

He hadn't looked merely irritated, he'd been furious. His strike had been so fast and vicious that Sofia was half surprised that the man's hand was still attached to his arm at all.

Had it been because it was her, because she was a woman, or would he defend any member on the team that way? Had she actually found a military team that treated women as equals rather than some tolerated lower species? Watching Carla and Melissa woman-handling the wounded asshole out the door and toward the infirmary—the men on the team not even offering to assist—made her think that maybe she had.

She wasn't sure how she felt about working with a team in the field.

The whole purpose of Activity was teamwork—collaboration between intelligence services, both domestic and foreign. Yet out in the field on reconnaissance, they were often loners. Even in the office, one ISA agent typically equaled one project. Only the information flow was collaborative.

Suddenly she was on a team again, and she wasn't sure why. Especially because it wasn't the sort of team she was used to—not intelligence gathering, but Delta Force action. Not a chance that she'd be admitting to anyone how much she was enjoying herself while doing it. Who knew that kicking in doors could be so satisfying?

The ship's captain, in his cultured, Danish-accented English, had killed Chad's idea of using his brig. "It is only big enough for to hold a few of drunk sort of people. I do not think you could fit them all in the sides, even standing up." *Ohp* was how he'd pronounced it—a dignified man who was still upset with the destruction of the wing bridge doors and the mayhem caused to one of the luxury suites.

Carla had suggested tying the rest of the "dead" up and leaving them in a pile like old driftwood until the CIA came to collect them.

Twenty-three mock-hostile casualties to...none of their own.

"You owe me, soldier!" Sofia turned to Duane and crowed with delight. They hadn't agreed on the payout, just the bet itself, but she'd think up something good. The CIA's SOG had committed over a third of their manpower to this training op. "They must have wanted it *ba-ad!*"

Duane nodded, being a good sport about losing, but she could see he was thinking about what lay ahead. Now that started to worry *her* as well.

Melissa's more rational head prevailed and the SOG operators were released and left to sulk at one of the midship buffet lines—

except for the one with the shattered wrist still down in the infirmary. He actually was being treated for two broken wrists, apparently not learning his lesson the first time. She couldn't imagine someone dumb enough to underestimate Carla, but apparently the SOG idiot had tried to fondle her breast from the treatment table.

The Filipino crew, who'd been told to stay safely below decks during the exercise, were now at their stations, feeding the SOG operators. They were apparently glad to have something to do—not used to having no passengers aboard. It was certainly an interesting break from routine all around.

Delta set up at the far end of the ship in a small Italian restaurant. They'd just placed their orders when Duane recalled the FAST ropes they'd left in the pool and the two tactical lines down to the ship's bridge.

"Least we can do is retrieve our own gear," Duane had headed out and she'd followed along. He studied her as they wandered out of the luxury restaurant with its white linen tablecloths and fine cutlery, such a contrast with their own black t-shirts, slacks, and the pile of Simunitions-adapted weapons and armored vests stacked on several of the tables. They both wore live sidearms again. Duane picked up his rifle and slung it over his shoulder as he headed out, so she did the same with her G28.

"What?"

He shook his head. "Just trying to puzzle you out."

"I am not some Rubik's Cube."

"No. You are a beautiful and skilled woman who is far too used to being alone."

"Why do you say that?" She walked beside him up the grand staircase that curved up to the next deck. Red carpet and gold-painted railings. She half expected to see a chandelier above, but it would probably make passengers seasick as it swayed with the boat and that would never do.

"Why are you following me? There's only the two FAST ropes and I can carry them myself."

"Maybe I like you," she went for her driest tone.

He snorted out a laugh and she liked that her joke had worked. Liked him for getting the joke. Liked that he—

Sofia chopped off that crazed train of thought before it could completely run off the tracks.

Maybe Duane understood that she was actually escaping the crowded restaurant, loud with stories and laughter. Even though they had all fit around one table—there were only four men and two women on the Delta team—and the rest of the tables had been vacant, they had overwhelmed the space. Including her own personal headspace.

The silent warriors.

Maybe around others. But with only her and the waiters there —and riding high on kicking some serious SOG behinds—the Deltas were suddenly loud, laughing, and...larger than life. Duane was the only one who seemed even close to normal-sized. Yet he had taken it all in stride: blowing up a Venezuelan prison one night and spending the next taking downing a large team of pretend hostiles, who hadn't been pretending very much.

He pushed out onto the upper deck at the ship's stern. The lights were off except for little kicker lights so that she could see the walkway. They didn't interfere with the stars that filled the night sky. A long trail of phosphorescent green followed behind them. The glow of Colón, Panama, hadn't yet come over the horizon. Only the deep-ocean tug, far ahead on the line it was using to tow the disabled cruise ship, lit the dark ocean ahead. It was breathtaking.

"Where did you go?" Duane called from farther down the deck. He hadn't even noticed her stopping.

She waved a hand toward the sea and the sky.

He spent about zero-point-three seconds looking around.

"Nice," he offered before continuing toward the pool.

"Nice? *Nice!* You dimwitted Delta!" Sofia stalked after him. "It's spectacular. Not even from the vineyards of home can I see such stars. Open your eyes! Look around you! Not everything is battles and—" Hardly aware of her own actions, she had stalked up until they were toe to toe and she was jabbing a finger against his chest. Without the armored vest filled with ammunition and explosives, she was driving the tip of her finger against equally hard muscle.

"I've got a question," Duane asked with a calm that she certainly wasn't feeling.

"*What?*"

"Am I going to regret this or not? I'm thinking *not*, no matter what happens."

"What are you talking about?" She stopped with her fingertip resting on his breastbone.

"This."

∾

DUANE RESTED his hands on that amazing waist of hers, pulled her the last quarter-step closer, and kissed her.

Sofia made a sound of surprise, but not of complaint.

Her finger slowly shifted from poking against his chest to palm flat. Then, with a long, slow pressure, she eased him back, even as she bent forward to prolong the kiss.

Once they were too far apart to continue kissing, his hands on her waist were the only thing that stopped her from retreating until she disappeared into the darkness. He shouldn't have done it but he'd be damned if he'd say he was sorry. She tasted exotic, like she was made of foreign lands and strange places to explore.

She felt—Christ! Had he ever held such a woman? A fighter, an exotic beauty, and a mind sharp enough to have helped him create an entirely new tactic for taking back a pirated cruise ship. Even holding and kissing her for such a brief moment had shifted something. Or maybe the cruise ship had caught a stray wave too big for the stabilizers too dampen out.

"That," Sofia pushed him just far enough that he pulled his hands off her waist, though her palm still rested against his chest —fine-fingered, strong, very feminine.

He could feel his heart beating against her palm.

"That… should not have happened," her voice was barely louder than the night.

"Why? Don't tell me you didn't enjoy it?" *Please don't tell me that.*

"I did. You have a very nice kiss, Mr. Duane The Rock."

Duane tried not to feel a foot taller and totally failed.

"But I will be gone soon and…"

"I don't care," he cut her off.

"But—"

"Any chance I get with you, sugar, I already know is going to be a thousand percent worth it."

"'Sugar' isn't helping your cause."

Okay. Good to know. He'd cross that off the list along with sister.

"Nor is using any percentage over a hundred. Percentages don't work that way."

"Sure they do. A thousand percent is ten times better than simply a hundred percent incredible," even if he hadn't meant it that way when he said it. It earned him a smile and an eye roll, though he couldn't tell if they were additive or if they canceled each other out.

"And you say 'any chance I get with you is going to be worth it'? Is that also simple hyperbole? I've heard it a thousand times before."

"Now who is exaggerating?" Duane teased her.

"I only wish I was," her sigh was not a happy one. He wondered just what she'd had to put up with in her life, especially looking the way she did in a Spec Ops world.

"Well, you haven't heard it from me before." And as soon as he said it, he knew it wasn't some line no matter how much it sounded like one. He'd be truly sorry when she was gone—rather than his usual not-so-sorry when a relationship ended because he was headed out on deployment. Women had a shelf date that always seemed to expire way too soon. Kyle and Carla, along with Richie and Melissa, appeared to be somehow different, but not in any way that *he'd* ever experienced. Or understood. Or believed in.

"Too bad," she tapped one of her fingers still resting on his chest.

"What's too bad?" He'd feel the outline of them for days.

"It's too bad that I almost believe you." Sofia took the final step back that had her hand slipping off his chest. Then she walked the rest of the way to the pool and coiled the first rope that had landed mostly out of the water.

Duane wanted to do something to lighten the mood. How had it all gotten so damn serious so fast? All he'd done was kiss her—that shouldn't alter the world. He fished the other FAST rope out of the pool where it lay like a swimming Anaconda in a pristine but no less dangerous swamp. The damn thing weighed a lot when it was wet. The helo was long gone, headed back toward its ship, so it was up to the team to clear all of their gear.

"See," Sofia hefted her own rope. "It is a good thing that I came along to help you or you must carry this as well."

"I'm thinking that anything you do is a good thing." Now *that* sounded too much like a line.

For some reason she stumbled and almost plunged back into the pool. Odd. She'd been so surefooted all day.

≈

Good thing?

Her commanders had always complimented her on her skills.

But Duane's simple statement of unquestioning belief in her skills had stopped her cold.

She'd spent most of her childhood snarled up in trying to be the good girl, trying to do the right thing, and her mother had always been very clear that she wasn't succeeding. Her brothers could get away with anything, but her? Not even a chicken scratch worth.

Why did *his* saying it make so much more difference than all of her previous commanders?

They were halfway to the bow of the ship to recover the light tactical lines they'd used to reach the bridge when they passed beside a wide-open skylight. It sat forward of the pool, filling the space between the two sides of the running track they'd raced along previously to attack the bridge. The skylight was the same width as the pool and just as long—the opening was at least thirty-feet square. With the storm gone and the training exercise over, the captain had reopened it to the warm night.

She and Duane stood in the darkness of the top deck. Beyond the inner railing, through the opening, they looked down at a well-lit, luxurious bar done in dark woods and lush leather. It was easy to see the SOGs who had gathered there.

She made the mistake of looking down. She and Duane would be invisible from below, especially due to the ceiling lights to either side of the skylight. The bar itself was a curved piece of walnut, shaped like a gentle sea wave. Behind it was ranged a truly impressive collection of liquor bottles. Correction, of whisky and scotch bottles. The ship's whisky bar. All of the stools were of the same wood as the bar; comfortable chairs of red leather with elegant walnut side tables were placed throughout the room, and it was populated by two Filipino bartenders and twenty-three SOGs—one in double wrist casts. All drinking, though it appeared to be first rounds, so a long way from drunk.

Then she heard the first words and did her best to ignore them.

Ignored them so hard that she ran square into Duane's back where he'd stopped as if bolted to the deck. She could feel the tension, no, the *fury* as she bounced off him. How could he be so solid?

He was glaring over the pipe railing and down through the big skylight.

"Can you believe that bitch who took us down on the bridge?"

"Su-weet! Like to teach her a lesson or two."

"At least an eight on the FI."

"And those other two. Hot shit!"

"Don't, Duane," she whispered to him in the darkness. "Don't listen to them."

He didn't answer—or move—as the SOGs continued.

Instead, he keyed the mic on his radio, "We've got a rat problem." Then he held it out over the skylight. At the same time, he swung his rifle off his shoulder, turned on the video camera attached to the scope, and aimed it downward. He worked it back and forth across the room, jumping to each face as they spoke.

"Their guard will be down now," another SOG continued as he grabbed a whisky bottle from a suddenly reluctant bartender. "We should go kick some ass and throw us a three-woman party. Then we'll just claim victory. Besides, you saw what they did to Bernie. Both wrists, man," Bernie held up the dual casts like a champion fighter taking his lap. "That's got a price. Maybe they'll have a small accident afterward."

"I'll take the brunette," one called out.

Duane's scope zigged left.

"Blonde for me," another answered. "Blondes always have a higher FI."

His scope swept right.

"I want that Spanish bitch until she squeals."

He zeroed in on the commander, a big ugly dude with a flame tattoo on his arm and steroids in his bulging muscles.

"What's FI?" Sofia whispered to Duane.

"Fuckability Index," his voice sounded dead. No, like death.

"Just ignore them. We'll post a guard and—"

He released the key on his radio mic.

"Situation?" Kyle called back over the radio. Sofia had forgotten to take out her earpiece, so she could hear the flatness of his tone as well.

"Whisky bar amidships. We're up above the open skylight. Twenty-two rats plus one in double wrist casts. Two noncombatants behind the bar."

Sofia could hear them still egging each other on. She'd only give it a ten percent chance of getting ugly; she'd certainly heard worse.

"Duane," Sofia tried pushing against his shoulder but he wasn't going anywhere. "Let it *go.*" They were so alpha-idiot raunchy. She upgraded the chances of action to fifteen percent and climbing. Initially only four or five were being vocal, but it was up to half now. There had to be a way to—

"In thirty," Kyle called back.

"No! Wait!"

Duane shushed her.

Damn it! She knew better and lowered her voice—not that the SOGs could hear her. They were up to twenty percent and climbing on the probability-of-action scale. She'd listened to plenty of intelligence traffic over the years to know that there was no way this was going to end well, not at the rate it was escalating.

At some other time she'd have to reconsider growth rates of group pressure dynamics. At thirty percent it was fast becoming a certainty, so why were her trained instincts still classifying it as only thirty...now forty percent likelihood of action?

"Duane, you've got to find another way." This time she actually had to raise her voice a little to be heard over the escalating cloud of machismo.

He pulled something out of a thigh pocket. He leaned through the rail and attached it to the edge of the skylight. A micro surveillance video camera.

She checked it out. Nothing fancy, thirty dollars retail online. She liked the low-techness of it. The Activity had a similar cam that they almost never took in the field because it cost closer to a thousand. Probably with about the same performance specs.

"You can help or you can step aside. But no one gets to talk about women that way. Especially not around a Delta team." He unshouldered the FAST rope and tied one end around the rail.

"All you have is live ammo," she double-checked her own weapons. "The Simunitions are still in the restaurant."

"No one on the team will be using Simunitions," his voice was low and dangerous.

"But you can't—"

"Just don't shoot to kill...unless you have to."

Duane balanced the coiled FAST rope on the rail so that it could be deployed down through the skylight with a nudge. He sat on the top of the rail and hooked one foot in place to keep himself balanced.

Helpless, unsure what would happen next, Sofia scrabbled to get her own rifle in place. Some part of her had been counting:

Twenty-eight.

Twenty-nine.

Duane placed his rifle against his shoulder and aimed down.

Thirty.

∾

"Well, isn't this cozy?"

Duane watched Carla walk into the room as if entering a ladies social club—one for which standard attire included a pair of Glock handguns and an HK416 over her shoulder.

The sudden silence was deafening.

"You know, I have some really bad news that you boys aren't going to like."

"Oh, and what's that?" The big commander with the flame tattoo stepped up in front of Carla. He was at least a foot taller and each of the arms he had crossed over his chest was as big as her waist. He still had two paint splotches on his chest from his initial Simunitions death, and a line of six more down his back from when he'd shot Sofia after he was technically dead and Duane had decided to teach him a lesson. It must hurt like a line of wasp stings, at least Duane hoped so. The next time Duane shot him, it was going to hurt much more.

"We just started streaming a nice little video of your conversation to our commanding officer. I'm sure you've heard what a patient man Delta Commander Colonel Michael Gibson is. Is there anything else you'd like to say to him? Now's your chance." Carla sounded all sweetness and light.

She could bluff her way through a brick wall. Sometimes he wondered why he bothered with breaching charges when she was around.

Two years ago—on the first day of Delta Selection—Duane had watched her face down over a hundred macho wannabes by herself. But still he couldn't believe how cool she was standing alone in front of all these assholes. He'd bet that not a one realized Carla was already in command of the room though she was the smallest one by far. Several of the guys were chilling down fast.

Not the commander.

If he'd been pissed before, he was nearly apoplectic now.

Carla put a hand to her ear as if listening. "Oh, Colonel Gibson said that he recalls you, Captain Victor (such an unfortunate name in the current situation)."

Maybe she wasn't bluffing. He should know better than to underestimate Carla.

"He says that the court-martial was very memorable. Ooo, dishonorable discharge. Two years in Leavenworth," she made loud tsking sounds. "He now has the Director of the CIA online. Sounds like she doesn't appreciate being woken up at 0200 Langley time. Look up, Captain."

He did. Not quite in the right direction to see Duane leaning out into the darkness above, but his face was very clear in the rifle scope's and camera's video feeds.

His face shifted as he figured out why she'd made him look up and his expression twisted from pissed to mean. In a move so fast and liquid that Duane almost missed it, the leader snatched one of his sidearms as he turned toward Carla. Then he grabbed for her with his other hand—intent on hostage taking, or maybe being dumb enough to think he could teach Carla a lesson.

Three things happened simultaneously.

Duane used his sniper rifle to shoot the commander's sidearm away, through the back of the man's hand.

Carla grabbed the arm that the commander was trying to grab her with, and twisted it up behind his back hard enough to make him scream in pain.

And there was the sharp spit and the click of a bolt close beside him as Sofia used her silenced G28 to shoot the SOG commander in the knee.

There was a momentary pause, then five of the men leapt to their feet.

Duane pulled out his handgun, which wasn't silenced, and shot an entire magazine into the walnut bar, placing a round in front of every SOG still seated there. The sudden roar filled the space and everyone froze.

Except for the Delta team. Just as they'd been trained, they used the distraction to surge into the room from both directions, rifles up with the safeties off and sweeping from side to side.

Someone flinched and earned a round through the arm from Chad. Another swore and Sofia's shot shattered the bottle in his hand.

Carla stepped up to the former Captain Victor, kicked him in the shot-up knee, then disarmed him while he howled.

Chad, who was as big as any of them, snapped out an evidence collection bag—a big, heavily-reinforced green garbage bag—and began collecting weapons, knives, and—in a smaller bag— anything else he could lay a hand on: wallets, IDs, watches, rings.

Duane knew Chad well enough to know that it wasn't just for show and humiliation. None of these guys were getting shit back. They were being robbed in the middle of the night on a luxury cruise liner and just didn't know it yet. Chad would probably, once the cameras were off, give it all to the bartenders still cowering behind the bar. It would make up for scaring a decade off their lives.

Melissa stepped forward with a fistful of plastic ties and began binding them hand and foot. When one kicked out at her, Duane shot him in the foot. Melissa bound it with a sea-green linen bar napkin—after she finished tying him up.

CHAPTER 8

S ofia found a room by herself. It wasn't hard, the ship had a thousand passengers fewer than it usually did. The rest of the team had opted for a pair of facing suites. She had quietly asked one of the stewards for a simple room on a different deck.

The SOGs—still bound—had been extracted before dawn. No CIA bird to whisk them back into whatever dark recesses the CIA's Special Operations Group lurked. Colonel Gibson had called in a Navy MH-53E Sea Dragon helo from a nearby aircraft carrier group. There might be no love lost between the Navy and Delta, but they were more than willing to team up against the SOGs. Especially after Duane had played his soundtrack for the helo's flight crew. The Navy was the most gender-integrated service of them all and had a real penchant for protecting their own.

Delta was to continue ashore with the cruise boat.

Which left her in limbo.

There was a soft knock on her door...and she made the mistake of answering it.

She'd expected a steward and at the last second, when it was too late to stop, half-feared it might be Duane.

"Hi!"

"Uh, hi." Sofia had never expected Carla Anderson, a thoroughly daunting woman despite her being several inches shorter than Sofia. Sofia still couldn't believe how brave Carla'd been to walk into that room the way she had, and she'd done it as if it was the most natural thing in the world. Carla wore her cinnamon-brown hair long and loose and looked like the fashion model next door. She also wore camos, a black t-shirt, Army boots, and a Glock 19 in a holster. Her face was dead serious.

"Can I come in for a minute?"

"Uh, sure. Sorry," Sofia stepped back and held the door wide. "It's not much, but you're welcome to it." The room had a king-size bed, a single chair at a desk, and a private bath. How they'd fit it all into a space smaller than her own bathroom in the Forteza family mansion without making it feel cramped was an engineer's conjuring trick.

Carla dropped into the lone chair. Not sure what else to do, Sofia sat on the bed and folded her hands.

"Did Duane do something I need to know about?"

He'd done a lot that Sofia didn't want anyone to know about, including herself. His kiss. The way he'd gotten so angry on her behalf, for something that she'd accepted as just part of her role as a woman in Special Ops—at least she'd accepted it before tonight. The way...

"Did he—" Sofia could see Carla gearing up, and then just saying it fast. "Do anything that I should have him court-martialed for?"

"What? No! What made you think that?"

Carla just waved her hand at the room. "Not quite the pick of a vacant luxury cruise ship. The *Oceanwide Whisperer* is a top-of-the-line boat, yet you lock yourself away three decks down and most of the way aft in a common suite."

"It's not Duane."

"Then who? Who on my team?" It was a lethal snarl that made the jaguar's roar in the jungle seem welcoming.

"No one!" Sofia felt as if she was being backed into a corner that didn't exist. Unaware, she had shifted across the bed until her back was against the headboard, which was the limit of how far she could get from Carla.

"Then what the hell, Forteza?"

"I'm trying to get away from *me!*" She hadn't meant to blurt it out, but there it was.

Carla froze for a long moment, then leaned back in the chair and propped her boots up on the foot of the bed. "Doesn't work, does it?" Somehow she switched gears from cool Delta operator to thoroughly outraged, then to understanding woman in mere seconds without any signs of the transition.

Sofia could only shake her head at the sudden change that had come over Carla. Minutes ago she wouldn't have believed anyone that Carla Anderson could smile, yet here she was doing just that. It turned her from dangerously beautiful—like the lethal look of a top-quality butcher's knife—to suddenly approachable.

"Everyone on the team knows that I tried to avoid myself," Carla continued. "Didn't work for crap. You figure out how to do that, you damned well better let me know the trick."

Sofia nodded again because it was all she could think to do.

"Don't speak much, do you?"

"I'm trained to listen."

"Uh-huh. So what the hell *is* wrong with you?"

"What?" Sofia was having a hard time keeping up with Carla's conversational style.

"What is it that you're trying to hide from?"

"Telling you would defeat that purpose, don't you think?"

Carla shrugged, leaned over to the mini-fridge that took up half of the foot space under the desk, and grabbed a pair of

Sanpellegrino Limonatas and two Snickers bars, tossing one of each to her. "Too bad. I'm here. So spill."

"I don't know where to begin."

"You can begin by telling me that this isn't about a dead brother."

"I don't have a dead— Wait. What?"

Carla sighed, chomped down on her Snickers bar, and spoke around the mouthful. "Melissa and I both lost brothers. In different ways, but it's what drove us both into Delta. Why are *you* here?"

"I'm not Delta. I'm with The Activity."

"Uh-huh. That's why you turned out to be a top performer in the field. We have baby D-boys fresh out of the Operator Training Course who don't do as well. You kicked ass girl, both in Venezuela and a couple times last night, so cut the bullshit. Now give."

Whether it was the bludgeoning style of Carla Anderson's staccato speech pattern or the unexpected kindness from the toughest woman she'd ever met, Sofia found that she was ready to speak. But that didn't mean that she knew where to begin.

"Family," Carla prompted. "Maybe not a dead brother, but it's always about family."

Sofia sighed, "Got me."

~

"SHIT, if this ain't the life." Chad slapped Duane hard enough on the shoulder it was a surprise he didn't dislocate something. Then he made up for it by handing Duane a beer so cold that it was dripping with sweat in the warm tropical air. Chad dropped into the next lounge chair over on their suite's deck.

The sun would be rising soon and right now the entire horizon above the dark Atlantic was painted in the softest possible pink with a pale blue arch above.

Zero-six-hundred. Time to get some shut-eye soon, but Duane doubted that he'd be sleeping, even with a beer in him.

All Duane could see was red.

He'd seen that asshole SOG grab Sofia's butt and squeeze it hard enough he'd probably left fingerprints. And something in her past had made that somehow part of "normal" life. The satisfying crack of his breaking wrist hadn't been nearly enough payback. And then he'd tried doing the same thing with Carla, which made it even worse.

When he'd overheard the SOGs' talk—and it wouldn't have taken too much to turn it back into just talk—it had been one offense too many.

"You were hard on those guys. They can't help it if they just stupid SOGs," Chad wasn't usually one for being insightful. "Don't blame you, just being surprised, buddy. Not your usual style."

Duane only grunted.

"Too bad the shits are outside of any military chain of command." Chad's comment snapped Duane back to present. "Hate to say it, but I finally get why they put us through all those stupid-ass sexual harassment trainings. I got a question, bro."

"What?"

"Can see how you feel about her. Why'd you only break his wrist rather than his neck? Thought you were better trained than that."

Duane couldn't agree more. "Mistake I won't make again."

Even at his womanizing worst, Chad never did anything a woman didn't want. Most people didn't know that about Chad because he was so damn smooth that women seemed to fall in love with him faster than you could chug a beer. But Duane had seen—Chad always left them with a smile. A trick Duane had never figured out how to do himself. Ultimately most of them scorched his back with their anger when it came time to walk away. Then the "I'm sorry" letters, begging him to call them. He'd learned not to.

Chad was still grinning at him.

"What?"

"You got it so bad, you didn't even hear it go by, bro."

"Hear what?"

"Duane and Sofia, sittin' in a tree," Chad sang. "K-i-s-s-i-n—"

Duane stood up and emptied his beer over Chad's head while Chad kept singing, before heading into his room for a sleepless night.

~

"Colina Soleada Wines? Sunny Hill? *That's* your family? Shit, you're high-end, girl."

Sofia wished she'd kept her mouth shut.

Carla bit off another big chunk of her Snickers bar and softened it with a swallow of Limonata. "You part of the family? Like, in tight?"

Sofia sighed. "Eldest of four and named heir."

"Damn!"

"That's assuming Mama does not find some way to get control and run it into the ground first. I think that's half the reason my nana is still alive, keeping Mama from screwing it up. If she didn't, my brothers would. They're worse than her in some ways. She's self-centered and careless, they're low and mean." She'd learned hand-to-hand combat fighting them off. Thankfully, they'd been too lazy to stick with the martial arts classes that Nana had started each of them in. Her battles with her brothers never lasted more than a few seconds. She'd made sure her little sister had the same training. If not for Nana, both of their lives would have been so much worse.

"So, your grandmother is why you are the way you are." Carla stated it as simple fact.

"Are you telepathic or something?"

"No, I'm just interested in what drives people."

"What about you?"

"Me? I'm easy. I'm a crazy bitch." Then she paused and crossed her feet the other way on the bed as if suddenly uncomfortable. Her voice went so soft that Sofia had to lean forward to hear her despite the small room's deep silence. "Probably gonna get me killed someday. The idea never bothered me much, but that was pre-Kyle. I still act the way I always did, but I can see it worrying him."

"Like tonight?"

"I was pissed. We fight so goddamn hard to do what we do. I was the first woman to make it into Delta the hard way. Not because they needed a woman on the team so they 'borrowed' her from the Coast Guard's MSRT or somewhere and never gave her back. I walked in through the front gate and survived Selection and the Operator's Training Course. Melissa was Number Two. We women battle for every inch, and Delta welcomed us—most of them anyway. The five or six lead SOGs in that group here are like a concentrated slime mold of all the worst of the worst from the whole military."

She huffed out a hard breath—she had straightened up as she spoke until Sofia half expected her to leap from her chair.

"Guess I'm still pissed," she collapsed back. "Only reason I didn't kill the bastard was you and Duane had already put a couple of holes in him. Nice shooting, by the way. Where did you learn that?"

"Nana."

Carla just raised her eyebrows in question.

"She was part of the very first wave of Peace Corps, answering Kennedy's call even though she left behind a husband and a vineyard for those two years. She ended up in Nigeria, where they lived in squalor and were denounced as 'international spies fostering neocolonialism.' The only way they survived was to sequester themselves in a dormitory and stage a hunger strike—

which Nana claims was *not* much of a hardship with the food they were able to get."

"She sounds like a pistol."

"In more ways than one. That first crisis was solved peacefully and she ended up liking Nigeria a great deal. But not long after she left there were multiple, violent military coups that ultimately killed millions—helpless civilians, some of whom she'd counted as friends, mowed down by war and famine. After that, she became a crack shot and made sure each of us was as well. I was raised to it."

Carla fussed with her empty Limonata bottle, rolling it back and forth between her palms as she stared at it.

Now it was Sofia's turn to ask what Carla was thinking.

"Nothing."

"Liar!"

Carla smiled briefly at the speed of Sofia's rebuke. "Okay, how about I say, 'not yet'." She stood up, stretched, and tossed the bottle in the trash. It was only when Carla had opened the doorway and stepped halfway into the hall that Sofia remembered how removed her suite was from the others.

"Carla? Please don't tell anyone else about…you know."

"About who you are? Miss Gazillionaire Heiress to one of the biggest wine fortunes in or out of the Napa Valley?"

"Yes, that. Men can become very peculiar when they find out."

Carla grinned. "You mean total shitheads. Safe with me. Won't even tell Kyle. But you won't be able to hide it forever. 'Til then, just me and Melissa will know."

"Why Melissa?"

"In case you ever need someone to have your back. She's good people. The best. The only kind of women we let on this team."

Carla stepped the rest of the way into the hall and let the door swing closed.

Sofia grabbed it before it could latch and stepped half across the threshold.

"Carla?"

She turned back to face Sofia. A lone woman standing in a never-ending corridor of soft blue carpet, pale yellow walls, and a line of doors longer than the freaky hotel hallway in *The Shining*.

"Didn't you come here to ask me why I'm at the other end of the ship?"

Carla just smiled. "Nothing gets by you, Ms. Forteza. I like that about you, a lot. But I'm not the person you need to be talking to."

Then she was gone as if she'd been whisked down the hall by the storm they'd flown through to get here.

If Carla wasn't who she should be talking to, then who the hell was?

CHAPTER 9

*D*uane stood at the threshold of the *palapa* and blinked against the sudden shade. Coming out of the bright sunlight while running on negative sleep wasn't helping shit. Visibility wasn't helped by the Panamanian noonday sun glaring harshly off the water that lay in every direction. The *palapa* stood on the end of a dock reaching well out into Portobelo's harbor. The small town and the ruins of its ancient forts were lost in the shimmering haze.

"Goddamn it."

"Chill, bro," Chad thumped him cheerfully enough on the back to drive him forward out of the tropical blaze and into the shadowed interior. He slammed into an unoccupied table that his eyes hadn't adjusted enough to see. It was only by chance he hadn't slammed into one of the stout wooden poles that held up a heavily-thatched peaked roof over the entire end of the dock.

On their approach, he'd been able to see the silhouettes of a bar and two people seated at one of the otherwise empty collection of tables. It looked like a restaurant, which should be busier at midday if it was any good. Once in the covering shade, the open sides to the *palapa* still allowed the painful glare in, but at least it was now "out there." On the plus side, "in here" the temperature was about a thousand degrees lower beneath the thatch—down to merely fucking brutal.

He rubbed at his forehead but it did nothing to ease the pain.

The tugs had nudged the disabled cruise ship against the dock in Colón at the mouth of the Panama Canal at straight-up, cook-your-brain noon. By noon plus twenty they'd turned in all of their training gear, been stuffed into a pair of minivans with no air conditioning, and driven ten kilometers north to Portobelo. The run-down harbor town wavered in the heat haze along the edge of the river.

He rubbed his eyes again, and then realized that his sunglasses were still perched on his head. No wonder his eyes hurt—Delta operators weren't designed to function during daylight hours.

Especially not after nights like last night.

Women like Sofia were *supposed* to be attracted to smooth guys like Chad. It had been that way since the moment he'd walked away from the family fortune. That's when he'd learned just how interested women were in money and not in him. But she was gone now and his life officially sucked.

Chad nudged him ahead into the dim cool shadows. A restaurant, big enough to hold twenty parties, had just the one table occupied. No one at the bar. Too bad, he really needed a beer.

"Well, look what the shit dragged in!" Chad sounded pleasantly surprised—the kind of joy he might show moments before taking out a major drug lord and all of his lieutenants with a Mother of All Bombs.

Duane's eyes finally adjusted enough to see who was at the table. "SOG Agent Fred Smith! I'll give you points for bravery, showing up after that fucking fiasco." He was completely on board with dropping a MOAB on the bastard and screw launch authorization.

"*Misplaced* bravery," he heard Carla's field knife slipping out of its sheath as she spoke.

"Sit," the other man at the table spoke in a flat monotone.

"Whoa!" Carla whispered from somewhere near Duane's shoulder and resheathed her knife with a slick, metallic sound.

Duane was finally able to focus on the second man at the table. *Holy shit!*

It was the colonel. How had he not seen the commander of Delta Force sitting there next to Fred? Because Michael Gibson was the most seasoned warrior Delta Force had ever seen and if he wanted to be invisible, he was.

Without any fuss, the team sat around the table. Kyle and Carla, Richie and Melissa, and he and Chad—too often tagged as the Odd Couple. Then Sofia Forteza slipped into a seat, almost as quietly as Colonel Michael Gibson would have.

Thank you, Jesus! He had been so sure that she was gone. No sign of her at breakfast or at the dock ramp. She must have gotten in the second minivan at the last second.

She moved like a shadow among the shadows, but her black eyes were clear and bright as she glanced over at him. He wanted to get up and change chairs to sit by her, but that would be... He wasn't sure *what* it would be, but he knew it wasn't right. Or practical. Instead he smiled at her.

She returned it in only the most tentative way. *Shit!*

Duane felt the vibrations on the floating dock under his feet before he saw the approaching waiters, coming down from the onshore kitchen. They served quickly. A large bucket filled with cans of soda and coconut water—he grabbed a Guaraná, made with one of the local fruits. A big spread of dishes were set family style in the middle of the table. A monster bowl of *sancocho* chicken soup, piles of *empanada* turnovers, a platter of banana leaf-wrapped *tamales,* and a big stack of his most recent weakness, *patacones,* twice-fried green plantain—he took a fistful—served with blazingly-hot *aji chombo* pepper sauce.

In moments the waiters were gone and they were alone at the end of the dock under the *palapa.*

Whatever the hell was going on was way above his pay grade, so he'd just keep his mouth shut. And whatever was going on with the woman across the table was even more mystifying. She'd evaporated after the incident with the SOG hardcores like a wisp of smoke and he'd half expected never to see her again. *Expected?* Hell! It had struck fear into his heart and left him thrashing in his luxury bed. He'd finally chucked a pillow on the carpet and found a little sleep on the deck.

Now, magically, like the stealthy Activity agent she was, Sofia Forteza had appeared out of thin air to sit down across from him. Across from him and offering only the chilliest of smiles. He—

Time to shut up his brain as well.

If only it could be so easy.

~

SOFIA WISHED SHE HAD A PILLOW, though she couldn't be sure where to place it. Under her butt, where the hard chair pressed painfully against the large bruises she'd received from the SOG agent who'd grabbed her? Or over her face so she didn't have to look at Duane?

She'd been so preoccupied when he smiled at her that she'd hardly returned it. This morning she'd barely caught the second van—the steward had forgotten to wake her, in that room off by herself at the stern of the ship. Duane must think she was avoiding him, or upset about his taking action last night against her advice.

By the time she saw the bastard leader gearing up to take a swing at Carla, he was lucky she hadn't shot him in the head— twice, plus one in the heart. She might have if Duane hadn't already made the crack shot of hitting his gun hand. She'd always been proud of her skills on the range, something she'd been singled out for time and again. Watching a Delta-trained sniper like Duane made her realize just how much more there was to learn.

She'd looked up the team's action reports last night after Carla left her suite—just out of curiosity so that she'd know exactly who she was dealing with...and *not* looking up Duane...at least not specifically. She had tried not to be disappointed that most of their individual records were, like any Unit operator's, behind a need-to-know wall; and she couldn't think of a good enough reason even if her clearance allowed it. The team itself had formed straight out of training over a year before and had been instrumental in devastating losses for drug cartels from Mexico to Bolivia. Their success rate was phenomenal even by The Unit's standards.

So how did an operator, especially one of Duane Jenkins' caliber, end up looking like a wounded puppy dog because she'd been too busy thinking to smile back properly?

The other's reaction to the table's two occupants had fore-warned her as she was last into the *palapa.* From that moment on, she'd been struggling to sort out the current situation's factors.

A top Delta team that had beaten the CIA's black ops team despite an overwhelming disadvantage in manpower and strategic situation—boarding an already "taken" ship.

Agent Fred Smith's presence this afternoon despite his team's recent loss.

The unexpected appearance of the Delta Force commander. It was hard to believe that Colonel Michael Gibson—the most deco-rated soldier currently serving in any branch of the military if the truth was ever known—had seen fit to come down and meet with this team.

His presence said that either there was real trouble brewing over last night's events or—as she previously postulated to Duane —there was a very dicey mission in the works.

She knew his face from the files, but hadn't ever met him before. He seemed the most unlikely version of himself. He wasn't big like Chad, not even as big as Duane. He had dark brown hair down to his shirt collar and was dressed in slacks and a black t-shirt. He looked harmless and a little lost.

It was hard to believe that he was the most dangerous man alive, even if the others were treating him that way.

Factoring in her own continued presence here didn't shed much more light on the topic, but spoke *against* the likelihood of this being a punishment or dressing down.

The other thing she couldn't piece together from the team's profile was their *modus operandi.* Delta Force was known for its mastery of the unexpected, using a small force to leverage huge results. But Carla's squad—already Sofia, too, was falling into that habit even though Kyle Reese was unquestionably the team leader —didn't even operate as if there was a box to go outside of. Their solutions, like the retaking of the cruise ship, had never come from any book or prior training. It was as if they were making it up as they went along—though that didn't make sense either.

"Thanks for coming," the colonel called the meal to order.

Sofia realized that she hadn't served herself and she had the only empty plate. She quickly did so to at least *appear* to fit in.

"About last night…"

Then she felt the tension snap around the table. Forks went down and hackles went up. Duane's hands balled into fists. She carefully set down the spoonful of *ceviche* she'd been about to bite into.

"I believe 'well done' is enough said."

Sofia was on the verge of protesting—there was a hell of a lot more to be said. Then she saw the team's faces. They looked as if they'd just been given the Congressional Medal of Honor by the President himself.

"But—" the word slipped out.

The colonel turned to face her, his soft brown eyes so calm she could read nothing in them. His hands—at least as big and strong as Duane's—were folded lightly. The dictionary definition of passively waiting.

She managed to hold on to her silence, which earned her a slow smile.

"This team," the colonel spoke softly, "created a wholly new attack methodology for one of the most difficult scenarios we train for—ship recapture. It will be fully incorporated in all future trainings. Most Unit operators will see it as a new tool in their toolbox rather than a point of departure for creating new tactics as this team does. These people are aware of this fact."

"What about—" slipped out before she could stop it.

"The CIA's Special Operations Group," the colonel continued somehow knowing exactly what she was going to say next, "lost six of its personnel last night—deemed unfit for duty. Though I fear they will next resurface in one of the contractor security firms. And not one of the decent outfits, because those have all been warned off." He glanced at his watch. "Right now, the Director of that agency is instituting a retraining of all SOG personnel, a training to be led by a Delta Force cadre, all of whom have been briefed with last night's events and recordings. She has stood down the Special Operations Group from all future global operations until I personally sign off that they are capable of meeting The Unit's minimum standards of conduct."

This time she waited him out. There was no smile but there was a brightness to his brown eyes that said he was enjoying himself immensely.

No one else spoke, of course. She now understood why. Colonel Michael Gibson embodied everything that a soldier—a very highly decorated soldier—was supposed to be. His few words carried...*gravitas*...and meant more than a thousand from any other man.

"I've told the instructor cadre they were also welcome to teach them some manners along the way. Though we will not be sharing how you beat them. That will be left as a lesson for the student."

That earned him laughter from around the table as everyone started eating once more.

CIA Agent Fred Smith looked far less distraught by that speech than she'd expected.

He noticed her attention and sighed. "I'm a field liaison, not an analyst like you and definitely not part of the action teams."

Was she still an analyst? Two actions in forty-eight hours, three if she counted the two separate encounters aboard the cruise ship. And clearly another pending with her still in the field.

Was this somehow her interim team? She certainly didn't belong. The Unit were the top combat fighters. Five years active military followed by the six-month Operators Training Course— they were in a league she could never belong.

"I am concerned with the operation, not necessarily with who is doing it. Am I disappointed? Sure. Once I saw the videos? Pissed might be a better description. I know this team's reputa- tion—I helped build it, for crying out loud. So I stacked the cards against this team, against *you*," his nod included the others around the table. "Minimum intel on the ship, four times your number on board. I might even have let drop exactly who was coming." He shrugged and bit down on an *empanada*.

The others waited while he chewed. They didn't look happy about it.

A flock of gulls circled above a returning fishing boat. Their cries were so loud, Fred had to wait a minute before continuing. He was the only one eating during the pause in the conversation. Once the boat passed, the midday heat once again pummeled the world into silence, other than the soft lapping of waves against the underside of the dock.

"My boss isn't so cocky about not using 'outside assets' anymore. I bet him that you'd win, and lose under half your team in the process. I should have gone for double or nothing if you didn't lose *any* team members but I never thought you folks were *that* good. I thought at least Ms. Forteza would go down. Nothing personal, I assure you, just a lack of field experience. Should have known," Fred shook his head sadly for the lost opportunity. "Still, I made a quick three hundred bucks last night betting on you—not that I'm likely ever to see a cent of it."

Sofia looked over at Duane. She'd survived because of how much he'd taught her, and how quickly. Ever since storming the gate of General Aguado's compound, he'd been feeding her a constant stream of tips.

Here's a 9mm tactical rope. This is a descender brake. Hold it like this and descend on the other side of the bridge.

Here's a breaching charge in case they've locked the bridge wing doors. Trigger it like this and stand with your back to it when it blows so that it doesn't mess with your night vision. The shaped charge shouldn't have any blowback—no shrapnel—except the small pressure wave of the detonation.

He'd also treated her as if he simply assumed that she'd succeed, which had made all of the difference in the world.

And then, when it had really mattered, the moment before the second attack on the group-enhanced machismo of the SOG in the elegant whisky bar, he'd given her permission to stand down on moral principles. Still no question of her capability.

His final comment before he'd descended the FAST rope to clean up a last-ditch altercation? A soft "Well done."

Now she truly understood. It was The Unit's highest form of praise. And that was all a Unit operator needed. They didn't want publicity or bestselling tell-all books. They wanted to do the job and fade away.

Her answer? To slink away into the darkness and try to analyze what had just happened. *Yep! That was definitely her. Analyze the shit out of everything, girl.* Much like Carla's "crazy bitch," it had earned her a reputation as a cold bitch—an epithet that she'd embraced because it was true. *Damn straight!* became her standard reply. It had served as her only method of survival in her family and it had served her just fine so far in the military.

Duane, however, was not looking at her. Instead, he was still watching Fred Smith.

"So," Duane toyed with a fried plantain *patacone* and managed to make it look like a steel martial arts throwing star that he might be embedding in Smith's throat at the least temptation. "What's the mission they wanted so badly that they'd risk so much to get it? And what dragged the colonel down to Panama?"

And Fred Smith, Mr. Unflappably Affable, suddenly looked grim for the first time since she'd met him.

~

"BY THE TIME we're done, you may regret last night's success," Fred was inspecting his plate. He'd finally stopped eating like the complacent bastard he'd been making himself out to be.

Duane checked in with Gibson—absolutely no expression at all.

A glance at Sofia—he still couldn't believe that she'd surfaced out of nowhere—revealed that she didn't know either. *That* he found particularly unnerving. He'd watched her put seemingly random facts together so many times over the last two nights that he'd wondered if she was psychic. He'd given her the absolute minimum training for each action—because that's all there'd been time for—and she'd picked up everything perfectly.

The one-two attack on the bridge had certainly saved his hide. He wouldn't have even come up with the attack plan in the first place if she hadn't pushed him.

And her backup at the skylight had been both perfect and remorseless. She'd fired without hesitation, even when the men in the crosshairs had technically been friendlies.

Michael started to speak, but Fred held up a hand to stop him. Man liked living dangerously.

Fred looked up slowly, inspecting each person around the table carefully before speaking.

"Any of you know about Operation Prime Cause?"

Nothing Duane had ever heard of.

"More CIA hush-hush shit?" Chad tossed out, then looked to him, waiting for Duane to drop the next line.

But he noticed Carla and Sofia both looked up quickly. Fred had their full attention, so he kept his mouth shut.

Fred nodded. "Ex-CIA field agents—"

"Special Operations Group?" Duane nearly spat on the table to clear the awful taste out of his mouth.

Fred's shrug neither confirmed nor denied. "They've been joined by other ex-Special Ops personnel from several branches, not all of them US."

"Another rogue contractor," Chad didn't sound any happier than Duane felt.

"Yeah, buddy," this time he was completely in Chad's court. "Why are we always cleaning up their shit?"

Yet Sofia, his reality check across the table, was having a different reaction that he couldn't read. She certainly didn't add the third line to their banter as she'd taken to doing.

"Quiet," was all Gibson said and they all shut the hell up. Duane tried not to feel sick that he'd spoken at all—like his mother's iced stare when he spoke out of turn at one of her dinner parties. It was no wonder he didn't speak much, he'd been trained in shut-the-fuck-up since the cradle. It had probably been engraved on his silver baby rattle.

"Not contractors. Not mercenaries," Fred Smith spoke into the void of silence. "They're a strictly non-profit group. They make contact through the US ambassador and receive full in-country cooperation from judicial and police—military if the others are too corrupt."

"What's their target?"

"Children."

"What the hell?" Not what Duane had been expecting at all.

"OPC, Operation Prime Cause, is a team of ex-field operatives who rescue kids from human traffickers, prostitution-supply rings, and brothels. They get the kids out and into an aftercare program, and they get the traffickers' asses on ice."

"Kick ass!" Chad's highest form of praise.

"Doesn't sound like a Delta mission though," Duane just couldn't see what it had to do with them.

"It's not," Colonel Gibson agreed.

"So, you're telling us this shit because..." Chad was watching the wrong person, which was weird because he always watched the hot women.

Duane could see the answer on Sofia's face. Could see the hot anger beneath her Latina skin. But it wasn't just anger. There was a hunger there. The kind of hunger that came from the sudden realization that having a real-world impact on something she felt passionate about was finally in her power.

She'd heard of OPC. Knew about them. Was—

Duane laughed aloud and everyone spun to stare at him.

"What?" Carla snapped.

Okay, maybe a laugh hadn't been the right response, but he'd just had the tiniest flash of insight into what it must be like to be in Sofia Forteza's brain. She worked for The Activity, which meant she was one of the best intel analysts in the business. She was also trained in field tactics. Was brave as a Unit operator and performing above the profile of many of them.

Add to that, the powers-that-be choosing to embed her here. In their team. At this moment. It was the power and clarity—the pure certainty of the vision that had evoked his laugh. There was a far larger plan running in the background here and he could actually hear the gears meshing as they were all caught up in it.

Was *that* what her mind was like? All the time? It sounded pretty damn busy to have all that going on constantly in her pretty head.

He thought back through his experiences of her and decided that the answer was an emphatic yes. He'd been trained by his mother, Carla, and Melissa to never judge a woman by her looks. Sofia Forteza was a stunning woman, one who blew him away. And that brain of hers that never stopped moving was equally, or maybe even more impressive.

Except perhaps for that sudden stillness of one soul-searing kiss. Then, there had been a deep silence as her eyelids had fluttered shut and for just that instant she'd given in to him.

He offered her the briefest nod of acknowledgement—that was one damn sharp lady sitting across the table—which only earned him a squint-eyed scowl.

"The reason," the colonel spoke up when it was clear that Duane was going to be keeping his mouth shut, "that you may wish you had not succeeded so well last night is because a mission that OPC *can't* handle is about to become yours."

"Which is?" Kyle's steady voice made sure no one else was going to interrupt. He'd done one of his leader things and suddenly the whole team, even Carla, had become an instrument for his command.

"The agents of OPC only go in with the full support of the government. They don't take down the traffickers themselves—in fact they come in posing as buyers of services and are very careful to be arrested right alongside the traffickers to protect their cover. Local law enforcement—or federal if the locals aren't to be trusted—and national courts make the arrests and dispense the punishments."

"Dead clean," was Kyle's assessment and no one argued. Not mercenaries. Good men with a serious cause.

"However, they do hear of situations that are outside their carefully circumscribed ROE. Situations with potentially national impact."

Rules of Engagement for a standard military op had elements like: you may not fire until fired upon, no return fire if it will put civilians at risk, and so on. It sounded as if OPC's ROE was dead sharp as well.

Whereas ROEs were always an interesting area for The Unit. The Unit's standard ROE was much looser: do what's necessary and don't let anyone know you were ever there. Civilians were rarely at risk from Unit operations because Delta Force didn't drop five-hundred-pound bombs, they typically took out villains one sniper shot at a time.

"General Aguado," Sofia stated flatly in one of her gestalt jumps that Duane realized was typical for her—and was exactly correct now that she'd said it. "Human trafficking. He's been talking."

"He has," Fred Smith agreed. "OPC are the ones who tipped us to them in the first place."

"No. I've been chasing him for six months. We..." and then she tapered off to a silence Duane didn't understand before swearing lightly in Spanish.

"OPC tipped me. I met with your boss, and he suggested that it be assigned to your desk. Colonel Richards thinks very highly of you."

"He doesn't tell me this," Sofia was inspecting her untouched meal intently. It was hard to tell in the shady *palapa* whether or not she was blushing.

Smith covered for her, which made Duane think a *little* more kindly of him. "We're here in Panama for planning and training. The geopolitical problems of Venezuela are escalating and desta- bilizing the region. My department," he was smart enough not to mention the failed CIA team directly, "and now—because of your victory last night—this team have been tasked with fixing that. The general was our first key in that lock."

No one else was eating, but Duane felt more relaxed than he had all morning and grabbed another *patacone,* then dredged it in the *aji chombo* sauce.

This was exactly why he'd signed up. Why he'd fought to get into Delta. *This* was what had driven him to survive the testing that culled over ninety-five percent of applicants.

He'd known from the first day that The Unit was home. But this? Taking on a foreign government who thought abusing its population, especially the women and children, somehow made sense. This fucking rocked!

He bit down on the *patacone* and gasped. He'd forgotten the lethal heat of the *aji chombo* sauce.

CHAPTER 10

"*W*hat has changed for you, Duane Jenkins?"

He leaned on the railing of the *casa* over-looking the Portobelo harbor, looking to her as if he was searching far beyond the horizon. A gigantic flock of pelicans flew in, skidding onto the water close by the building The Unit had taken over until the surface was dotted gray and white as much as it was turquoise water. Swallows soared above, feeding on the evening bugs in happy loops and swirls.

Sofia had seen the moment he'd shifted from curious to committed. Duane Jenkins was two people as surely as if he was twins who kept trading places before her eyes.

Duane One was the easy-going Delta shooter. Laughing with Chad, patient when giving her new techniques she hadn't known, holding her close and showing her the detonator the moment before he blew the crap out of something—she would bet much money that he had thoroughly enjoyed that. A comfortable man who had kissed her without permission. It had been a long time since a man had gotten past her defenses far enough that she didn't break his nose or at least take a good shot at busting his balls for doing such a thing. Quite why she'd allowed that from Duane One still eluded her.

Duane Two she'd only met twice. Once above the skylight open to the whisky bar below. It had been a fierce and brutal warrior who had called in the second attack on the SOGs. In retrospect, Sofia wondered at the immense control he'd shown in not simply laying waste to them all.

The only other place she'd seen such fury was in her own mirror the night before she left home to join the military. The night her mother had slapped her—Sofia had been too shocked to defend herself—and wished that she'd never had such a useless bitch of a daughter.

The second time she'd seen Duane Two had been at the lunch table under the breezy *palapa*. Something had transformed him. Everyone had gone somber. She could *feel* the oppression suffered by the women. Had seen it on the faces in General Aguado's compound. Had seen it...many places. She knew about OPC, donated money to them. Had read the stories about the children—

And suddenly Duane had started eating with a large appetite and glowing smile—an avaricious one. One she couldn't make sense of and she postulated it was greed for vengeance. That, alarmingly, fit Duane Two well.

Tonight, she could see Duane One hauling his thoughts back from wherever he'd gone until, finally, he was standing beside her on the *casa's* balcony, looking out over the bay.

The sun was dropping over the hills behind them. Sailboats, fishing trawlers, and an odd selection of luxury yachts were anchored out in the sleepy town's harbor.

She'd asked about those because there were far more than such a small town would justify. It seemed that a lot of the yachts had belonged to over-extended travelers who had simply abandoned them here after they'd gone broke. Coastal cargo freighters were anchored when they couldn't find another contract—left to float or sink. The wide bay floor was apparently littered with several thousand wrecks spanning the last four centuries. Luxury yachts were sometimes docked and a check arrived each year for their upkeep, but the boats were never retrieved. Eventually, when the checks stopped arriving, the boats began their long decay toward a final resting place at the bottom of the bay. Or a hurricane slammed ashore and took care of a large number of them all at once.

The old forts, burned by pirates four hundred years ago, were a UNESCO World Heritage site and dominated the waterfront with its old stone and rusted Spanish cannons. Once *the* great trading port for shipping Peruvian silver to Spain—and the most fortified town in the Americas when it had boasted ten separate forts—only UNESCO's attention had saved it from abandonment and total ruin.

Duane looked breathtakingly powerful against the backdrop.

"What changed for you at the table?" She asked the question again. Asked it before she could do something she'd regret later, like reaching for him.

"How much do you know about me?"

Leave it to Duane to understand her role as an Activity analyst and that, of course, she'd have done her homework. "Nothing prior to you entering Delta Selection except your rank and a listed home city of Atlanta, Georgia."

He nodded and leaned back on the rail, still facing away. They were on the *casa's* middle floor, at one end of the long balcony.

"Dad works for a major company there."

"Coca-Cola."

"Atlanta isn't just Coke. We have Delta (the airlines, not The Unit), FedEx, UPS, Home Depot, AT&T Mobility… Bunch of others. They're all bigger."

"Okay," that would teach her not to assume.

"But you're right."

She punched him on the arm hard enough to make him flinch. All he had the decency to do was laugh—it had been a good punch. Again she was overwhelmed by the solidness Duane represented.

"Dad's way up. Mr. Third-generation Major Corporate. I was following in his footsteps, Mr. Goody Two-shoes Fourth-gen Junior Executive-in-training. Just about had my goddamn MBA. Wrote a thesis on Coke, one the whole board read—changing several long-term growth policies. They made my thesis professor sign a nondisclosure before the company would let him read it."

He went back to brooding on whatever had brought him out here into the sunset.

"What made you walk away?"

Duane cricked his neck as if it was suddenly paining him. "Shit!" He turned and dropped into one of the creaky wicker chairs that faced the water. She sat in the one close beside him and waited.

Silence was one of the best tactics she'd ever learned for extracting information. Gregarious people couldn't stand the void and felt a need to fill it with words. The more reticent ones, like Duane, needed to be left the space to gather their thoughts before they spoke. The sky darkened visibly before he spoke again.

"My Dad took me on a tour. International sales. Twenty cities in thirty days. Multiple meetings every damned day—showing me his job and also my introduction to the major players, country by country. You know how the poorest people often live by the airports?"

She nodded, not quite following the subject change.

"Mexico City, Panama City, Bogotá, Quito, Caracas was particularly horrid, Rio might have been even nastier, Joburg, Nairobi, Cairo, Mumbai…It was like some crazy rollercoaster ride of all the worst the world could hand out. I remember sitting in the back of our limo—sometimes our *armored* limo with a police escort because Coke is that important to their economy and Dad is that high up—and just watching out the window. I like a cold one as much as the next Georgia boy, but I kept thinking that there was no way in hell *Sharing a Coke* was going to fix any of that shit. I took to skipping the fancy dinners after all the meetings and walking through the cities instead. Only the 'nice' neighborhoods at first, but it didn't take me long to buy tattered jeans, tennies, and a poor-man's t-shirt and start walking into the worst of them. What I saw out there still gives me nightmares."

"So you joined the military."

"I figured I could help more people that way. Actual, real-life help."

But Duane's reaction today had been stronger than that. "There was something different for you today."

For the first time since lunch he looked right at her. His eyes were a honey-gold and she couldn't look away from them. "You are direct, aren't you?"

"I am not a woman who likes unsolved puzzles."

"And I'm your current puzzle."

His statement surprised her—because it was true. *He was.* Duane was very attractive. And he'd proved a deep kindness in how he'd helped her along. But there was something about him that she still didn't understand.

He slouched lower in his chair, the aged wicker complaining bitterly. The sun had set beyond the mountains and the fast tropical night was slamming into place. It felt as if Duane was fading into the dark.

"Why did you laugh?"

"What? When?"

"At lunch, with the colonel. You laughed while we were talking about human trafficking." Sofia recalled the whole team flinching as if they'd been slapped.

"Well, shit. That doesn't sound very good, does it?"

"Then what were you laughing at?"

"You," he grunted it out as if it pained him.

"Excuse me?" There was still enough light to see Duane's smile at her arch tone.

"And that would be *at* and not *with*. Just so we're clear on that point."

~

"You were laughing at me?" Her tone of justifiable outrage just cracked him up.

Duane could do this all night. Teasing Sofia Forteza was the best thing. Well, second best, after fighting beside her. Third best after holding her. Fourth after kissing her…

And he'd wager good money that bedding her would be a whole new level of wonderful. So, the teasing was sliding down the scale fast, but it was still undeniably worthwhile.

"I got to see inside your brain for a moment."

"You what?"

"Your thoughts are very busy, Sofia Forteza. Do you always think so hard?"

"It's my brain that sets me apart."

"That combined with your million-dollar looks."

Even in the fading light he could see her jolt as if he'd slapped her.

He managed to catch her wrist before she could bolt from the chair. She made it to her feet, but stopped. With her back turned to him, only his hold on her wrist kept her anchored in place. "You've got to know that you're incredibly beautiful."

She remained. Frozen like a statue. But she didn't pull to free herself, leaving him to feel her pulse racing beneath where his thumb had landed.

"Sofia?" What had some bastard done to her? If he ever found out who, Duane would fry him, mash him, and fry him again just like a goddamn *patacone*.

"You were only talking about my looks?" Her voice was small, too small to belong to Sofia Forteza, and that bothered him a lot.

"That *and* your brain. There's a whip-smart lady in there. To this Southern boy, that's at least as charming as anything else you have going on. Ma'am."

He could feel her pulse slowing, could feel the tension sliding out of her wrist muscles. Some lights had come on in the town, but not enough to cast more than a soft glow up to their balcony. Against the darkest blue of the sky, he could see her tilting her head just enough to call bullshit. Her defenses were coming back online.

"Okay, it's your killer body that has me completely charmed. Nothing else. I swear," he raised his free hand as if taking the Officer's Oath. "Well, maybe your smile. It's a hell of a smile, ma'am. Lights you up right purdy," he went for a slide into good-ol'-boy and was pleased with the tone he hit. It also seemed to halt her hardening defenses in surprise.

"Give me one good reason to keep listening to this baloney you spew out so simply."

"Easy," Duane decided what the hell and went for the truth. It wasn't like he had anything to lose. "I can't stop thinking about you. I keep expecting you to be gone and I'll never see you again. After Venezuela and again after the debriefing. After the cruise ship. After today's meeting at lunch. *My* brain doesn't seem to care. It just keeps thinking about you."

Sofia remained very still in the darkness. He could no longer see her features. No longer see if she mocked him with an eyebrow raise. All he could feel was the soft heartbeat in her wrist.

He pulled her toward him with a slight tug. She stumbled forward as badly as if he'd yanked on her arm hard instead of barely holding her wrist between his fingertips.

She recovered her balance and finished the step forward until they were toe to toe, her standing, him sitting and sliding his thumb on the soft flesh inside her wrist.

Then her shadow leaned down to him.

"You'd better be worth it, Mr. Duane The Rock." Her breath a warm brush on his cheek. Her scent sweet and heady. And rich with a depth that promised wonders. When her lips brushed his he learned that, indeed, honesty was the best policy.

~

SOFIA WAS QUESTIONING every single moment.

Duane's nailing her with his "million-dollar looks" comment. His number was far too low, but she'd certainly heard the phrase before in much less inviting ways. Had the fact that he came from money caused him even half as much trouble as it had caused her? She hoped not.

But she actually believed him about the innocence of his remark, which was a first.

Innocence? Ha! He was turning her knees into jelly, making her forget how to stand or think coherently. His gentle hold on her wrist—that she knew he would release at her slightest tug—sent shivers up her arm. Good shivers. As if he was waking up the dormant nerves one by one that had felt nothing for too long and now were in shock from his simple touch.

It was like that brief kiss on the cruise ship. It had wiped her brain and left her standing there, helpless to stop something so good. Is that what a kiss was *supposed* to feel like? Warm, tender, questioning? She was far more used to demanding, manipulative, and coldly calculating.

She gave in to his gentle tug on her wrist, but held on to at least a shred of her common sense. Without breaking the kiss, she managed to sit back in her chair rather than in his lap. It was a good choice. One, these chairs were questionable for one person —if she sat in Duane's lap, twice the weight was sure to dump them to the decking. Two, if this small contact with Duane was affecting her so much, curling up in his lap into a melting girl puddle generated an unacceptable risk factor.

The low chair arms were little enough barrier as it was. One hand drifted up to cradle her cheek—a big, hard hand, rough with calluses. He slipped his fingers around her neck. But rather than dragging them closer, he used his fingertips to trace the line of neck and shoulders.

His other hand never released her pulse. She didn't need to feel it, she could hear it roaring to life, far louder that the music drifting along from the *taberna* coming to life next door.

Sofia had long ago stopped telling men about her family and her wealth, yet still it was the first time she felt as if a man was kissing her and not her fortune.

He rose slowly to his feet and, helpless to do otherwise, she followed him. If he swept her into his arms and dragged her into one of the bedrooms, would she complain? In her current mood, she didn't think she'd mind if he slammed her up against the wall, tore off her clothes, and went at her hard and fast in the darkness of the night.

"Duane?" she managed. Though she didn't know what she was asking. Men only ever saw two things about her: her money, before she stopped telling anyone, and her body. Duane had seen her fight, offered her comfort to face her first field kill, and had complimented her mind. It even sounded as if he somehow understood her—which put him in a minority of one, because she most certainly didn't.

She wound her arms up and around his neck, ready to hang on for whatever came next.

Where had her willpower gone?

When had her absolute conviction that she wasn't the sort of woman for a short term fling fallen by the wayside?

When was Duane going to make the next move?

Then strangely, impossibly, with their arms wrapped around each other in the Panamanian night, Duane "The Rock" Jenkins began to dance with her. The balcony was too narrow. The wicker chairs too close.

Yet he whirled her about in a dance that started slow, but soon had them apart.

He was...masterful. She followed his lead, feeling as confident in it as she had racing along the upper deck of the cruise ship with him—too wrapped up in the moment to think.

He twirled her out, guided her back with a tug on her arm, spun her in a quick pirouette, with his arm still holding her hand but raised just enough for her to slide under it with each turn.

"I don't know how to dance," she managed on something closely related to a giggle of delight.

"Me either."

She snorted out a laugh in response.

"I'm just making it up as I go along, genius lady." He twirled her out again.

Let her hang at the end of the spin for a moment.

She was tipped out over the balcony rail, held from falling in for a swim only by his lightest hold on her fingertips.

Then he guided her back with a hard enough tug that their bodies slammed together and his arms were suddenly tight about her. So tight she could barely breathe.

"How long do we have, Sofia?" His voice was low, dangerous, and she didn't need any light to know Duane Two—perilous, dangerous—was now holding her.

She could only shake her head. "A night? A week? No one is telling me."

He stroked a hand down her: hair, back, hip, and behind.

What was she willing to do? Right now she couldn't think straight. Her senses as well as her arms were filled with him. He smelled like the tropical night, redolent with spice and promise and hot with a passion that could consume her, and a taste like a 2009 Napa Merlot—a solid structure with a lively edge to grab her undivided attention.

He kissed her hard, so hard that one of her legs wrapped around him of its own free will to draw them closer together.

His hand slid along her leg, caressing the length of it, until he reached behind him and slowly unwound it. Only when she was solidly back on her own two feet did he start to disengage.

"Sofia?"

"Uh-huh."

"I don't believe I'm going to say this."

"Uh-huh," she'd rediscover speech soon. Maybe after she discovered fire and invented the wheel.

"I don't want you like this."

"Uh—what?"

"You're not a one-night stand kind of woman."

She wasn't. "Is that what this is?" She leaned in to taste his lips again for a moment. Maybe for Duane she could learn to be.

"I don't know," he leaned his forehead against hers. "But as much as I want you, I don't want to have that between us."

I do! Her body practically screamed it aloud without passing through her vocal cords. The fog that he cast on the turbulent waters, churning alive inside her, was making it very hard to see what was happening. She dropped her head down onto his shoulder and hung on for a moment.

This is not like me. This is not like me.

And it wasn't.

How could a kiss...unwoman her? She'd spent a lifetime learning to stand up and be strong. Since birth, her grandmother had indoctrinated in her a woman's strength. And all she wanted was...

"Try that again? Why don't you want to make love to me?"

"Welcome to the conversation." It took her a moment to recognize that Duane was using her own words from their first meeting in the sniper position above Aguado's camp.

"Throwing a woman's words back at her is not a way to win points."

"The way you're holding me, I'm not too worried about the score."

So she let go of him. It was harder than peeling away a double-wide band of military-grade Velcro. She could feel the tearing of it as she did: lifting her head, shuffling back until their bodies were no longer layered together like sniff, sip, and savor at a wine tasting, and finally unwrapping her arms from about his neck where they'd entwined like a centuries-old grape arbor.

When the cooling sea breeze finally had space to slip between them, her sanity wended its way back to her.

She couldn't believe it was happening, not until their positions from last night were reversed—his two strong hands on her shoulders, stepping her back, even as he leaned in to tease out a last kiss.

Her knees slowly gave way. If Duane hadn't guided her landing, she'd have been on the deck rather than one of the creaky wicker chairs.

"What was that?"

"I know what I'd call it." How could he sound so calm and rational? She'd had sex that didn't measure up to that kiss. Actually, maybe she'd *never* had sex that measured up to that kiss.

"And?" she prompted him when he didn't answer.

He creaked into the chair beside her and took her hand. "A taste of heaven."

Pure and utter hogwash. But she couldn't think of a better word for it.

～

DUANE LAY in bed but had no idea how he'd gotten here or why he was in it alone.

The Unit typically fought at night and slept during the day. But the short sleep on the cruise ship and nothing else for forty-eight hours wasn't his problem. Sleep deprivation and Unit operators were old friends.

Intelligence Support Activity Agent Sofia Forteza absolutely was the problem.

"Since when do I resist a woman who throws herself at me?" He whispered it into the darkness.

"Bro!" Chad hissed from the next bed over. "You didn't?"

Shit! He'd forgotten about Chad. They'd landed in the same room.

"You turned down Forteza? She's a hot chick, bro. You're telling me she opened the goddamn door and you didn't walk through it? Didn't I teach you shit?"

Duane sighed. Apparently not.

Chad shuffled around in the darkness. They were shifting over to daylight operations while they were in Panama, but sleep wasn't any closer despite the darkness.

He could feel that Chad had twisted round to face him. "Tell me one good reason why."

Duane could think of a dozen reasons, all true and none of them relevant. The only thing that mattered was that a woman like Sofia Forteza actually *did* throw herself at him. And, oddly, that was what had stopped him cold.

"C'mon, bro. You try to hide shit from me and you'll be getting the noogie to beat all noogies," the bedsprings pinged as Chad began climbing out of the sheets.

"Okay!" He knew that Chad would deliver. "Remember when you were in college and—"

"No college, bro. I got my higher education in the Army."

"Sorry," he'd forgotten. "Remember back in high school—"

"Didn't have much of that either."

"Shut up, Chad!"

"Yes, sir!" Chad had gotten his GED during Basic Training. Self-educated—mostly living in the library when the Detroit streets got too cold in the winter—he'd sat all the tests back to back and they'd stamped him as way smarter than the average bear.

"You wanna hear this?" Duane resisted pummeling Chad in the

face with his pillow. Chad was close enough, but then he'd keep the pillow for himself.

"Fire away! Gotta hear why you turned down the hottest babe to ever offer you the whole enchilada."

"That's the problem," Duane sat up and looked across at Chad in the darkness.

The ancient concrete floor was rough and pitted against the bottoms of his feet, but pleasantly cool.

"Before…" He could barely remember the man he used to be.

"When you were being Mr. Rich Playboy?"

"Yeah, back then. I'd roll up in my ragtop Corvette—"

"Always buy American," Chad chimed in. They knew each other's stories too well. To Duane's way of thinking, of course a kid with a Coca-Cola endowed heritage bought American.

"Take them out for a ride and they'd give me a whole different kind of ride later." Hard to believe he'd ever been so crass. Or maybe not. Rich, mostly left on his own as long as he aced school and a sport—captain of the track team had only enhanced his ability to sweep up the girls.

"Sure, they'd screw you until your eyeballs fell out. Mr. Rich Happy Boy. All the debs hoping for the golden ticket by going to the one-man ball."

Duane shrugged uncomfortably. "Yeah, that was about the size of it."

"You showed up with your Vette and your bottomless bank card and *I* might have done you."

"Thanks for a mental image that now I'll never be rid of."

"Glad to help, bro."

"Why am I telling you any of this?"

"One of two reasons," Chad sounded entirely too cheerful. "Either you're fucked up enough to think I'm gonna help you…"

"Doesn't sound like something you'd do, does it?"

"Nope! Or, you fucked up. Period."

But Duane didn't buy that. It *had* been the right thing to do.

Step back. Slow it down. He just didn't know why. "Maybe I just don't want to watch the best time of my life walking away from me at the end of this mission."

"Maybe you'll never know if she *woulda been* your best time because you, you damned fool, said no to *that*. She's the hottest thing since corndogs with ketchup." It was easy to imagine Chad waving his hand about in the dark toward Sofia's room. "Don't even know why I'm speaking to someone that dumb." He heard Chad thump back down onto his pillow.

Duane thought about it for a while. "I didn't want to mess it up."

"If you can tell me what 'it' is in that sentence, I'll give you twenty bucks and a kiss. Else you'll owe me the same."

"How much to not get the kiss?"

"A hundred. But I'm worth it. The ladies definitely tell *me* I'm worth it." Implying Duane definitely wasn't.

"Shut up."

"I would if you'd stop yammering and just go lay the woman."

Still, Chad had a point. What was the "it" he didn't want to mess up? His and Sofia's "relationship" so far constituted blowing up a jungle prison, taking out a CIA team—twice—and a hellaciously amazing pair of kisses. The "it" was some unimagined, undefined future…something.

Duane thumped back down onto his pillow himself, no closer to an answer.

"So, do I get my kiss?" Chad asked softly.

"Go to hell, Chad."

"Aw, bro," Chad offered his sympathy and, not long after, his snores.

CHAPTER 11

*S*ofia couldn't help admiring Operation Prime Cause's jump team leader, also OPC's founder, because he was putting his life and limb at risk for something he believed in. Steve—who was at least former CIA Special Activities Division, if not former Special Operations Group (he wasn't saying)—looked completely normal. Blond-haired, blue-eyed, Steve embodied the friendly guy next door who was glad to lend you his lawnmower. And the instant talk shifted from introductions to operations, the change had swept over him—pure business. Even sitting in a circle of Unit operators he didn't pale by comparison: very driven, very committed.

He and Duane also took to each other right away, which she interpreted as a good sign.

Now she was in the jump team's operations center. It was in the back corner of a warehouse in the Colón, Panama, port. Outside, on the next pier over, the disabled cruise ship they'd arrived on stood out ostentatiously along the industrial section of the waterfront across Manzanillo Bay.

Inside there was just enough room in front of the communications gear for her, the OPC's man, and the lieutenant assigned by the local chief of police. She wasn't quite sure of her role here, but appreciated a chance to talk intelligence gathering with another professional. OPC's man was very forthcoming about their field data collection methodology—something she was glad to reciprocate as much as she could. He often made notes on tactics she mentioned that he said he was aware of but wanted to be sure to incorporate in future operations.

The police lieutenant rapidly grew bored, which she didn't like. In his job he should be as eager as she was for this type of information.

Today was the actual take-down operation. OPC had already been on the ground for several days prior to The Unit's arrival, making contacts and being careful not to spook the target.

The rest of the team were gathered around in folding steel chairs or standing—they at least were paying close attention. She'd been unable to read Duane's expression this morning, his dark sunglasses weren't helping. No man had ever refused her so graciously.

It hadn't taken much to figure out that Duane was many things in addition to being a Unit operator. Duane One and Two embodied the aspects of the helpful fellow soldier and the pure warrior. Duane Three was—against all chance—a Southern gentleman. She hadn't even known that such men existed anymore. If they ever really had. Sofia expected that history had been filled with far more Rhett Butlers than Ashley Wilkeses.

She still didn't know whether to be charmed or irritated.

"We're going in," came over the radio.

In moments, everyone focused on the flat-screen monitors fed from the hidden video cameras they'd planted yesterday in a small house just four blocks north of the warehouse. Sofia could see the jump team entering the living room. They were posing as four Americans, fresh off the ships in Colón's Free Trade Zone and after a little virginal companionship.

Sofia didn't know if she'd be able to do that—pretend for even a moment that it was something desirable. They set out food and a small gift table in the dining room. Then they sat down to wait.

"We never know if they're actually going to show," OPC's man said. He hadn't offered any name other than Joe. The way he was so slow to answer to the name made it obviously not his. Who knew what the leader's real name was? They were all strictly on a first name basis.

"How often do you get no-shows?"

"Roughly one in four. We do a lot of prep before we get to this stage. Typically five hundred dollars or so has changed hands for promises to deliver. Virgins run three to ten thousand. And—" He tapped a monitor focused on the street outside the house.

A car and then a pair of vans pulled up. Four men climbed out and began opening doors and shooing out girls. Sofia had to put her hand over her heart as she watched. They were of several races, mostly Latina and black with a few Chinese. None of them could have even been sixteen.

"Uh-oh." Joe didn't sound happy.

"What?"

"I'm counting fourteen girls so far. This happens sometimes. When the traffickers think they have deep-pocketed buyers on the hook, they'll try to sell as many girls as they can at once. We bring extra cash, but making a new deal slows things down."

"Can't you take them down now?"

"No. They will just say these are all sisters and cousins and they were invited to bring them to a party. The food and gifts support that. We need the deal itself, on tape, before we can act."

Sofia zoomed in the images, zeroing in on the men herding the girls up the front walk. "They're armed. Handguns in their waist-bands under their shirts."

"All four?" Joe didn't question her. Just took it at face value. "I only spotted it on the leader and one other."

"All four," Sofia confirmed. "See how this one bends strangely at the waist when he leans forward? The hammer is jabbing him in the gut. These two carry it in back, you can see their untucked shirts aren't sliding freely across their backs as they walk. The leader in the jacket either has a very strange chest or he is wearing a twin shoulder rig."

Joe transmitted all of the information softly to the team.

"What is your team armed with?"

"Their wits."

Sofia could only stare at him in disbelief.

Joe grimaced, "Firefights on foreign soil aren't what we do anymore. Also, we can be fully frisked if the sellers get paranoid. Which is almost always."

In moments the girls, some so young that they probably really were virgins, went in to the "party" set out in the dining room. Even after a confirmation by one of the OPC guys that it was all for them, they were very hesitant about touching the food or gifts. Finally, the smallest girl reached out and pet a small stuffed dog. That seemed to break the ice as much as anything.

With the girls safely isolated, the men got down to business.

"Where are your men place—" Sofia turned to the police lieutenant, but his seat was empty.

"Maybe he had to hit the bathroom." Sparing only a quick glance, Joe kept his eyes on his team.

She spun around to look at the Delta team. Duane shook his head and pointed toward the open door.

"The boss seller's cell phone is ringing," Joe spoke up.

Duane didn't even hesitate. He slapped Chad and they both sprinted to the door.

There was a loud yelp of pain from close outside the warehouse.

Sofia turned back in time to see that the bad guys' leader was just reaching for his phone. His hand stopped inches away from it, then he visibly shrugged when it stopped ringing.

She saw Chad and Duane dragging the battered police lieutenant back into the warehouse.

"Ring his captain," Duane called out. "We need to know where his men are and how to reach them. Hope to hell that he's not bent as well."

Chad turned to Duane. "Twenty and that kiss you owe me says there aren't any police on station."

Duane's grimace said he'd lost some kind of strange bet. He then dug into the lieutenant's pockets and came up with a badge.

"You," he pointed at Sofia. "Call the captain and get a squad there on the double."

She grabbed her phone and had to hunt around for the number. Joe finally found it and handed it to her. Lesson: next time have all essential contacts on speed dial.

"Everyone else," Duane called out as he tied and gagged the lieutenant, "you're with me."

Even before the captain picked up his phone at the station, the entire Delta team was out the door.

This is what Sofia did: live intelligence in the field. But it felt wrong to watch her team sprint out the door and not be with them. Wait! *Her* team?

The captain answered and she'd have to think about that later.

"He was one of my best," the captain sounded furious. "How did those bastards get to him?"

She didn't need to remind him to focus on the immediate problem because, in between imprecations, he was screaming for a strike team.

∾

AT THE LIEUTENANT'S van in the warehouse parking lot, Duane paused. It would help if they had some more authentic gear than one measly badge.

It was locked.

"I should have grabbed the keys." A Delta team's flexibility meant that he was the mission leader because he'd taken first action. It was part of their deeply-trained unpredictability.

He glanced at Chad and then at the side window on the van.

Chad rammed a rifle butt against the window—and it bounced off. Bulletproof glass. With a curse, Chad whipped a jimmy tool that he just happened to have in his thigh pocket—there was a reason he liked teaming with Chad, who slid it between the glass and the door. The van unlocked with a snick. In moments they were loaded up with handcuffs and bright yellow jackets that said *Policía* across them in large letters.

When they'd come up to the van, there had been a couple of forklift operators in the area, running cargo from one warehouse to the next. In the twenty seconds they spent rifling through the lieutenant's vehicle, this whole area of the warehouse yard had emptied.

As they started running out of the warehouse district, Duane clicked on his radio and called Sofia.

"I'm here," she responded immediately. "The deal is going fast. Hurry."

"Already hustling, ma'am."

The light traffic at the edge of the residential district didn't even flinch at the sight of a phalanx of six heavily-armed individuals in yellow police jackets, sprinting across the road and racing up the sidewalk. Kids playing soccer in the street were soon a noisy band following along behind them to see what happened.

"Young boys got no sense of self-preservation," Chad huffed out from close behind him.

"Don't we know it."

"Too bad so many of them survive anyway," Sofia added in one of her punchline tones that forced a laugh out of him.

"Just make sure that the real cops, when they get here, don't shoot us."

"Worry. Worry. Worry," Sofia teased him even though they were in the middle of an operation.

It was the most heartening thing he'd heard all day. Last night he'd turned her down cold. She could have easily decided that he was a jerk and she wanted nothing to do with him.

He'd worried more as she'd descended into her element with the OPC team. She and "Joe" were soon talking about things they never taught mere Unit operators—at least not in any parlance that he recognized. Was it just a subject they were both passionate about, or was she trying to make him jealous as both she and the OPC guy got wound up about intelligence operations? He was finally hoping it was the former, but it didn't stop one bit of the jealousy.

"Hold short," Sofia called. "The deal isn't closed yet. Police are still eight minutes out."

"No sirens 'til it's done."

"I have told them this, but I am not one to be making any promises."

At the end of the block, he turned to the crowd of boys who'd followed them and pointed emphatically at the ground. "*No pasado aquí!*"—Not past here! The eldest nodded and stopped the younger ones from following.

He held up three fingers and flagged them to the right around the corner. Half the team split off to go up the next street and cut off any escape that way.

Their team of three continued along the block until they were just two doors from the target house. They quickly ducked down behind a trio of trashcans. Chad and Carla had followed him. That meant Kyle, Melissa, and Richie were covering the back.

"So why are you scaring the daylights out of Sofia?"

Duane twisted around to see Carla watching him from the next garbage can over. He hoped to god she'd turned off her microphone. He doused his own.

"He's not scaring her," Chad spoke from behind his own trash can to Carla's other side. "She threw herself at him and he totally dissed her. Not nice, bro."

"I didn't—" Why was he even trying?

"No woman likes getting all wound up and then being told her man doesn't want her."

"I didn't dis her! I just—"

"—didn't take her to bed," Chad pointed out, happy to hoist Duane on his own petard.

"You don't want her?" Carla glared at him.

"Of course I do."

"They why did you say no?"

"Yeah, bro, why?"

Duane leaned out from behind his can just long enough to glance at the target building that had once been white but was now a mildewed gray. He begged them to get the damn deal done.

Chad hit him in the head with a wadded up ball of old newspaper that smelled like it might have once been wrapped around a fish. Carla pinged him with an old sock.

This wasn't happening.

He checked his six—back along the block—but the young boys were still down at the end of the street. The more bored ones had restarted the soccer game while they waited for some action.

His watch said there was at least five more minutes before any cops would be arriving, so they weren't going to save him from Carla's interrogation either.

"Hey, I'm the good guy here!"

Duane barely managed to duck an old sneaker that Chad threw at him. Which earned him Carla's toss of the other dirty sock square in his face.

"Because I like her too much to risk hurting her! Okay?" It snapped out of him hard enough to make his two attackers freeze even though their arms were cocked back with more ammunition.

"Was that so hard?" Carla asked softly.

"Yes. No. I don't—"

"Go! Go! Go!" Sofia called over the radio.

The other two dumped their garbage and the three of them

sprinted up the street side by side, unslinging their rifles as they ran.

He didn't even bother slowing down but hit the front door at full speed with his shoulder. The frame blew apart as he dove and rolled to a kneeling position, his rifle tucked against his shoulder and aimed at the circle of men and the small knapsack over-flowing with money.

Chad dove through an open window as Carla stepped in from the next room that she must have reached through a side window.

The B team came in the back before the bad guys could even brace to run. The girls' screams shattered the air as Kyle turned aside to make sure they stayed put. But Melissa and Richie were there with rifles at the ready.

By the time the real police arrived, the Delta team had everyone disarmed and cuffed: the four traffickers and the four American "buyers" from the OPC jump team.

Then Carla used her rifle butt to crack the lead trafficker in the balls, hard. He crumpled.

"Resisting arrest," was all she said.

Duane didn't argue.

He tasked the others with escorting the jump team outside (with believable shoves and curses). Chad grabbed the knapsack filled with OPC's seed money and dumped it into an evidence bag that he took away from one of the real police. He and Carla hung back until the aftercare team arrived to transport the frightened girls to safety. No way was he relinquishing anyone other than the traffickers to the real police. Duane dragged the police captain aside when he complained.

Once they were out of sight of the captain's men, Duane slammed him against the wall. "You said that the lieutenant who tried to betray our team was one of your best. You want to impress me, get him and those four bastard traffickers, who think selling underage girls for profit is a good time, incarcerated.

Maybe I'll trust you after you've sent me the balls of all five of the bastards in a baggie. *Comprendes?*"

"*Sí,*" the captain looked almost as pissed as Duane felt.

He hadn't even been aware of pulling his sidearm and ramming it up under the man's chin. He reholstered it. "*Mis disculpas.*" But not very sorry. "I'll be sure that your bosses and the justice department are notified if you let any of them slip through your fingers."

The captain straightened his uniform and glared at Duane before stalking out of the room. By the time Duane reentered the room, the head trafficker had to be carried out; now his face was bloodied as well. Maybe he really hadn't known about the lieutenant—who'd jolted to his feet the moment the traffickers' faces had come on screen. Should have been Duane's cue. He wouldn't miss it again.

Sofia rolled up in the corrupt lieutenant's police van and they hustled the jump team into the back before driving them all back to the warehouse.

~

THEY DID this for five setups over two days, all within a ten-block radius around the warehouse to either side of the Free Trade Zone.

Sofia tried to take some reassurance from the fact that Panama was a Tier 2 country on the US government's human trafficking categorization—which meant not the best, but making an effort to fight and prosecute it. It was the tier in which the United States ranked forty percent of the world's countries. An almost equal number of countries' citizens lived in Tier 2 "Watch List" (which was way worse than Tier 2) or Tier 3 conditions. Tier 3. The twenty-seven worst countries in the world for human trafficking. A level that Venezuela recently had fallen into after a long and painful slide. Much worse and they'd end up joining the three "specials": Libya, Somalia, and Yemen.

The US average of four trafficking cases per hundred thousand of population sounded awful—roughly four thousand per year. Then Joe had showed her Venezuela's and other Tier 3 numbers, mostly in the one- to three-hundred per hundred thousand.

"And you guys are going after them one trafficker at a time?"

Joe had shrugged and replied, "It's what we do."

Seeing the terrified girls they'd rescued over the last two days made her ill. And this was a good country? An ally in the war against trafficking humans?

Operation Prime Cause had arranged five separate "buys" while in Panama. Twenty-three traffickers in jail and one-third of them were women, which was beyond comprehension, selling off other people's children. Fifty-three girls and eleven boys rescued —none of them over sixteen and many with over three years "experience" in the trade. Plus one goddamn police lieutenant who she'd been promised wouldn't see the light of day again in his natural lifetime—apparently a first cousin to one of the traffickers. The captain had personally overseen all the successive OPC missions himself, earning him a handshake and a "well done" from Duane after the last one.

The fourth of the five jump team missions had been a no-show, which had disappointed her at first.

"Actually," Joe had explained, "that's good news. It means that word was getting out that there was a hard crackdown by police in progress. That's one of the reasons we try to plan multiple assignations and why we also make sure that we're arrested as well. We don't want the bad guys waiting until we're gone; we want them to think this area sucks for business and then shut down their operations. We'll spend tomorrow doing training sessions with the local forces on how to set up stings like these. Hopefully they'll keep it going too."

"Won't the traffickers just pop up somewhere else?"

"Not twenty-three of them. And probably not a bunch of others. Wouldn't make bets, but the perimeter of the Free Trade Zone in Colón, Panama, is going to be a much less popular place for sex-traffickers for a long time. And buyers are going to be warned off by the locals talking about the heavy police presence, so it should decrease overall."

It gave her some hope…and made her feel guilty as hell for sitting safe in the quiet town of Portobelo each night.

Tonight it wasn't Duane who sat with her out on the balcony overlooking the sunset-painted harbor, but rather Carla and Melissa.

"I'm not sure I'm happy with the change."

"What change?"

Sofia looked at Melissa, wishing she hadn't given voice to her thoughts.

"World view change? If that's it, then the last two days sucked," Melissa sounded grumpy.

"Us for Duane," Carla spoke with entirely too much insight as she slouched low enough in her wicker chair to prop her crossed feet on the railing.

Which made Sofia sound like a trivial airhead for caring more about the man than the young girls who were still hurting her heart.

A brilliantly red-blue-and-gold Amazonian parrot fluttered down to cling to a roof eave and inspect them.

Sofia showed her empty hands. *No food. No idea what comes next. No idea about anything.*

The parrot chittered at her, then swooped away in a glory of color.

"Duane Jenkins," Carla said thoughtfully as if tasting her Atlas *cerveza* and finding it particularly tasty, even though they'd already agreed it was the lamest beer they'd ever had.

"Heck of a fighter," Melissa agreed.

"You have to forgive her," Carla turned to Sofia. "She's born and raised Canadian, which make her far too polite. Vancouver, BC, which is even worse. I'm surprised she even said 'heck.' Lord knows I've tried to teach the blonde wench better."

"Whereas you pride yourself on being a foul-mouthed girl from the wilds of the Colorado mountains," Melissa shot back.

"Fuck yeah!" Carla raised her beer in a toast. "What about you?" she turned to Sofia.

"What about me?"

"Come on, Sofia. You're like this total rich bitch from Oregon. What the hell are you really like when you aren't being all Agent of ISA? Are you really a Miss Hoity-Toity under your ISA skin?" Carla said the last in a fake English accent.

"That's *Ms.* Hoity-Toity to you," Sofia snapped back more fiercely than she'd meant to, but she didn't like her past being bandied around.

"She's rich?" Melissa asked in surprise.

"Top tier," Carla answered before Sofia could stop her. "But don't tell the boys. They'd get all weird about it."

And, Sofia realized with some surprise, Carla was treating her exactly as she had since the first day. Sofia wasn't used to her money making no impression on someone.

"Just rich? Or there's-a-bridge-I-want-to-sell-you rich?"

"Bridge category," Carla answered for her.

"Sweet. Sounds wonderful."

"It has a few moments," Sofia admitted. "But most of them suck."

"Yeah, like we believe that shit. So what are you doing slumming with us, anyway?"

"Duane's rich, too."

"He is?" Carla and Melissa echoed each other as they turned to her in surprise.

Sofia didn't know what to do with that. They'd been together for over two years as a team and she'd been around for about four days. How could they not know such a simple thing about him?

"Only person he ever talks to is Chad. I mean we're supposed to be the silent warriors, but Duane really takes it to a whole other level."

Sofia remembered the helicopter pilot teasing him for speaking in whole sentences. "He speaks to me..."

"Other than bragging about being rich? Is that how he was trying to get into your pants?"

"No. He was explaining...something." He'd been talking about why he'd chosen to go Delta, but it was as if he'd never quite finished the story. Instead, that kiss had happened. Using "kiss" to describe the groping, full-body clench that had swept over them wasn't right. Duane had elevated "kiss" to a *duende*—a mad passion, as if they'd been creating art between them.

"Explaining things?" Carla sounded worried. "Melissa, you'd better call a medic. I'm thinking Duane Jenkins is unfit for duty if he's actually explaining things."

"On it," Melissa raised her beer in acknowledgement but took no other action.

"How can you not know this about him?"

"You know," Melissa was watching the flight of pelicans swirling down onto the water, this must be their standard night-time habitat. "It makes him and Chad even more of an odd couple than you'd think at first. What with Chad being a street kid from Detroit and Duane being an Atlanta rich boy."

"Coca-Cola," Carla stated.

"There's more to Atlanta than Coca-Cola," Sofia found herself echoing Duane.

"I guess. Never been there."

"But," she sighed, "you're right. His Dad is a Coke exec and he was supposed to be one also."

"Why would a man like that go Delta?" Melissa asked the descending night.

"Why would Ms. Rich Bitch here go Activity? Bored with her prom dresses and BMWs?"

"I will *not* be telling you about my BMW Z4 Roadster then," one of the few things she'd taken with her when she left Oregon—currently parked in her condo's garage in Maryland.

"Present from her sweet mummy and daddy on her sixteenth birthday," Carla cooed at her.

"Actually, a present from my kick-butt grandmother on my sixteenth birthday."

"Kick-ass," Carla corrected her. "Serious car envy while I'm at it."

"Now *that's* a grandmother," Melissa nodded.

Sofia couldn't agree more.

~

"SHOULDN'T we be including the women?"

"You've lost it, bro! Did you see them together?" Chad pointed back in the general direction of the aging *casa* they were all staying in. "I'm sure not gonna mess with that level of shit storm."

Duane *had* seen them. Carla, Melissa, and Sofia sitting together on the balcony, beers in their hands, and talking too softly to be overheard. Maybe clearing out was a good idea.

Fred Smith was back from wherever he'd been the last two days and was leading all four of the guys into the small town. He walked right past Restaurante Casa Vela, which smelled just fine for dinner—had a number of tourists who looked like they were enjoying themselves. Chad was definitely eyeing the ladies, but Smith didn't stop. Past three *tabernas* and a half dozen small hotels along the water front.

There wasn't all that much to Portobelo. It was about three blocks wide and barely a kilometer in length—mostly strung out along the waterfront. That included the two historic forts. At this rate they'd run out of town and be tromping in jungle shortly.

"Hey!" Chad called out in protest as they passed another target-rich restaurant.

"Thought you guys might enjoy this one," Smith ducked through a battered door of a covered marina slip—the boathouse framework so aged that it was a miracle it still stood. The next heavy rainfall—which happened all the time in the tropics—might bring it down.

"Wow!" Richie sounded as if he was going to give birth to kittens on the spot. Duane's eyes finally adapted to the shadowed interior.

"Cripes!" He felt as wholesome as Richie, but Duane didn't know what else to say.

The boat inside the shelter was long and low. Actually, it wasn't that low, but it was so long it was difficult to get perspective on it. It was a hundred feet of sleek. Its three decks—waterline with portholes plus two upper decks—were swept like a racing car. A racing car made of an equal mixture of carbon fiber and evil.

"Any particular reason you wanted us to see this one?"

"Why are you always so damn practical, Kyle?" Chad opened his arms wide to the boat. "Come to Daddy, you sweet thing."

"Leave it to Chad to be horny for a piece of Kevlar."

Duane felt the same, but he was duty-bound to harass Chad. The boat was part James Bond-villain gunmetal-gray with tinted windows as if no light could ever escape, and part Bond-girl hot. It lurked in the dim interior of the floating boathouse. It was a dangerous, sexy thing of shadows and suggestions.

"How fast?" Chad punched Duane's arm.

"Mid—"

"Fifty-three or -four sustained," Richie cut off Smith. "Range of about a thousand miles. This is an AB Yachts 100, the *GoldenEye*—spelled as one word just like the James Bond movie, with a capital E, at least the second one. The first and third are still lower case."

As if they couldn't see her name painted right there on the hull.

"It's the fastest production super-yacht anywhere. Might be the fastest period." Richie sighed happily. "Way more than just a speedboat, the inside is seriously high-end."

"Why show us?" Duane found himself echoing Kyle's original question.

Smith paused and gave an answer that didn't strike Duane as his first thought. "I watched Richie nearly wet himself over some of the abandoned boats anchored here at Portobelo. We can't go on this one, but I wanted to watch you guys drool a bit."

Duane didn't buy it for a minute, but didn't see any use in trying to call an SOG agent on his shit. They'd already learned just how slippery Smith could be.

Though he did sound as if watching them drool was a close *second* reason and that he enjoyed rubbing it in their faces as he continued. "Valued at over eight million—that's Euros, not US. It's been parked here for almost three years. Someone's paying every month to have it kept up but hasn't visited it once."

Richie groaned with the travesty of the waste.

"I was amazed myself, when I found it here." Smith led them out of the boathouse and deeper into town, this time away from the waterfront. Maybe Smith was trying to show them he was just "one of the guys" even if he was CIA.

They had gone several blocks, one more and they'd be in the jungle, when Smith turned in. There wasn't any obvious sign at the door—it looked like any other. A two-story building, painted white with a red tile roof, and an aged wooden door. Inside was a *taberna*—not one intended for tourists. This was obviously where the natives came to *get away* from the tourists. Nine locals were lounging around mostly open tables—slow night. There was a lazy card game going on at one. Somebody else was plucking a wandering melody on an undersized guitar.

At a small bar in the back, Fred Smith simply said *"cinco"* to the bartender as he held up five fingers. "*Y empanadas*" he pointed at a greasy-looking stack of the turnovers on a plate that was probably cleaned every Christmas...and now it was October. With a nod, the five of them headed to an open table well away from the others.

"Not the most subtle of places to meet," Kyle observed as they all jockeyed to end up with their backs to the walls and facing the entry.

Duane gave up first and sat with his back to the room. He'd just keep his eyes on Smith—who had claimed the best seat—and when Smith reacted, he'd know it was past time to get moving.

And still only he and Smith were seated while the others jockeyed for the strategically safest position.

"You're doing a shit job of blending in, guys." At Duane's statement, they finally settled. Kyle next to Smith, Chad and Richie to his own left and right.

"Not a real subtle place for five gringos to hang out," Chad kept twisting around to check out every noise. "Why here?"

"Good beer," Smith answered with his normal cheeriness as the bartender delivered five liter-size glasses. "And the best chicken *empanadas* this side of Guadalajara."

The bartender merely grunted his appreciation as he set down a big plate of them.

Duane tried one—and his eyes nearly blew out of their sockets. "Holy shit!"

Smith took one and bit down on it and chewed. "Good, aren't they?"

Duane grabbed for his beer to put out the three-alarm fire in his mouth.

"After the first bite or two, the heat settles to a dull burn. Then you can really taste the flavors," Smith cheerily kept eating.

Warned by his example, the others took a firm hold of their beers before carefully tasting an *empanada*. The first round of beer disappeared quickly, but the *empanadas* were really good, once you got over the surprise and the pain.

"What happens to the girls after OPC frees them?" Duane was the first to recover.

"OPC has an aftercare system all set up. Runs them through medical and psych evals, arranges counseling if necessary, then tries to either get them back to their families or placed in a good home if they can't. Recidivism is under five percent. They get their lives back."

Duane could see joining up with them after he was done with Delta. He probably still had a decade to go but, with the notable exception of the colonel, Delta was not an old man's game. Kyle might stick it out, try to follow in Colonel Gibson's footsteps, but Duane was enough of a realist to know that wasn't him. The Unit didn't have a lot of field guys past forty, or even their mid-thirties —the toll on the body was just too high.

"Why are we here?" Chad held up his pastry. "Other than the joys of a near-death experience. Your mouth made out of iron, Smitty, or what?"

"I wanted to get your read on the last two days." His beer was barely touched as he reached for a second lethal pastry.

"Operation Prime Cause's tactics were good," Kyle started. "From seeking initial leads through setup and execution, they're pros. Even maintaining the after-action debriefing, they're solid. Can't see much I'd change of OPC's operations, they—" Smith cut him off with a gesture abrupt enough to earn him a dangerous scowl from Kyle. He appeared to not notice the imminent threat of destruction, but a CIA field agent couldn't be that oblivious.

"Their operation is no longer our concern."

Duane looked around the table but no one seemed to have any idea of what Smith was after.

"You want *our* reactions?" Duane tossed out. Knew he was right as soon as he said it. "That's what you're after."

Smith nodded and, for once, held his silence.

Duane wasn't sure where to go next.

"You're on a roll, bro," Chad nudged his elbow into Duane's ribs almost hard enough to topple him over into Richie's lap.

"If you want to know what I think about what they're doing, I thinking they're goddamned brilliant. The look in those girls' eyes when they got even the least sliver of hope was amazing."

Then he recalled what had been said at their first meeting with Smith and Colonel Gibson.

"Oh, fuck!" Everyone turned to look at him. Again, Smith uncharacteristically nodded and kept his mouth shut.

Duane rubbed at this face. He took a swallow of beer. He foolishly grabbed another *empanada* and bit into it without thinking. But the roaring in his brain made it so that he barely noticed the blazing heat on his palate.

"What is it, Duane? What am I missing?" It wasn't like Richie to miss making connections and it always made him crazy. Duane knew he wouldn't put this together because he was too sweet a kid at heart. Maybe that's what had swept Melissa off her feet—the sleek blonde warrior and the truly decent geek.

What would sweep Sofia off her feet? She wouldn't be—

Everyone was still looking at him. He half expected Richie to start tugging on his sleeve in his frustration.

Duane flashed two fingers at Smith, then three.

His slow nod confirmed Duane's guess, but left it for him to explain to the others.

"At lunch," Duane started slowly. "Colonel Gibson said that OPC heard about problems that they couldn't address. Maybe they couldn't get agreement from the host country or couldn't find a reliable contact—like the corrupt lieutenant on that first job. He could have gotten OPC's, or our, team killed. Imagine a whole country of that shit."

The lightbulb went on for Kyle and he looked ill.

"Panama is a Tier 2 country," Smith filled in, holding up two fingers in imitation of Duane. "Good laws in place, trying to make convictions that will stick. Maybe not the best at finding the bad guys. Some corruption going on. That's Tier 2."

Chad and Richie both had furrowed brows still.

"Venezuela," Duane picked up the tale, "recently fell off the next lower grade, the Tier 2 Watch List. That placed them solidly in Tier 3. Heinous abuse of citizens. Rampant trafficking as drug mules, slave labor, and big-time into the sex trade. And based on the laws they *don't* have, it's all effectively government sanctioned and..."

But Smith was shaking his head, actually smiling that Duane had gone off the track.

Duane cursed again, but this time everyone just waited.

"That's what they found? What OPC found?" Duane asked.

Smith nodded.

"So, the trafficking isn't *effectively* government sanctioned. They found where it *is* run and operated by the government."

"Fuck!" Chad was not happy. "I thought General Aguado was just a bad egg. Took everything I could do to not chuck the bastard overboard. I was hoping we were done with that place. Venezuela is coming apart and their president-dictator *hates* America."

"He does," Agent Smith stated. "The connection they found doesn't necessarily lead to his office, but it definitely hits high in the government. Specifically in SEBIN, their secret police. SEBIN is also their CIA, FBI, Secret Service, and US Marshals all rolled into one. With a level of nasty that even our own SOG doesn't go near. What he hates even more than us are dissidents. If a person is imprisoned by SEBIN, they rarely are seen again. And their families, especially their wives and children, are believed to be trafficked into sex and labor by the government in retribution."

"And what they must do to those women and children..." Duane couldn't even finish the sentence. Everyone, even Chad—who'd definitely seen more awful shit than the rest of them combined—looked queasy.

He finally understood why the team's women weren't here at the bar with them.

It wasn't because the idea was too gruesome. It was because the women would already be on board. It was the men that Smith had to be sure of.

CHAPTER 12

"*W*hat are we doing here again?"

Sofia was amazed that Richie didn't have every detail about why they were flying back to the States.

Fred Smith opened his mouth and Sofia glared at him until he shut it. He'd taken the men away and told them something that had changed every one of them. The unflappable Kyle had turned grim. Richie—who was always a little clingy—was glued to Melissa's side. Chad's fierce silence made him appear truly dangerous despite his Iowa farm boy looks.

And Duane hadn't met her eyes once since they'd been awoken at dawn and shoved onto this plane. The unmarked Gulfstream business jet was covering the ground from Panama to Washington State in a little over six hours and they were getting close.

"ECHELON," Sofia explained, "was partly based here in central Washington—out in the Yakima Training Center at a location called the Yakima Research Station."

She, of course knew about it from her time at the Activity.

"ECHELON was part of the Five Eyes agreement set up in 1941. Us, the UK, Australia, New Zealand, and Canada created a cooperative, intelligence-sharing service during World War II.

Full access to shared intel, no matter who got what. It was run on our side by FBI, CIA, NSA, and a couple of others," that she wasn't authorized to mention because their identities hadn't been made public by the thief-turned-traitor Snowden.

"Yakima? What did they do here?" Richie never stopped until he had something pinned to the ground and throttled within an inch of its life.

"Gathered signal intelligence from Soviet satellites mostly."

"Let me guess," Richie might be the one geeking out, but everyone was listening closely, even Duane, who had sat a row back across the aisle by Chad rather than with her. "You're speaking in past tense. That implies that it has been shut down because Soviet intel is no longer on the satellites, it's all cyber and Dark Web games now."

She nodded. That and they'd consolidated the intel gathering at a new, vastly more capable facility in Colorado at the Air Force Space Command. It was rapidly becoming the nation's Number Two intelligence agency headquarters after Fort Belvoir, Virginia, where The Activity was based among more than a dozen other agencies.

"So what are we doing *here?*" Carla asked suddenly over-loudly as the engine roar eased down.

Sofia's ears popped as the cabin pressure changed and they began their descent.

"Well!" Richie jumped in before Sofia could speak. Clearly he now had the missing pieces he'd needed. "They may have shut down the Yakima station for ECHELON—you all remember that scene in the second Jason Bourne movie when Landy calls for an ECHELON package to observe Bourn? So cool! Don't know how I forgot that. And when—"

"Richie," Melissa called on him to focus.

"Right," then he plowed his way back to the topic at hand. "But the facilities are still there. Did you know that Venezuela has just two satellites in orbit? The new one is for land, agriculture, mapping—that sort of thing. Max resolution is over two meters and it's in a fast and low orbit, so it's no good for following people. But their first satellite, the Simón Bolívar, is up in geosynchronous orbit and totally belongs to SEBIN. It's a hot signals intelligence gathering machine that the Chinese put up there for them. Supposed to be as secure as hell. This means that we've cracked it and can hear all of—"

"We didn't crack it," Sofia hated to burst Richie's balloon.

And sure enough, he looked like a little kid holding an empty string.

She glanced at Melissa, who patted Richie's arm in sympathy.

"Their codes are still secure," Sofia repeated. "But Yakima is listening and it has also become the center for most of our intel on SEBIN."

That appeared to placate him some.

Melissa was apparently attached to Richie's sweetness—which would never work for her. Sofia wanted… She turned to Duane and caught him watching her. At least he had the decency to not look away immediately. But after a few seconds, he did turn toward the window and look out at the approaching landscape.

Sofia didn't want…anything—though Duane had been working down the path to convince her that maybe she did.

And then Smith had done something to him.

~

ALL DUANE COULD SEE every time he looked at Sofia was what happened to women in screwed up, ultra-macho, horridly repressive regimes like Venezuela. Smith had laid out for them just what horrors it took to be a Tier 3 human trafficking country. Then he'd started breaking down the known abuses by SEBIN.

Nothing about the mission.

Nothing about when the team was inserting, where or what their mission might be.

Way too much about what was happening to the civilians and protestors. At first it had seemed like he was laying it on too thick. Then Duane had started looking at the reports and wondered if Fred Smith wasn't treating the guys just a little bit kindly.

Way too easy to imagine Sofia there. And how much value such a beautiful woman would have to a trafficker. He wanted to shoo her home, back to whatever safe, quiet corner of the country she never talked about—not drag her out into the field where—

It wouldn't be right to lock Sofia away somewhere secure, even if she'd let him. But that didn't stop him from wanting to try.

"Dude?" he whispered to Chad after Sofia had turned once more to face the front of the plane.

"Yeah, bro?"

"Any of this making sense to you?" There were pieces on the move here. Big ones. Ones the SOG had been willing to stage a battle on a cruise ship for. But none of them were fitting together.

"Shit. Why ask me? You need to ask Richie or your girlfriend—they're the thinkers on this team. I'm like you, just along for the ride."

That was one of the things about Chad.

He was always low-key, always had your back. Steadiest guy you'd ever met. And up until now Duane had been comfortable in that role himself. *Just along for the ride.* Glad to take down the bad guys and have a cold one at the end of the day. There was a reason that neither of them was a leader.

Kyle was the natural leader, keeping all of their rampant personalities focused on the same track. Carla was the driver—the force behind all their butts that shoved them ahead at full tilt. Richie and his *girlfriend*—

"Wait!" He nudged Chad, who was pretending to sleep even as the airplane's wheels squealed on the runway. "What did you call Sofia earlier? My *what?*"

"Fuck, you're being slow. Not like you, bro. Not like you at all." Chad didn't even bother to open his eyes.

Sofia had changed him. A couple goddamn kisses and his brain was warped somehow.

He watched her profile as she chatted with Melissa.

What had she done to him?

He'd been happy just being a Unit operator. And the team he'd landed on had some serious grit—so damn good he was always amazed that he was part of it.

But Sofia Forteza called up something deeper in him. Reminded him why he'd walked away from his life to join up in the first place. Made him want to know, understand, be involved at a new level.

Then he thought about what Smith had been telling them and he decided that maybe just being along for the ride wasn't a bad thing.

CHAPTER 13

"I thought the Pacific Northwest was supposed to be so green," Duane was looking down out of the Bell JetRanger helicopter Sofia'd rented in Yakima. After days of complete immersion in Venezuelan intelligence gathering, she had needed a break. And, gathering her courage, she'd invited Duane along to the family home.

At first it had been for support, something she hadn't realized until after she'd asked, otherwise she never would have. She wanted to go see Nana, but really needed someone to bolster her courage to face the rest of her family. Sofia had never needed anyone, but this time she did.

But she'd also wanted him to see her home…except she hadn't warned him. And still hadn't as they flew west-southwest toward Dundee, Oregon.

"Yakima is in *eastern* Washington," she explained. "There are big mountains up ahead, and the rain stays on the west side." The low morning sunlight made everything look so fresh and alive. The higher hills were already dusted with reds and golds on the trees of early fall. The valleys were still lush with the end of summer. She loved watching the turn of the seasons.

Duane grunted an acknowledgement and continued to stare down at the landscape. And Sofia was now third-guessing her invitation.

She was so looking forward to some time off. The Venezuela team, buried in the heart of three hundred thousand acres of achingly dry scrublands that made up the Yakima Training Center, had been so excited by the team's arrival. For once, instead of simply collecting and feeding data to some far-off facility at Fort Meade, they had a real-life Delta team onsite. The team had been inundated by the enthusiastic researchers. They'd delivered briefings on everything from police vehicles to SEBIN's dreaded La Tumba. The Tomb. A place political prisoners disappeared into and were rarely ever seen again.

There had been no chance to talk with Duane. They were all quartered together, trained together, and fed meals together. It was amazing they weren't all showering and going to the bathroom in unison.

Sofia's thoughts were awash in too much information and too many grim images.

Duane looked as tired as she felt.

But he wasn't avoiding her. At first she'd thought that's what it might be—morning after such an incredible kiss, as if they'd really had that one-night stand that she was sure she wouldn't have regretted. But, more often than not, they sat next to each other for meals. He laughed at her jokes, though he rarely spoke above a one-line banter.

And when they'd been given time off, she'd decided to go home. Four hours by car without traffic—but it was only a ninety-minute flight.

She wasn't sure what had possessed her when she'd asked Duane if he wanted to join her. Sofia had suggested it quietly, when they had a brief moment apart from the others so that she wouldn't be too embarrassed when he turned her down.

He'd searched her eyes for a long moment, then simply nodded. "That would be great."

Now that they were finally alone and flying around the mass of Mount Hood, a mostly dormant volcanic peak, she didn't know what to say.

Maybe she should change the plans. Timberline Lodge stood on the southern slope of the mountain. It was a grand, Depression-era timber lodge known for its skiing and hiking trails. But she'd wanted to go home. It had been too long since she'd seen her grandmother.

How could she be taking Duane there? He didn't know about her family. He didn't know about...so much. Like how she felt every time she came near to him.

"Duane—"

"Sofia—"

"You first."

"No, you."

She used her I'm-busy-being-the-pilot prerogative to wait him out.

"Why am I here?" He finally asked over the intercom that connected them.

"Don't you want to be?"

"No. Yes. I do want to be with you. I haven't been able to think about anything else. But I—"

"That's fine then," and they stumbled back into silence. It had never struck her as a strange disconnect before, but it was. In a five-seat helicopter, the two pilot seats placed them shoulder-close. Yet they spoke over the intercom headsets as if they were using cellphones across the country.

She concentrated on passing between Mt. Hood's eleven-thousand-foot peak and the four thousand feet of controlled airspace around Portland International Airport. Not hard really, there were thirty miles between the two.

"So you live near here?"

"Uh, yes, Oregon. Outside of a small town called Dundee."

"Where they teach beautiful intel analysts to fly helicopters?"

"I have a nana who believes very definite things about a woman's capabilities."

"I've seen you shoot. That doesn't just come from military training. Was that her, too?"

"Yes." Monosyllabic responses. Next she'd be down to male grunts if she didn't do something about it. "My family owns some vineyards on the other side of Portland."

"Oregon grows wine?"

Sofia actually had to turn to look at him and see if he was joking. He didn't appear to be. "Number Two region in the country after Napa Valley."

"I'm more of a beer guy. Isn't Oregon the place they thought up microbreweries?"

"I thought you were more of a Coca-Cola guy."

He barked out a laugh, "Doesn't my dad wish. He was so damned angry when I joined up, I'm surprised he didn't disinherit me."

"My grandmother named me the heir the day I joined."

"The heir to what?"

Sofia wished she had flown more slowly or reached this point in the conversation sooner. But I-5 flashed by below them. She followed the Willamette River as it wound its way through some of the country's lushest farmland. Leaving the valley at Dundee, she climbed them up over the deeply rolling, vine-covered hills. The autumn golds of the vines, bordered by the dark green conifers that carpeted so much of Oregon, was like a soothing balm on her nerves and eyes. The brilliant blue sky was glorious and always an additionally cheering sight for any Oregonian, far too used to the fall, winter, and spring rains.

"This," she nodded downward, "is the Dundee Hills AVA. That's American Viticultural Area—a very prestigious designation. There are several internationally recognized, award-winning vineyards here. My family owns the top-rated Colina Soleada Wines as well as seven others. Though we don't advertise that relationship to avoid any perception of diluting our brand."

And now was when the change happened. When men found out who she was and their entire attitude about her changed. It was too late to unsay the words. Too late to turn back to the Yakima desert and pretend that—

"Colina Soleada? Spanish for Sunny Hill?"

"Not long after the war, when they were newly married, my nana and *abuelito* came over from Penedès wine region near Barcelona. It is one of the oldest and best grape regions of Europe and has been making wine for over twenty-seven hundred years. They settled here."

"You grew up in a place called Sunny Hill?"

"*Sí*. Colina Soleada."

"Huh," Duane grunted thoughtfully as she flew one more lap above the golden vineyards she had grown up in.

They spread in every direction. There were two hundred wineries in the rolling Dundee hills, ranging from tiny, twenty-acre dreams to major operations like their own. Beyond lay the wide flats of the Willamette River Valley stretching from the nearby pine-green Coast Range over to the snow-capped Cascade Mountains some forty-miles to the east. The sunset-colored vines. The blooms of rose bushes planted at the end of so many rows. Small patches of orchards thick with apples, pears, and hazelnuts. It was still the most beautiful place she'd ever been.

He remained silent as she circled down to the helipad behind the grand Spanish villa close by the vintner's buildings. They were barely twenty feet up when he broke his silence.

"Sounds nice," as if he'd never heard of their wine. "Hope you're not upset, but I'm more of a beer man."

Sofia almost bobbled the landing, but managed to get the helicopter's skids settled onto the grassy helipad without looking too awkward. She didn't know whether to be shocked or ecstatic. The vineyard was such a part of her life it was impossible to imagine someone not knowing it. It's revelation had reshaped or destroyed every relationship she'd ever had.

But on the other hand, Duane would make no assumptions about who she was or who her family was. And coming from money himself, actually, having walked away from money to join the Army, meant that maybe her family's wealth wouldn't twist him either. That was a gift beyond imagining.

∼

COLINA SOLEADA? The heir? Then what the *hell* was she doing in the military?

Shit! It was one of Mama's favorites at parties—"This darling little Oregon winery I discovered. They send me a case of their private reserve whenever I need one." She didn't entertain often, but when she did, it was one of her pat lines. But she meant it. Their Pinot Noir and Chardonnay had frequently graced the family's dinner table as well.

But it didn't take a genius to read Sofia's body language. He'd felt it right through the helo as she spoke. She'd flown so smoothly until they began discussing her family, then she'd tightened up, almost as jerky as a beginner pilot. It screamed her unease with what she'd been telling him—a feeling he completely understood. He'd regretted telling her about his family, wishing he could take it back. The least he could do was not let her own revelation change anything for him.

Wouldn't Mama just shit a hissy brick if she knew who he was sleeping with.

Except he wasn't sleeping with her.

Except he wanted to.

Badly.

"Sofia?" He asked her softly while she was shutting down the helo.

She didn't respond.

The intercom sounded flat, dead in the headset's earmuffs. She'd already shut off the power. He peeled his off.

Then waited for her to finish shutting down and do the same before he tried again.

"Sofia?"

"Yes?" She placed her headset on the console before turning to him.

He tried to find the right thing to say.

It eluded him.

Rather than hunting it down, he kissed her. For the first time in days, he kissed her.

And, thank god, she kissed him back. No hesitation. Faster than a bullet to a fifty-meter target, they went from first contact to full ignition. The lower radios on the console and the collective control lever between their seats was all that stopped them from crawling into each other's laps.

Sofia wrapped her arms around his neck and leaned into the kiss as if she was trying to drive him out the far side of the helicopter.

To hang on, he got one hand around her back. Because they could only turn toward each other but not manage a full-body clench, he managed to slide the other hand up and over her breast. Its shape had hinted at wonderful in her full field gear. It had looked incredible across the table, masked by civilian attire, and felt plenty amazing when pressed against his own chest during a full-body kiss. But in his hand, full and shapely without tipping over into either generous or lush, it was goddamn perfect.

The outline of her bra through her light blouse gave him lines to tease as she groaned against him.

"Now!" She broke the kiss just enough to gasp out the word.

"Here?" If she was willing, so was he. He'd never done it in a helicopter before, didn't know if it was possible. But taking the time to get her out into the grass was too damn long. She leaned in to press her breast more fully into his palm.

"Yes. Sure. Whatever. Just...now!"

Buttons. She had buttons. Take too much time. He'd buy her another damned blouse. He slipped his fingers inside the collar of it to tear it out of his way. He had to see if she looked as good as she felt.

His fist clenched as one of her hands slid up the inside of his leg and grabbed him through his jeans. Grabbed him hard enough that he had to gasp for an instant before he could rend.

Had him opening his eyes in surprise, just enough...to see the two horses looking in at them through the front windshield. A windshield that exposed them from their knees to above their heads.

Then he managed to focus on the faces of their two riders. One was a handsome young man who looked amused. The other could have been Sofia's twin—an older, very well-tended, furious twin.

CHAPTER 14

*A*fter they'd ridden off, Sofia couldn't seem to stop laughing about it.

She'd just get it under control, but it burst out each time she looked at him. It was a nervous, girly giggle that she'd only ever defeated by teaching herself not to laugh at anything. But it kept slipping out.

"If it tickles you so goddamn much, maybe we should try the same thing when I meet your grandmother." She wasn't sure if he was more upset by how he'd met her mother and eldest brother or by their interrupted intentions.

Personally, she was leaning toward the latter. Sofia had long ago given up caring about what her mother thought.

Camila Forteza had ridden off before Sofia could get her shirt back under control and clamber out of the helicopter. Her brother had at least stayed long enough for introductions and a knowing smirk.

"I can see how close you aren't." Duane helped her tie down the rotor so that it wouldn't windmill in the breezes that wrapped around the tops of the Dundee Hills.

"We've been that way ever since…well, not birth. But not long after."

"Why?"

"Mucho ruido y pocas nueces."

"Lots of noise, very few nuts? What are they, squirrels?" But his smile said he knew the idiom.

Sofia sighed. "My family, other than Nana, are about the most useless lot you can imagine but, as Shakespeare says, they love making much ado about nothing. *Abuelito,* my grandfather, Nana says was a good man. The rest of my family? Feh!"

She leaned back against the helicopter. Off to the left were the big vintner's sheds. It was the harvest season and the trucks were rushing great mounds of grapes from the fields, so lush and darkly purple that they seemed ready to burst forth and fill the air with their dark flavors. Straight ahead and up the hill was the *Corazón de las Vides*—the Heart of the Vines tasting room, restaurant, and an elite, members-only lounge that filled the entire upper floor. To the right was *La Casa*—the family home. A grand villa. All were done in deep yellow faux adobe with red Spanish tile roofs so that they were the colors of the Spanish flag.

"I haven't been here in a year, but it smells like home." She breathed in again. She could taste the richness of the soil at the back of her throat. The dry hills of early fall before the rains came in to reshape the scents.

Duane fetched their overnight bags, dropped them at her feet, and leaned beside her.

"Why?" He wasn't going to let her get out of this one.

"Mother will never forgive us, all four children, for the travesties we caused upon her body."

She could hear Duane thinking about Camila Forteza's looks, even if he was decent enough not to say it. Ever since her mother had turned thirty, she'd done her best to remain frozen in time—and had done a very good job of it. At sixty-one there wasn't a sag or bulge out of place.

"The best surgeons money can buy and a ruthless commitment to her personal trainer," Sofia answered his thought anyway. "I should say trainers, as she grows bored with their other, more personal services fairly quickly."

"Uh-huh." Somehow he knew it was only a half truth.

"Also, Nana made me the heir, not her. Mama has an allowance and that's all. She has no business sense and a great desire to acquire things. She is always broke by harvest time but must wait out the rest of the year before Nana will release her next year's quarter million of pocket money."

"Tough life," he sounded disgusted.

Oddly, his tone said he wasn't disgusted at the amount of money but rather the attitude with which it was handled.

"I have a cousin like that. Collects sports cars and very expensive ex-wives. Where's your father?"

Sofia shrugged. "Mother grew bored of him, too, when I was seven or eight. She waited until he had a fresh affair—not as if it was news even then—and used it to drum him out of the family. A payoff of a few million and he was gone. We never hear from him. He never even came back to see his last child's birth, assuming Consuela is even his."

"How did you turn out so normal?"

"Normal?" She pushed off from the helo. To pick up her bag, she bent at the waist with her behind facing him just to torture him.

A casual glance over her shoulder showed that it worked perfectly. Duane was looking right where she wanted him to. At her— She straightened, hating herself. That was her mother's game, not hers.

"I work for The Activity, where I am appreciated for my skills and sharp brain." *Not for waving my butt at beautiful men.* "I have just been on multiple missions with a Delta Force team in exotic countries—all for truth, justice, and the American way. And you call me normal?"

"Not how a little girl pictured herself growing up, huh?" Duane Jenkins backed it up with that good smile of his.

She laughed and didn't care that it was her happy giggle sound. "Truthfully, almost exactly what I pictured."

Duane offered one of his surprised grunts. Sofia enjoyed doing that to him, keeping him on his toes. She kissed him lightly, but didn't lose herself in him this time though it would be so easy to do.

"Nana filled my head with such ideas from the time I still thought peekaboo was a wonderful game. I have told you she is *una pistola.*"

~

MARIA ALICIA FORTEZA Y BORGA DE OLIVELLA was a wizened woman who didn't even come up to Sofia's shoulder despite standing ramrod straight. Duane didn't expect a "pistol" to look like she'd be blown away by the next breeze if not for her cane.

Apparently Sofia didn't either by her hard stumble. If he hadn't caught her arm, she might have gone down to the marble floor. They had found her grandmother—"you may call me Ms. Forteza"—in the estate office. It was a grand, wood-paneled room designed to impress visitors. He was certainly impressed. His family's home was modern, pretentious, and custom-built—with a complete lack of personality.

Even though Sofia had said this estate was younger than the woman standing before them, it felt as if it went back forever—rooted as deeply into the soil as the vast vineyards that had lined the hillsides, curving like contour lines of a topo map. This place belonged in *Architectural Digest.*

And this room, with the tiny woman standing in the center of it, felt like the anchor to it all. White marble floor. An aged, oaken desk faced with a handful of wine-colored leather chairs. A small circle of couches and armchairs around a quietly crackling fireplace lit against the cool October morning. And portraits that began with what could only be a young Maria Alicia Forteza standing above the first plantings of her vineyard. No question where Sofia and her mother got their fine looks—straight down the matrilineal line.

Though the warmth had skipped a generation. No matter what Camila Forteza did to maintain her body, nothing was going to hide that her eyes had all the warmth of a Venezuelan pit viper.

But the room didn't overpower Maria Alicia Forteza—not even standing in front of her own portrait. Instead it was the other way around despite her frailty.

Sofia hugged her very gently.

"I'm not dead yet," the woman snapped, but returned the embrace kindly.

Sofia nodded quickly, but it was easy to see the shock in her eyes. Maria patted Sofia's arm consolingly.

"I was thrown from Diablo, my horse," she explained for his benefit. "I broke my hip. At eighty-seven I do not heal as quickly as I once did."

"Why didn't you tell me?"

"Because you would have worried. I was just a sick old woman who hated giving up her morning ride. I wasn't fit company for anyone."

Then the woman's black eyes, emphasized by the pure whiteness of her hair, turned to inspect him.

"So, this is your *gigoló*. Camila seemed quite bothered by you, young man."

"She may not have liked that I was in the midst of manhandling your granddaughter at that moment."

A ghost of a smile touched the woman's lips. "Was she enjoying it?"

Sofia opened her mouth, whether to answer or protest, he wasn't sure. Maria Alicia Forteza cut her off with little more than a raised finger. And Duane could see that smile grow ever so slightly at her granddaughter's discomfiture.

"We both were, ma'am. Quite a bit as I recall."

This time Sofia blushed, her golden skin deepening toward a ruddy sunset.

"Camila always was the jealous sort."

That made Duane blink in surprise. And now Maria's knowing smile had his own cheeks heating up.

"You, my good boy, are very handsome, yes. But you are also very real. Any fool, even my daughter, could see that at a glance. Far more interesting than the pretty young men Camila uses. Come, sit with me," she waved toward the chairs. "Or would you rather go finish what Camila and Emilio so rudely interrupted?"

While it was tempting, Duane didn't need to see Sofia's near-panicked expression to know the latter wasn't an option at the moment. She was truly thrown by the change in her grandmother.

They followed her to the seating area. Maria did not protest when he held her arm as she settled into a chair. She felt no bigger around than a toothpick. Before Sofia could start fussing, Duane took her hand and pulled her down on a couch beside him. Her clasp was strong, fiercely so, and she didn't ease up.

Maria glanced down at their joined hands and then back at him. "I think you are an interesting man, Mr. Jenkins."

"For what reason, Ms. Forteza?"

"You two have not slept together, but already she depends on you greatly," she hummed to herself for a moment as she studied the painting over his head. "That is not something I can ever recall my granddaughter doing."

"What are you talking about, Nana?"

Maria clasped both hands atop her cane. "Your mother and father taught you quite young that men were not reliable. Your grandfather died in Vietnam, long before you were born, which was a great loss to me and my baby daughter; but I could have wished that he lived to meet you. You both would have benefited by it."

"Yet you never remarried?" Duane couldn't help asking.

"No. Some lovers…"

He could feel Sofia's hand jolt in his. Her grandmother didn't miss it.

"I remind you, Sofia, I am not dead. Far more discreet than your mother, which is saying very little, but still a woman."

Duane could see where Sofia had inherited all of her spine.

Then Maria shook her head and inspected the low mahogany coffee table set with yellow roses. "You and Camila were both raised without male role models. Perhaps, by not remarrying, I also did not give you an example of what a good man could be. Perhaps," she looked up at Duane. "Perhaps *you* will."

~

SOFIA OPENED the door to her bedroom, and hesitated. She had brought boys here before, even some young men. Neither of those described the man waiting close beside her no matter what Nana called him.

She wasn't sure if she'd have survived seeing the vast change in her grandmother without his support. Once again she was reminded of Duane's impossible solidness; rooted where he stood, with roots deeper than the oldest vine.

Giving in, she let the door swing open the rest of the way. After Duane had stepped through, she closed the door and leaned her back against it. He didn't glance back at her for permission before prowling the room. She could feel the Unit operator assessing everything about the situation. She could feel him learning things about her so rapidly that it was spinning out of her control. She—

Remembered her training.

Managed a breath.

Another.

And then she watched him. Her first impression was wrong. He wasn't a soldier assessing a new environment as she'd first thought. Instead, he was a man curious about a woman's private room.

She had always liked to think it was an accurate reflection of her. Rich with warm golden colors, a dusky carpet the shade of the Colina Soleada rosé. Though she'd never noticed before quite how much the Moroccan blue duvet made the large bed stand out, as if she'd wanted to draw special attention to it.

At the dresser, Duane paused to study the photos of her on Esperanza—her first pony. And later, Bandito with various show ribbons and trophies. The posters that now made her blush. Thankfully, the shirtless David Beckham had come down a long time ago, but the shirted one still hung next to Adam Levine— Maroon 5 had been her first concert and it was signed to her.

But *was* this room still her? The more she learned about Special Operations' targets—not just since liaising with this team, but through her work at The Activity as well—the more it had changed her. There was a softness to the woman who lived in this room that she no longer recognized. She couldn't reconcile her younger self with the one who knew as much as she now did about terrorists' and various governments' motivations.

Duane whispered a soft, "Damn!" He was looking out the window. It was one of those crystalline fall days. The flats of the Willamette Valley were commanded by the lone tower of Mt. Hood in the distance. The view from the family bedrooms had always been the best.

He finished his inspection, then came to a stop in the middle of the bedroom, looking right at her.

"You're not feeling self-conscious, are you?"

His amused smile had her shaking her head no just to keep him from being too smug. Besides, she'd stopped breathing again and couldn't speak.

"I can think of a way to cure that?" Duane made it a question. No, an offer. Leaving the choice up to her. Which was decent but she already knew the answer.

She nodded yes.

He strolled up to her as casually as he walked when on a mission. Silently. No wasted motion. Not looking away from her face for an instant.

Pinned. Trapped. She couldn't move. All she could do was lie back against her own door and wait.

He stopped inches away, reached up...and past her. He brought his hand back, and it was filled with pink silk. Her bathrobe hung on the back of the door. He let it run through his fingers.

"I can't imagine how incredible you would look in this. Just this," he held it out until she reached for it. He reached past her other side and locked the door with a soft click. He barely brushed his lips on hers, then he stepped back to the middle of the room and faced the view once more. Offering her privacy to change right there. As if. Yet she planned to be naked beside Duane very soon.

Sofia looked at the robe, then at Duane's back, then back at the robe in her hands.

Well, he was welcome to his fantasies, but this was *her* bedroom.

She hung the robe up once more, kicked off her sneakers, then walked silently across the carpet to stand behind him. When he started to turn, she placed her hands on his shoulders to hold him in place, then ran them down his back, appreciating his muscle definition.

Skimming her hands around his waist, she slipped his black t-shirt up and over his head.

He wasn't built like Chad, who could be used as a human tank in a pinch, but still he was powerfully built. His back was better than most of the cover models on her mother's romances—which she'd hijacked plenty of as a teen.

And, as Nana had noted, Duane was impossibly real.

His skin was warm beneath her touch, and much more marked than she'd expected. Duane always gave the impression of being impregnable. He was just this guy showing up to do his day job—which happened to be as a Unit operator. Which meant, by definition, that he worked in the worst places in the world.

She slid a single finger down a long slice over one shoulder blade that must have taken dozens of stitches to close.

"I always was crap at climbing trees as a kid," his voice was rough.

Sofia traced a line of three bullet wounds low on his back.

"You know what they say about playing with pointy sticks."

She leaned against him, sliding her arms around his waist and holding on. He stroked his hands along her arms. Duane was built of earth, of stone, of the hyper-compressed core of the planet. With her cheek against his back and her ear on his shoulder, she could hear his heartbeat. Through her arms, his breath.

She could hide here. Right here. Bury her face and forget about her mother the bitch. Her smug brother, who she'd had to teach the hard way to leave her alone in the quiet nights. And most of all forget Nana's transformation over the last year. She seemed to have shrunk inches, bent over her cane as if she could barely stand upright.

When she sniffled too loudly, Duane turned in her arms and in moments she lay against his chest and *he* was the one holding *her*.

"Whoa!"

She turned to plant her nose directly against his breastbone and hung on tighter. Sofia didn't need anyone, but she needed Nana. One of the pillars of her life was teetering, and for the first time ever, she was truly afraid. She'd thought that Duane might teach her fear—even if she didn't believe in it. Now, suddenly, he was the only thing holding it at bay.

Rather than pushing her away, he held her. Stroking a hand down over her hair, down her back.

She sniffled again, but it was for a different reason.

She was afraid, despite not believing in fear.

And she also felt safe, perfectly safe in Duane's arms.

It wasn't that she didn't believe in feeling safe—it was that she'd never felt it before.

∾

DUANE KNEW that throwing Sofia over his shoulder and tossing her down on the bed wasn't the right answer at the moment, but he needed to do it soon. To see what she had become from the sweet girl with her pony, her smile, and her prize ribbons was like a supercharged lightning bolt to the libido. How such a magnificent woman came from such an innocent was beyond impossible. Having that beautiful woman curled up against him, despite all she'd seen and done, made her even more incredible.

He buried his face in her thick dark hair and breathed her in.

Maybe this *wasn't* the time for self-restraint.

He inhaled deeply, stretching her embrace, then exhaled abruptly and squatted down before she could compensate.

Shoulder into her gut.

Arm around the backs of her knees.

Stand.

She was so damn light. Such a substantial presence as Sofia Forteza should not weigh so little.

Three steps, lean forward, and shrug.

Sofia flopped from his shoulder-carry onto the bed with a squeak of surprise.

She let out a half laugh as he finished the work he'd begun in the helicopter—with a single grab and yank, her blouse was torn open as several buttons pinged away as fast as bullets.

And he stopped. "Your skin," he could barely speak. Her skin was the same perfect golden color all the way down to her waist-band, only her bra interrupting the view—an impediment he dealt with quickly.

Then he could only stroke a hand down her in wonder. He'd had his share of hot lovers, but Sofia was something else entirely. Duane had to see more.

He began stripping off her pants.

"No, wait."

Her fly open, his hands curled in the fabric to reveal her in one long pull, he stopped and looked her in the eyes.

Her breath heaved once, twice, a third time, her magnificent breasts riding up and down on each successive wave.

"No..." she heaved another beautiful-to-watch breath. "Don't wait."

He didn't.

Nor did he waste time in getting naked himself. Holding Sofia was always incredible. Holding a naked Sofia against his own bare skin was a revelation.

There was no holding back. There was no slowing down.

Yes, it had been a while since his last port of call.

Wasn't even a part of the equation.

Sofia lit a fuse in him that burned so brightly it was a wonder he didn't spontaneously combust. The body of a fighter—strong, flexible, perfect—was a hundred percent pure woman.

Ha! Used that percentage right.

They feasted on each other. Caress, taste, feet winding together testing the curve of a calf against an instep. No quiet foreplay. No gentle teasing. No male-female roles. Just two greedy needs coming together and crossing an instant ignition point.

One memory stood clear of all the others. One instant when they both hesitated, paused to appreciate the exquisite wonder of the moment. Safely sheathed, he slid inside her in a moment of utter silence. Her black eyes watching him steadily as her body arched up against his.

Their rhythm built together, their gazes locked, until her eyes finally rolled shut as her entire being strained one last time against him before exploding. She cried out as her body thrashed and her arms clung. Her legs locked so hard about his waist that his own detonation—for there was no other way to describe the power of it—somehow blew them closer together rather than farther apart.

And still she writhed, finally burying her face against his neck as the last of the roiling aftermath rattled through her.

For timeless minutes, neither of them moved.

He slowly became aware of one hand tucked under her butt. Of the other buried deep in her hair and cradling her head. Her own hands—one on his own butt and the other still locked about his neck.

"Sweet Jesus," he managed on a gasp.

"I have never been called that before," Sofia mumbled without unburying her face from his neck. He could feel her smile.

"I'm sorry I couldn't take more time. Later, I promise. I just…" He didn't know what "he just." Needed her? Wanted her? Had to be buried deep inside her? Had lost all goddamn control for the first time since Cindy Sue had introduced him to the wonders of sex as his sixteenth birthday present?

"I am filing no complaints with any persons," the Spanish influence was richer than usual in her voice. It rose and fell like music on the morning light.

He managed to roll onto his back, keeping her tightly against him. She made no effort to move away. He slipped his hands over her; from butt to hairline she was blemishless.

"We are going to be needing to do this again."

"Give me a couple of minutes on that. You've tripped all my circuit breakers, lady. Need a little time to reset them."

"Really?" she wiggled against him like a serpent uncoiling from a nap in the sun. "That is such a pity. And I thought you were a real man." She nipped at his shoulder.

He got his hands around her rib cage and lifted her into the air. "Behave, you."

"Never!" Sofia cried and reached down to tickle him under the arms.

In his surprise, he dropped her and she landed squarely back on him, knocking the breath out of both of them.

But she didn't stop. In moments his arms were full of squirming, fighting woman. Except she wasn't fighting to get away, she was fighting to make him completely crazy.

He finally captured her wrists in one hand, but she used that as leverage to sit up over him. He used her momentum to carry her right over onto her back, which had her hanging head and shoulders over the foot of the bed. By a miscalculation of center of gravity, caused by a well-placed knee to his gut worthy of a yogi contortionist turned street fighter, combined with the slickness of the duvet, they both toppled off the end and onto the carpet.

By some secret ninja method he'd never seen before, she ended up kneeling astride him as he lay on the carpet.

"Now," she declared, leaning in as he cupped her breasts. "I think I need to go have a shower since you are no real man."

Impossibly she managed to slip away from him and stride naked to the bathroom.

He'd had fantasies like this this one—Duane was sure he had. But if so, he knew he'd been lacking in imagination. She moved with a spring in her step and a soft swish of tangled hair that had him starting to his feet.

By the time he reached the bathroom door, she'd closed it. The click of the lock sounded clearly in the suddenly quiet bedroom. His knock went unanswered. He could hear the shower start.

He pounded again.

He was answered by the opening lyric to Paula Abdul's *Opposites Attract*.

If a naked Sofia Forteza was dancing to that music in the shower and he missed it, he was going to have to kill himself.

174

He tried the handle again.

No joy.

It only took him a moment to locate his pants and his pick set.

Five seconds later all he could do was stare in wonder as Sofia danced within the glassed-in shower enclosure. The russet and golden tiles highlighted her as if she was the most precious thing ever, poised in a life-sized display case.

∿

SOFIA LOVED her control over Duane. It seemed trite, selfish, and egotistical.

But she watched him through the curtain of spray and the glass. One of the most skilled warriors anywhere stood frozen in all his naked glory in the middle of her bathroom. How was a girl *not* supposed to feel good about that?

Maybe it was okay to tease him with her body.

She turned a slow circle in her dance as she broke into the refrain.

Opposites attract?

But how opposite were they?

Intelligence agent versus Unit operator—both at the top level of Special Operations. Both rich. Both repulsed by their parents. Both...

All she was coming up with was similarities.

Yet by the time she'd circled around, Duane still hadn't moved. No, at least one part of him was moving. He had delivered the most powerful sexual experience of her life, and it was clear he would soon be ready to prove that it wasn't a fluke.

"I once dated a Greek military officer—" she called out loudly enough to be heard over the pounding spray.

"I didn't need to hear that," Duane's growl carried into the shower enclosure just fine.

"He said that no day is a complete day if there isn't dancing in it." She kept dancing by herself—torn between embarrassment at her display and a primal joy at Duane's on-going paralysis. "He was right! Some people sing in the shower. But I know better, I sing and dance."

Still nothing.

"We were showering when he taugh—"

"Enough already! I surrender!"

Duane stepped in quickly to join her.

"Holy hell, woman!" He reached for the temperature controls but she slapped his hand away.

"I like my showers the way I like my men. If you are one who cannot be taking the heat, you had better be getting out of my shower," she ran a soaped hand down his chest.

"If you can take it, so can I!" He snatched the bar of soap away from her. "I need to check on some things."

"You need to what?" But her next breath was snatched away as he brushed a soaped palm over her hip.

"I was in too much of a hurry before to notice the shape of this curve. Or this one," he brushed a thumb along her jawline, then leaned in to kiss her. Unable to do more than groan, she leaned into him.

As strong and willful as she'd felt a moment before, now she felt helpless, unable to respond, to move without Duane's guidance. He took control of her body until once again her voice rose to echo from the walls.

She lay against the cool tile as the heat washed over and through her.

Her grandmother was wrong—Nana had provided all the role model she would ever need. She would stand alone. In the Activity, and someday the vineyard, she herself was all Sofia needed.

But this. She clung to Duane's broad shoulders to keep her sanity—for her self-control, it was too late; it had left the shower long since—as he found yet a higher place to force her to climb.

She would definitely have to make sure she always had time for this and a man to take her there.

Unable to bear the impossible tower he was making her ascend alone, she bolted from the shower.

Duane looked upset by the time she came sprinting back to the shower, still soaking wet. Her wet and soapy feet had her skating across the tile floor. She hopped through the open shower door and slammed into his arms.

Then she slapped a condom into his hand and in moments they were seeking the heights together.

They finished that dance, then Estefan's *Conga* and Maroon 5's *Sugar* before they were too waterlogged to move.

An hour later, the shrill scream of the phone beside the bed yanked them from a slumber that was more boneless collapse than sleep.

There wasn't even time to dry her hair. When Nana ordered them not to be late for lunch, she didn't dare delay.

～

DUANE COULD GET USED to this. His parent's place had a territorial view of the local neighborhood and the high-rises of Atlanta. Ansley Park allowed the wealthy to look at the city they ruled.

The stone-flagged patio of the Forteza estate house had a hundred-mile view of rolling vineyards, a sweeping river valley, and towering mountains. It was a humbling view, the beauty keeping even the lushness of the family mansion in perspective.

He also liked the simplicity of the meal despite the setting—a meal his mother would never deign to let out of the pantry. A generous platter of cold cuts and other sandwich fixings. Chips, beer, pickles…yes, he was indeed a happy man.

That and looking at Sofia.

The woman in the sapphire blue blouse and jeans was overlaid by his memory of the naked woman gyrating about the shower

177

for the simple joy of it. She had unplumbed depths of joy that were so unexpected. In the field she'd been, by turns: serious, concerned, fierce, and competent. Away from all that she was playful, exotic, and the damn sexiest thing he'd ever laid eyes or hands on.

Now, seated beside her Nana, she was practically prim. A woman of dazzling contrasts.

The rest of the table was a train wreck of spectacular proportions. There was the youngest Forteza—the silent sister. Consuela was pretty enough in a slender way, with none of the flash of her older sister or her mother. She concentrated on the meal, but Duane would bet that she didn't miss a thing. There was a sharpness, an awareness in her eyes when they briefly met his. After that, she was careful not to look at him directly. He wasn't sure what she was hiding from, but the other family members were fair candidates. If she didn't want to be noticed, she did an excellent job of it throughout the meal—apparently she was wholly invisible to everyone but him.

Offspring Number Three, Humberto was presently doing three-to-five for dealing coke—the other kind of coke than his own family dealt—to a couple of DEA agents.

That left Sofia's mother—apparently between fitness trainers until her allowance was restocked at the New Year—and Offspring Number Two—the smug, handsome, snake-in-the-grass Emilio he'd met earlier at the helipad.

"You're in the Army?" Asked with a dripping disdain—implying Duane wasn't qualified for anything better—that tempted him to put on his good-ol'-redneck suit. He considered it, except he didn't want to embarrass Sofia. Then he saw her roll her eyes just the way Chad would, as if saying, "There's fresh prey. Go kill it."

"Yeah-sir!" Duane let the South roll off his tongue and go for a stroll. "Fightin' for my country and proud" pronounced per-*owd* "to be doin' it."

"He's good at what he does." For a moment he thought that Sofia was trying to defend him.

Until her brother stepped on the straight line, "Oh, I'm sure he is, sister," with far too knowing a tone.

"Yep!" Duane eased back and sipped the last of his beer before thumping the glass back on the table. Then he made a show of flexing his hands into fists for a moment as if they were a little out of practice from lack of use—like a pianist warming them up. "Why, I haven't beat the shit out of anyone since..." he looked over at Sofia.

"Thursday," she provided. Man but she cracked him up.

"Right, Thursday. I only fractured his jaw a little."

Emilio eyed him skeptically.

"A'course, that ol' boy is now inside La Joya prison with a lot of other folks that he put there. That's in Panama, by the way, just in case you didn't know." Carefully implying he was too stupid to.

The Panamanian lieutenant who had tried to sell out Operation Prime Cause's operation to the drug dealers might well be dead already for his deeds. La Joya placed plenty high in the World's Worst Prison contest. The lieutenant's trip there didn't make Duane's heart bleed in the least. There was a phrase in-country that, roughly translated, said the only way out of La Joya was feet first.

"And Duane hasn't shot a soul for at least a week," Sofia added helpfully. Damn, all he needed was a Chad-casual move, but he didn't have a weapon on him to pull out and begin cleaning.

"Been a whole week?" Duane let his surprise show. And he hoped that the CIA team leader's hand and knee were healing slowly and painfully.

Now Sofia's grandmother was rolling her eyes. Maybe they were laying it on a little too thick.

"Who are you with?" Emilio hadn't thrown in the towel yet. There was something odd in his dynamic that Duane couldn't pin down. He'd have to ask Sofia later. He wasn't gay, that was obvious from how he looked at his own sister's breasts—Sofia had told Duane about beating the shit out of Emilio when he tried to put action behind that look. But Duane couldn't pin down what was out of sync.

"Have you heard of the Green Berets?"

"Sure. They're the guys who wear green berets. Like John Wayne."

"They are," Duane agreed amiably. He'd been 75th Rangers, but he didn't want even the stain of this shit's thoughts on his old unit. Chad had come to Delta out of the Green Berets. Too bad for him that he wasn't here to defend their honor.

"How many people have you killed?" Sofia's mother was as disdainful as her son.

Duane was so goddamn sick of that question. Civilians never understood what it took to keep them safe. It wasn't how many he killed; it was killing the right ones that mattered. General Aguado's guards counted as proper takedowns. The bug hunt in which his team had knocked down twenty percent of the US supply of cocaine at its source had been a righteous one as well.

A glance around the table revealed varied reactions to the question.

Maria Alicia Forteza y Borga de Olivella watched him closely. She appeared to be waiting to see how he would handle the question rather than what the answer might be.

Sofia blushed and looked down, ashamed of a family that wasn't worthy to lick her boots.

Camila and her son, Emilio, poised in unison to label him murderer.

And the quiet Consuela looked up just enough to show her smile as she watched him. It was her amusement that gave him the right answer.

He rose slowly and put on his best mosey around to Sofia's chair, helping her to her feet. Duane had to tip up her chin to make a slow, clear, delicious point of kissing her in public. He led her a step away, then, as if reconsidering, he left her there and returned to grab Camila's and Emilio's shoulders.

A wink at Consuela was rewarded with a particularly nice smile—one that looked as if she wasn't used to other people seeing it, or even noticing her existence. He turned his attention back to the pair of pit vipers.

"Y'all gotta understand something. I'm trained to protect good people, at any cost to myself."

Then he dropped the Southern from his voice and let it go harsh.

"That doesn't include you," he squeezed Camila's shoulder hard enough to ensure her undivided attention.

"Or you," he clamped down on Emilio's hard enough to go right through his gym-trained strength and earn a gasp—the pressure of Duane's fingertips pressing on the pectoralis minor nerve trigger point distracted Emilio too thoroughly to permit anything as trivial as speech.

He held the pressure for a count of five, then eased just enough that Emilio would be able to hear him. Duane let his voice go back to good-ol'-boy.

"As to how many people I've killed up until today? Well, hell, y'all. The day ain't over yet. I'll jes' have to keep ya posted."

Emilio let out a whimper when Duane let him go abruptly. The sudden release would be nearly as painful as the pressure itself. His arm wouldn't work right for a day or two.

Camila moved in fast to console her son the moment Duane let her go.

Consuela was hiding her face behind her napkin, but her eyes gave away the look she was hiding.

Nana's infinitesimal nod accepted his solution to the problem without condoning or condemning.

He strolled past Sofia, taking her hand, and led her off the porch and out into the fields.

~

"WAS HE ALWAYS THAT AWFUL?"

Sofia could only shake her head. Emilio had never been friendly—perhaps due to being the oldest male in a matriarchy—but he'd never been so thoroughly pugnacious either.

"Your mother's influence."

Sofia guided him around the side of the house to get out of view as quickly as possible. She could feel the pressure ease the moment they were out of sight. A shaky breath was incredibly cleansing—the crisp fall air purging the worst of the experience.

Ahead lay the *Corazón de las Vides* tasting rooms and the wine lounge. Open to the general public, for a fee, it was focused on cultivating the big spenders. It had been built farther around the hilltop than the house, commanding an equally impressive view to the south and west. The Coast Range, while far lower than the Cascade Mountains to the east, was also much closer. Starting less than five miles away, its conifer-shrouded shoulders rose to impressive heights above the last of the Willamette Valley patchwork that surrounded the Dundee Hills.

It was a masterpiece of yellow faux adobe, heavy stone, and wooden beams, capped with red Spanish tile. Inside it offered seating for cozy groups by warm fires, and a luxurious old-world dining room where, for special events, a hundred could dine, and wine, behind the floor-to-ceiling glass walls. World-class chefs had created feasts here, all paired with the estate wines, of course. On summer days, the glass walls could be folded aside. No expense had been spared and buyers would be able to feel it just by entering the building.

Colina Soleada wines started at seventy a bottle and went up rapidly, so they'd expect no less. More affordable vintages were grown and bottled at other vineyards quietly owned by the Forteza empire, but here at the main estate only the best, show-piece wines were served and sold.

Her entry caused a familiar flurry among the staff and guests—familiar and, now, strangely foreign.

The appearance of a family member in the wine lounge was always an occasion. Isabel, the *Corazón de las Vides* manager, appeared moments after their arrival with her unvarying air of having been waiting specifically for the most honored guest. She offered the same to everyone from the beginner, who'd invested fifty dollars for a thirty-minute tasting, to the owner of a restaurant chain that placed a hundred-thousand-dollar order over a complimentary glass of the three-hundred-dollars-a-bottle Soleada Signature Reserve.

It was a standard practice that she'd learned at Nana's knee, for the family to visit any groups that happened to be there. It was a practice she knew well and had always enjoyed. A friendly handshake and a few words with a family member served to confirm to buyers that they mattered, that they were actually seen.

That was the wholly unexpected thing that Duane had done over lunch.

Certainly they'd had amazing sex, but she didn't need to be told that's all it was. He'd taken one look at her, ripped off her clothes, and they'd had a wonderful time. Startling, breathtaking, mind-bending sex, but she knew better than to think there was any real relationship behind it. Her family exemplified that there was no such thing.

She'd seen actual relationships, appropriate for the rare few like Carla and Melissa, but she and Duane knew better.

Yet if ever there was a man she would choose... Throughout the whole meal, Duane had remained pleasant and easygoing, leading conversation when it lagged—even teasing Nana about falling off a horse.

"You let your horse throw you? I don't believe it. I bet you were just testing our your flying skills," said with such charm that even Mother couldn't find an offense in it—something she'd striven to do at every turn.

Duane's background, which neither of them mentioned to anyone, showed in his every word and gesture—Southern gentleman to the very core. A Southern gentleman well trained in how to host a party and be the perfect guest—at least until Emilio went so far out of his way to be insufferable.

Unit operator Duane Jenkins had *seen* her family, with uncomfortable clarity. He'd made her feel seen as well. Despite her first expectation in the Venezuelan jungle, Duane hadn't been trying to charm her simply because she was a woman. When he spoke, which she now understood was less rather than more often, he worked to charm everyone. He *saw* them and let them know that.

Isabel acted as genteel escort, making it even more clear to guests that this was an occasion and just how lucky and special each of them were. Each time, she found a new way to slip into the conversation that Sofia was only here for one day after a year abroad—so they should feel even more privileged—and implied that she had been doing wonderful, wine-related things during that time.

In one of the more private rooms, Sofia greeted a buyer from Wolfgang Puck's restaurants who she remembered from when he'd started out as a wine buyer for Palace Station casino in Vegas.

She traded air kisses with Phoebe, a Michelin-starred French chef down from Portland. She was a slender woman who preferred to serve Colina Soleada wines over her native country's. When Sofia found out she was planning a second restaurant, this time in San Francisco, she introduced Phoebe to Wolfgang's buyer. Before she was gone, it was clear that the two were hitting it off on many levels—talking about wine, but thinking many other things as well.

A group of Japanese tourists had all sprung for the full tasting, tour, and trays of traditional *tapas* finger food created by the onsite chef. They traded low bows and then took dozens of selfies with her despite the mess her hair must still be from drying in the sun. At least it was back in a ponytail.

Through it all, Duane followed close beside her. Silent, powerful, she supposed that he appeared to be her bodyguard, as if she needed one. Or the perfectly solicitous assistant, holding Phoebe's chair, taking the group photo for the Japanese, and a dozen other small niceties.

Duane moved through it all with an ease and familiarity that belied his rough appearance and callused hands. Money didn't daunt him...or impress him. The more people they did a meet-and-greet with, the more she found herself watching him rather than the patrons. He was proving that he was magnificent out of the bedroom as well.

They finally made it through to her favorite place, the second floor balcony. She often sat here in any weather. A table umbrella against summer sun or spring rains and a standup heater close by the outdoor hearth against fall and winter chills. This had been her escape from the rest of the family. Always by herself. Now she took her favorite table by the railing and Duane sat with her.

Isabel provided them with two glasses of the estate reserve before tactfully disappearing. Sofia knew that there would be a waiter on alert watching for so much as a raised finger, but out of eyesight.

"You do that very well," Duane toasted her.

"It might be my very first memory, walking among strangers, reaching up to hold Nana's hand, and welcoming them here."

"Bet you were charming as hell as a kid. Cute too."

"It felt strange this time."

"Me or you?" Duane's perceptions were as clear as ever.

"I...don't know."

Duane sipped the wine and relished it with an unexpected practice. "Wow, that's a good year."

"The 2012, our best in over twenty years." She was halfway to tasting her own glass when the implications sank in. "Colina Soleada. You said you'd never heard of it."

Duane shrugged easily. "I didn't want to make you self-conscious about telling me who you were."

"You lying son of a bitch. You took advantage of me. I thought that for once I found someone who might like me for me, not for my heritage. You—"

"I only implied I didn't. Half truth," and the twitch of his shoulders said he regretted it. "We were already in the air on the way here before you told me. Besides, my interest is in the brilliant and beautiful intelligence analyst who kissed me on the balcony of a Portobelo *casa,* not in some wine heiress."

Sofia rubbed at the goosebumps on her arms. "Oh, as if I'm supposed to trust that."

Duane shrugged again, even less comfortably. He studied the dark red wine as he slowly twirled the stem in his battle-callused fingers.

Yet with him, perhaps she could trust it. He, too, came from wealth, true wealth. Her fortune would have less impact on him. "Most men I meet are more like Emilio, always hungry for more."

"If you are the 'more,' then yes, I seem to have an insatiable appetite. If your money is, I don't give a damn. The Army more than covers my expenses, never mind Mother and Father."

"Are they still together? Your parents?"

∼

NOW IT WAS Duane's turn to wish for a subject change. He wanted to shrug the question away, would have with anyone else. But he'd seen the disaster that had somehow created the wonder of Sofia Forteza and he could hear the pleading and hope in her voice, even if she probably couldn't.

"Yes, but not in the way you mean. Not 'The Real Thing.'" It was the best answer he had. "I don't know that they were ever 'together.' Well, except for the fact that I was conceived in there somewhere, maybe once was enough as I'm an only kid. They are the perfect host and hostess for each other's careers though: the Coca-Cola exec and one of the most powerful lawyers in Atlanta. They make an exquisite couple at parties. A couple who live in opposite wings of a seven-bedroom mansion with their mostly unnoted son living somewhere in the middle. Mother lost all interest when it became clear I was following in Father's footsteps rather than hers. He lost all interest when I followed in the Army's instead of his."

Sofia didn't look up at him.

"At least you have your grandmother. She's wonderful." Wrong thing to say, as the fear was once again back in Sofia's eyes. He wanted to reassure her, but couldn't think how. For all of her spine of steel, Maria Alicia Forteza was a frail woman who had barely touched her meal.

"I can't imagine how she fell," Sofia still didn't look up. "She and Diablo finished second in a major eventing seniors' competition just three years ago."

"Eventing?"

"Dressage, cross-country, and show jumping. It's a combined event that challenges all aspects of horsemanship. Think the decathlon for horse and rider, and Nana is an expert. There is an entire room in the house just for her awards."

"Oh."

Sofia was eyeing him carefully. "You do ride, don't you?"

"Some." Every Unit operator had at least basic horsemanship training. Ever since the very first troops into Afghanistan after 9/11 ended up deploying on horseback and mules to mix in with the hill tribes, Delta had added a one-week riding course. But other than that… "Not a lot of horses in downtown Atlanta."

"This," Sofia declared, "we must fix soon."

"Sooner than we go back to bed?"

Sofia's smile gave him some hope, but her response dashed that. "Absolutely!"

"This should be fun." *Not!*

Sofia sudden scowl told him that he needed to learn when to keep his mouth shut.

He went for a subject change. "So how long have your mother and brother been lovers?"

Sofia's wine glass flipped out of her hand and shattered on the flagstone at her feet. "They *what?*"

Duane really needed to learn to keep his mouth shut.

CHAPTER 15

Sofia took Diablo herself, suspecting that Nana's horse had been too long unridden. She placed Duane on Genuine—short for The Genuine Fake Copy of the Artificial Real McCoy, a name Sofia had given the mare when it was still a gangly foal struggling to find its feet for the first time. She had turned out to be a genuinely pleasant animal and an easy ride for even the least skilled riders. She and Genuine watched Duane closely. He might not be skilled, but he at least had the basics down.

She guided them into the woods, first at a walk, then a light trot. Duane's uncertain seat made her decide against a canter, though Diablo was begging to be allowed to run. Once well clear of the house, and circling deeper into the woods between Domaine Serene and Erath wineries on the uncultivated west side of the Dundee Hills, she slowed them once more to a walk. They were following a dirt road that let them ride side-by-side for a little while.

"What you said back there..." she couldn't complete the question.

"Uh-huh," Duane didn't sound happy.

"How sure are you?"

"Very," he was sticking with no more than two syllables, a restraint he'd shown since the waiter had rushed over to clean up the shattered wine glass and make sure she was okay.

"But…" It was pretty much the most disgusting thing she'd ever heard. And when talking about her mother and brother, that was saying something. It was even worse than when he'd come into her bedroom thinking he'd get some of that from his sister.

"Ask Consuela."

"What? Why?"

Duane was settling more easily into the saddle, loosening his hips to take on the horse's rhythm rather than continuing to force his own. Maybe they could canter later. After Duane stopped being so close-mouthed.

"Why ask my sister?"

"She doesn't miss anything."

Her confusion must have shown on her face.

"You two aren't close either."

"She was entering third grade when I left for college."

"Well, she's a grown woman now, with a very sharp mind."

"How do you know? She never even spoke at lunch." Or had she? Would Sofia have even noticed? Every time she looked at Consuela, all she could remember was the little girl in pigtails who had seemed bolted to her hip.

"Didn't need to," Duane stated, then apparently decided to throw caution to the wind and speak like a normal human again. "You didn't see the proof about your mother because I was blocking your view. It was the way Camila clung to Emilio the moment I released my hold on him. I wasn't feeling kind—still not —so he's going to be hurting for at least a day or two, but what Camila was showing had to do with far more than a mother's care."

"There's not a maternal bone in her body," Sofia wanted to spit to clear the foul taste of that out of her system.

"Making my point all the more. There'd been a puzzling dynamic all through the meal that I couldn't explain, but that's the piece that made it all fit. Your sister was watching me, not them. She already knew and wanted to see if I noticed. When I did, it earned me a sad smile as if she was saying, 'Welcome to my world.' Seems like a pretty shitty one to me."

Sofia couldn't believe that she hadn't noticed. Now that Duane had pointed it out, Sofia supposed that it was obvious—perhaps painfully obvious. Yet, despite her vaunted intelligence skills, she'd missed what was right in front of her face. She knew from training that the hardest thing to see was often the most obvious because it disguised itself in the world of the accepted "normal." Yet another lesson: there was always more to learn.

"*Mierda!*"

They rode in silence until the dirt track narrowed. Where it turned south, she picked up the single-file horse trail deeper into the Douglas fir and cedar woods to the north.

"Can we just pretend that I don't have a family?"

"I dunno," Duane rode easily as they took a small jump over a fallen alder. "Your grandmother is an interesting woman. And I suspect Consuela is as well."

"Consuela has some degree, an MBA maybe? I just never think of her as grown." Or think of her at all, really, which was pretty shameful. "The others are slime."

"Yep, the others are slime."

She could have done without his easy agreement reinforcing the truth.

"There's one other exception," he noted.

"Who?"

When he didn't respond, she reined in Diablo and turned to face him.

He sidled Genuine up alongside her until they were boot-to-boot. He had a strange half smile as she puzzled at it.

With his effortless strength, he plucked her from her saddle and set her astride Genuine's saddle facing him.

"Oh," was all she managed as she clung to him.

"Where are we headed?" He kissed her lightly, teasing her lips with his taste of fine wine and deep earth.

"Diablo knows the way," she leaned out just enough to slap Nana's horse on the butt, sending him ambling ahead. Letting go of all the madness, she lay her head on Duane's shoulder and let the easy rhythm of horse and man lull her until she couldn't imagine being anywhere else.

∼

"It is my favorite place in the Hills."

Duane could see why. Diablo had led them to a small lake tucked deep in the forest. It wasn't big, perhaps a hundred feet across. There was a clearing at one end, barely big enough for the two horses now grazing there. Medium- and old-growth trees circled the little lake, but the high afternoon sun managed to reach down to them from the patch of blue sky.

"Too bad we didn't bring bathing suits. I really wanted to see you in that bikini."

Then he turned and saw that Sofia was already stripping down.

Sofia Forteza naked in the bedroom was one thing. Sofia Forteza naked in the forest was something else entirely. This wasn't the lethal jungle of Venezuela; it was a haven in the gentle woods of Oregon. Here she was both the fantasy of the bedroom and the wonder of their first meeting in the wilderness.

The water was cool and they swam and floated in it speaking of nothing. When they grew too warm, they paddled into the dappled shade made by the tops of the highest trees. When too cool, they swam back beneath sun shining down from the cap of sky. And the entire time he could not take his eyes off the woman beside him.

"What the hell are you doing to me, Forteza?"

"This!" Sofia pounded a palmful of water into his face. She tried to swim off, squealing with delight when he managed to snag her ankle. She was as rough-and-tumble in the water as she had been on the sheets. They were both going to be bruised after this—if they didn't drown first.

Somehow she broke free and bolted for the shore. He wasn't a SEAL, but there was an honor to be upheld. They raced the length of the lake.

Their shared calls of hitting the shore declared it a tie. Actually, Sofia had him by a hand length, not that he'd ever admit it.

"My great-grandmother, she was a mermaid," Sofia proudly declared as she stepped ashore, knowing she'd won, and began wringing the water out of her hair.

"I'm descended straight from the Greek god Pan," he swept her up in his arms and carried her over to lie on his clothes. Where some protection was also handy in his jeans pocket. "Pan was a big fan of hanging out with stunningly gorgeous nymphs."

"Hmm," Sofia made a delighted sound. "Descendant of a lustful Greek god. Remember I was telling you about the Greek officer who I danced with in the shower. He—"

He stoppered her merry laugh with a kiss, apparently the only way to silence her. No, he soon discovered, there were other ways. Or at least ways to elicit other sounds aside from coherent speech.

Halfway through, Sofia rolled him onto his back and sat astride him.

"I want you to see what I've been seeing."

"What, your magnificent breasts?" He caressed them with his hands so that she knew exactly what he was talking about.

She clamped her hands over his to keep them there, but nodded upward. "No. This!"

Sofia, beautiful Sofia, framed against the pines and the blue sky as she slowly began rediscovering the rhythm they'd been building since the moment he'd dragged her onto his horse.

"You aren't of this world!" At least not any world he knew. His world was bounded by women fitting into a very clear role. Sex— sometimes good, sometimes great. Fun—while it lasted. Then safely gone. A space that Sofia refused to occupy. She kept bursting through the careful perimeter he'd staked and claimed as his own.

What if she became more?

She was going to be gone. After this mission or the next, she'd disappear back behind the invisible curtain of The Activity as neatly as the Wizardess of Oz.

And when she did, what was going to happen to him?

There was an easy answer. Keep it light. Keep it about the sex.

But even as she did something with her hips that should be stamped Top Secret and Potentially Lethal—maybe a move straight from Mata Hari for eliciting information from unsuspecting men—Duane knew this was no longer about sex.

She still clamped his hands to her breasts. He arched up his hips to reach deeper into her. She hung her head. Bracing on the edge, preparing for the moment of release. Her hair a wave darker than the oldest bark on the sheltering trees.

Then Sofia looked at him. Her fathomless eyes were watching him, puzzling at the same question.

If this wasn't sex, what the hell was it?

His release triggered hers, and this time she wasn't the only one to groan with the power of it as it swept over them. He'd heard women describing their orgasms as "shattering." For perhaps the first time, he understood. Those carefully constructed perimeter fences inside him were crumbling—fast.

Even as they both slid from ecstasy to shudder to collapsing together until they were as close as two people could be, the question remained.

If this wasn't sex, what the hell was it?

CHAPTER 16

*W*hen they returned to the house, Sofia went to look in on Nana. She was sleeping fitfully. She shooed Duane away and sat beside her. It was over an hour before Nana awoke.

"Still not dead yet," Nana greeted her.

"I'm not a ghoul. I'm worried."

"About what?"

"About you. About the winery. About Duane."

"Mr. Jenkins strikes me as a young man very skilled at taking care of himself."

She helped Nana struggle a little higher on the pillow.

"It will just take him some time to see the wider picture of how much he already cares about you."

"Okay. Now I'm *more* worried about Duane."

"You have the same problem, but you'll get over it. It only takes time." Nana signaled toward the glass of water at her bedside.

Sofia fetched it, unnerved by Nana needing even that small bit of help.

"I need to get you a nurse."

Nana flapped her hand at her. "Your sister, Consuela, already did. I gave the nurse the day off while you were here so that you wouldn't have to worry."

"Well, that didn't work, did it?"

Nana smiled wryly, "I suppose not. She'll be back in the morning."

Sofia chewed on her lip, unsure how to proceed.

"Spit it out, child." Sofia smiled at the age old advice.

"If you die—"

"You mean *when*. We all die, though I'm going to do so sooner than I planned."

Sofia couldn't ask the next question.

Nana asked it for her. "What becomes of the winery and your career?"

She could only nod and hated herself for thinking of anything other than her ailing grandmother.

"I do not have a good answer," Nana sighed and handed back the water glass after barely taking a sip. "You already know your mother and brother are going to cause as much trouble as possible."

Sofia could only nod. She hoped that Nana was spared knowing what else they were doing.

"You were always the smartest of us, my darling Sofia. You will find the answer," she was drifting back to sleep. "Or ask that young man…"

Sofia sat until she was sure that Nana was only sleeping.

At dinnertime Consuela, again proving that she was no longer a precocious, pesty seven-year-old, had a date. Mother and Emilio were nowhere to be found, which was definitely a good thing in Sofia's present frame of mind.

She and Duane gave the cook the night off and fended for themselves. She'd rustled up a pair of dry-aged T-bone steaks and built a nice reduction sauce on the back of a reputable merlot. Duane had grilled Brussels sprouts and made country-mashed potatoes with caramelized onions. After the day's many revelations, Duane was sensitive enough to keep the topics of conversation as far away from family as possible. They talked of past missions—what they could of them—but also about the people of the many countries they'd each been to. Food, music, favorite rifles—a topic Duane was particularly passionate about—and anything else that came to mind.

Then, for the first time, as the fall twilight had darkened outside her bedroom windows, they had made slow, tender love. In the past, her lovers had been either a good romp or gentle and considerate. Duane was the first that was both.

Now she lay curled up against him, listening to the sound of him sleeping.

It was the best sound she'd heard in a long time.

It calmed her nerves as thoroughly as his early efforts had calmed her body.

Now she could do what she did best—she could think.

CHAPTER 17

"Come down to see us off?" Duane sat partly in the parked helicopter, his butt on the deck of the open pilot's door and his feet on the grass. The early morning sun was warm and pleasant.

"Yes. Where's my sister?" Emilio's strident tone was not so pleasant.

"She's gone up to the house, waiting for things to come to fruition." Duane nodded toward the harvest trucks that had restarted the work hauling grapes at sunrise. Not that they were pertinent to anything, but it served to confuse Emilio. Duane'd missed his cup of coffee this morning and needed something to perk him up.

"Sofia said you had to be gone first thing. What are you waiting for?"

"Me?"

"Who the fuck else am I talking to?" Emilio waved a hand around. *It's in the details,* Duane reminded himself. A chipped nail, a grease stain on the back edge of Emilio's hand where it was hardest to see when washing up.

The nearby winery was just far enough away that no one was

paying them any attention. But they were close enough that the sudden roar of a heavy diesel engine momentarily smothered conversation. A truck dumped tons of purple grapes into a massive hopper at the side of the building. Duane could see Sofia on the balcony outside her grandmother's room, looking down at them. The truck clanked a few times as the operator shook the bed to empty the last of it, then eased to a quiet putter as the dumper eased back down onto the chassis.

"*Well?*" Emilio's anger was still hot.

"Well, Sunny Jim. Gotta confess, I be waitin' a passel, too."

"For what?"

Under different circumstances, Duane could get to enjoy this. He missed the double beat of Chad and Sofia's interjections. This conversation could use someone with a sense of humor—his own was wearing very thin this morning.

"I find it funny that you don't know how brilliant your own sister is."

"Oh, I can tell that from her selection of boyfriends. You're just a wind-up tin soldier."

"I suppose that's better than being called a Jarhead," he had yet to pay Sofia back for that particular insult at their first meeting.

"What?"

Duane ignored him. "You see, your sister started thinking last night. She thought up some very interesting things."

"Such as?"

"May I see your phone?"

Emilio had it half out of his back pocket before he could stop his reflexes.

Duane shifted to his feet, taking a quick double-step forward, and snatched it away.

"Hey! You can't—"

Duane swept his leg against the back of Emilio's knees, landing him hard on his back.

Emilio struggled only briefly after Duane managed to get a foot on his throat and pin him to the helipad.

"If I'm wrong, I'll apologize later." He grabbed Emilio's flailing hand and pressed his thumb to the sensor pad. The phone unlocked.

"That's illegal search and seizure."

"I'm not an officer of the law."

Duane tapped Photos and found nothing of interest.

"Do you see any police?"

Then he tapped Videos.

Bingo!

"This is between you and me, Emilio."

He hit play.

And there was the "accident."

Maria Alicia Forteza riding in a ring, practicing jumps on Diablo.

Just as she reached the jump, Emilio's voice sounded loudly from behind the phone, "Look at the camera, Nana." As she turned her head at the call, Camila, who had paused her horse on the far side of the jump, reached down and lifted the end of the top bar just enough. Diablo caught his hooves—knocking the bar from her hands. Horse and rider plowed to the ground on the far side of the jump. Diablo had stumbled to his feet, then bent down to snuffle at the woman who didn't rise.

"I was keeping that," Emilio sounded desperate. "Mother is vicious. I needed protection in case she came after me too. I can't believe she did that to Grandmother."

"I see."

"Honestly, I'm the innocent party here. She's crazy. She's—"

"Your sister said you'd be dumb enough to keep something like this. What about the helicopter?"

"What about it?" But Emilio's face went pale.

"You don't understand the level to which she and I are trained."

"What do you mean?"

He could almost pity Emilio, lying on the ground as his world came apart.

Two state troopers rolled up the driveway.

They hurried up without a word.

Once one of the officers had his own phone positioned to record video, Duane hit play again. The officers' faces became grimmer by the moment as they recorded and watched the scene unroll again. Maria Alicia Forteza was one of the seminal forces who had spent decades shaping the Dundee Hills into such a major wine region. Her popularity was immense throughout the community.

"And this," Duane snagged Emilio's hand, pointing out the grease and chipped nail.

The officer shot photos, then put a plastic bag over the hand and taped it in place until a forensic team could see it.

"You really should have worn gloves when you were sabotaging the helicopter, Emilio." Duane kept his foot on Emilio's throat even after the police cuffed him. "Even I could see the fingerprints you left behind. Your grandmother dying by your mother's hand, and your sister and me dead by yours when that linkage failed in mid-flight, would have set you up pretty. Leaving you and your mother to take over the estate."

"That's my mother. Not me. You're lying. He's lying, officer. Fabricating everything. I would never hurt my sister. Sofia is—"

Duane increased the pressure of his boot just enough to cut him off.

The officers did nothing to interfere.

"Sofia is the one who realized what was going on. I also have a nice video," he handed a thumb drive over to an officer, who bagged it separately, "of you with your hacksaw and flashlight last night sabotaging the helo. I didn't even need night-vision gear; your flashlight provided plenty of light. You really need to remember to look behind you when you're working on attempted manslaughter."

At that moment, a lipstick red Lexus ES sedan roared out of the garage. Apparently, Camila had gone to check on Nana's pending demise and run into Sofia, who had explained a few things to her mother.

"She won't get far," one of the officers stated. "On your advice, we have a roadblock at the end of the driveway." The sudden blast of sirens and the squeal of tires skidding on pavement as Camila slammed on the brakes answered that one.

∾

THE THREE OF them sat on the grassy hillside, overlooking the vines. The police had spent hours taking their statements and collecting evidence—including the mostly hacksawed control linkage on the helo.

"It's strange with them gone," Consuela said it softly.

"Good strange or bad strange?" Sofia looked at her sister and saw that Duane was right. There was a young woman there who she barely knew.

"Just strange," Consuela shrugged. "Like there's been a pernicious disease that's miraculously cured. I keep waiting for the relapse." Her tentative laughter was easy to join in on. "I still can't believe that Mother did that to Nana."

Sofia thought about that. About how their own mother had shut them out. "It wasn't us, you know. It was her."

"What do you mean?"

"We weren't the unlovable ones. Her heart was always *Más frío que culo de foca.*"

"Colder than a seal's ass?" Duane laughed once, harshly. "I didn't know that one. That *is* cold."

She could hear the double-beat of a Chad-Duane comment, but couldn't think of what to add—Camila Forteza had *never* cared about anyone except herself.

Consuela nodded but didn't reply. The silences tended to

stretch around her sister, but Sofia let them. They were comfortable and, Sofia was discovering, thoughtful silences.

"What now?" Consuela finally asked.

"I guess I have to quit working intelligence and come home..." Sofia could feel the wrench in her gut. "It could take some time. You can't just walk away from Special Operations, they have to let you out as well. At my level we are serving at the President's pleasure, not our own."

Consuela was silent for so long that Sofia turned to see what Duane was thinking. He wouldn't meet her eyes. Instead he was plucking stems from the perfectly mown lawn and tossing them away. They'd flutter for several inches before falling to the ground in the vicinity of his feet.

Leaving Special Operations would mean leaving a job she loved. And it would mean leaving Duane, even their temporary connection. She couldn't ask him to come be with her, not that they had that kind of relationship. He'd be no happier leaving his team than she would be leaving The Activity.

"I wish there was another way," she said softly to him.

He nodded without looking up from his task of trimming grass one blade at a time.

"What if there was?" Consuela's whisper was so soft that Sofia almost missed it.

"I'm listening."

"If Nana dies..." her sister's voice choked off, and for the first time in far too long, Sofia wrapped an arm around her little sister's shoulders.

"When," Sofia felt as if she was being wise in echoing Nana's own admonition—the feeling was horrible. "But maybe with the doctors who are seeing her now, we'll be able to delay that."

Consuela nodded but didn't speak.

"What's your idea?"

Her sister looked at her, took a deep breath, and then plunged in full force.

"Look. I know you care about the winery. About preserving and growing all this. And someday you'll care enough to come back home, but that isn't now. Let me do it. I have a dual masters: an MBA as well as Viticulture and Enology from UC Davis. I don't care about ownership. I care about our wines. Let me be your manager. Let me—" Consuela reeled herself in with a groan.

Sofia couldn't help but smile.

"Stop grinning at me. I'm an idiot." Consuela hugged her knees to her chest and put her forehead on them.

Duane was smiling too, his blue eyes sparkling. It wasn't the look of a man pleased that his lover wasn't leaving him right away. He was grinning at Consuela's intense passion. That was something else Sofia shared with him—without that passion, they'd never have gotten to where they had in Special Operations.

"You're really not an idiot," she reassured her sister. "I just don't know when you grew up so much. I still remember the little girl who followed me everywhere."

"I wanted to be just like you, Sofia. Beautiful, smart, you have breasts," she waved at her own slender figure in dismay. "And you knew so much about everything: horses, wine, people, the business. I remember following you into the *Corazón de las Vides* wine lounge and watching every little thing you did so that I could do half as well someday."

"I can tell you that you were a real pain whenever I brought a boy home. Always underfoot."

Duane's "Good!" had them all three laughing.

Laughing? She hadn't laughed in years, and on this crazy day of all days, she could feel her heart loosening as she did.

Sofia looked at her sister for a long moment and knew Duane was right about her. Here was a smart, passionate, *grown* woman who missed nothing. She was also family; the only family she had left other than Nana.

"Okay, Consuela. This is what we're going to do. As of today, you are the manager of the Forteza combined estates. Not only

Colina Soleada, but all of the other vineyards and labels as well. When you need advice, feel free to call me, but go ask Nana first. We need to ease her burden, but keeping her involved in the operations may help her recovery, too. Give her hope and a purpose. But don't bother her with the little things; those are yours to decide."

"Really?" Her beloved little sister—who in many ways she hadn't seen in years and years—was suddenly looking up at her with her childhood's disbelieving eyes.

"Really." There was something more. "What is it?"

"The Dundee Harvest Festival is next week," she was rushing out the words again. "With Nana's injury and moth—Camila and Emilio gone… Will you still be in the country? I've got it all organized, but without Nana to attend the booth, we need you."

It was one of the most important events of the marketing year for the estate. "Perhaps you didn't hear me. *You* are now the manager. You will represent the estate and the family. Isabel will help you."

"But what if I make mistakes?"

"You *will* make them. But you'll *learn* from them. So will I, in your monthly status reports to me. Be sure that you include the bad with the good. But if you're half as successful as I think you will be, in two years you get a quarter interest and in five you get half ownership."

Consuela stared at her in blank shock for so long, Sofia was starting to feel self-conscious.

She wasn't ready when Consuela threw her arms around her and burst into tears. She kissed her sister on top of the head and held her close.

She *did* have a family! That was a surprise beyond any others on this trip.

What would she have in two years? Or five?

She couldn't help but look at Duane as she wondered.

CHAPTER 18

"*N*o plan," Duane scratched at his chin.

"Nope," Fred Smith offered cheerfully.

It was classic Delta, without being classic Delta.

"Usually you at least give us a damned target," Chad's growl filled the small, highly secure conference room at the Yakima Research Station with a dangerous sound.

The Unit was typically provided with very specific tasks, but not specific methodologies. The *how* was their specialty, achieving the impossible. But this time they weren't being told *what* they were supposed to be achieving in the first place.

Smith finally spoke up, perhaps to avoid destruction-by-Chad. "We have spent a week introducing you to all of the intelligence we have on Venezuela's current regime. It's a vicious dictatorship only marginally cloaked in due process. The judiciary is a puppet of the state and the parliament—dominated by the opposition party—risk their very lives every time they show up for work. It's so bad that even members of the hyper-loyal military and police are protesting, though only a very few."

"Sure," Chad put in. "We heard about the guy who flew over

the Supreme Court building and dropped a couple of hand grenades on them."

"Right," Duane agreed. "He should have dropped some five-hundred-pound bombs on the Palacio de Miraflores if he wanted to make a real impression. Smack in the courtyard while the President and First Lady were in residence."

"At least," Sofia put in, but her response sounded more force of habit than from really paying any attention.

Smith shook his head. "The President of *our* country has ordered that there is to be no direct action against the official government of Venezuela, which includes the President. The US can't be seen as staging a coup."

"No matter how awful the man is?" Melissa offered one of her rare questions.

"No matter how awful *we* think he is," Smith agreed. "If you—"

"The government," Sofia spoke slowly, as if she hadn't heard anything else going on. "Is only propped up partially by the military. It is really underpinned by SEBIN."

"Yes," Smith tapped the closed files on the table that they had memorized inside and out. "Their secret police has its fingers everywhere."

"So, let's take them down!" Carla thumped a fist on the table.

"No obvious direct action," Smith repeated.

"They're not the government. They're the secret police."

Duane watched Sofia and waited. This was what she did. He had known he was within minutes of losing her at the vineyard. She would walk away and run her estate and protect her grandmother and sister. They might get together a time or two, but they'd drift apart as he fought new battles in new places.

What had surprised him at the time was how much that idea had hurt. Another shocker had been his pleasure at the simple solution that had presented itself. No, that Sofia had conjured up out of thin air with Consuela's help as if it was the most natural thing ever—something the two sisters had created between them.

"Make it up as we go?" he asked. "It worked once."

Everyone looked at him curiously. All he or Sofia had told the team was that their helicopter broke and they'd been delayed waiting for an FAA-certified repair tech to get the part and show up at Sofia's home. The estate's marketing machine had kicked into gear, minimizing the news and keeping Sofia and Consuela's names out of it completely. The two attempted murder trials, if Camila and Emilio were too stupid to just plead guilty, would make the news at some later time.

Sofia started nodding. "First we need to get their quietly."

"The boat!" Richie jumped in immediately. "Let's go grab the boat. Guys, we gotta see what it can do, don't we? I mean it's an AB 100. We just gotta."

"That ain't real quiet," Chad was laughing. Clearly he wanted it too.

"Sure it is," Duane wouldn't mind a boat ride. "Because it looks like it belongs to a rich idiot, not a Delta team."

The women started asking what boat, and Richie and Chad began filling them in about the super-yacht abandoned in the Portobelo, Panama, boathouse.

Only Duane was watching Fred Smith, who was smiling happily. Of course he'd known exactly what he was doing when he'd showed it to them. This moment was his first reason for showing it to them. The *GoldenEye* was the perfect way to infiltrate the country—the arrival of wealthy and powerful business people.

"You with us all the way, Smith?" Duane asked quietly while Richie was busy lecturing everyone else about the nineteen hundred horsepower of each of the three MAN engines versus hull design factors in super-yachts capable of exceeding a fifty-knot speed.

"Me?" Smith sounded shocked. "Oh, I'll keep you company back to Panama, but I'm just an analyst desk jockey."

"What about her?" He indicated Sofia with a quick swing of his eyes that wouldn't draw anyone else's attention.

"That's up to her," Smith said quietly with a worried expression. "I hate to send her out into the field again, but—" His shrug was very expressive.

Yeah. Duane would hate it too, but he'd wager their odds of success would increase drastically with Sofia along.

Also, he'd wager that there wasn't a chance of stopping her.

～

SOFIA DECIDED that the boat tucked away in Portobelo, Panama, was everything the boys had advertised it to be. It was the middle of the night and no one wanted to turn on the boathouse's interior lights for fear of attracting attention. And even in the dim glow of the flashlights, it was amazing.

The boat roared with testosterone, even sitting dark and vacant inside the aging boathouse. It was a boy toy that no macho Venezuelan would be able to look away from. Arriving in Caracas —the capital city—aboard this vicious-looking beast, not a single man would ever remember how many were aboard, much less what they looked like.

Sofia felt like some rich, jetsetter, party girl from the moment she stepped aboard. The low dock was level with the swim deck, which had a garage that held a Zodiac inflatable boat and a pair of jet skis. Across the middle of the garage door, *GoldenEye* had been emblazoned in what might actually be gold laid into the Philippine mahogany.

Up a flight of stairs, the aft deck was a great expanse of teak, with a cushioned area big enough for ten people to lounge in the sun and an outdoor glass dining table for an equal number. The interior carpeting was a thick, charcoal gray that invited a girl to take off her shoes and wiggle her toes in its lush depths. The inside was as sleek and macho as the outside. Chrome, granite, indirect lighting, leather…definitely a boy toy.

Someone risked turning on the boat's interior lights, soft and low. A great sectional couch curved in a large U-shape and faced the rear view and a monster big-screen television set close by the aft door. Forward of that was a formal dining table and a two-seat command station clearly intended to humble the uninitiated. It also made the boys completely geek out.

She decided she'd wait until they were safely away before exploring any farther and did her best to stay out of the way.

All of them, even Duane, were swept up by the excitement of it. In minutes, it was clear that she and Carla were completely superfluous. They retreated to the vast lounge sofas to watch the show.

Richie, Duane, and Chad were all over the boat. Checking everything out, including the wiring, and getting ready to quietly steal it.

"What's with her?" Sofia asked. Melissa was right in there with the boys.

"She's a boat gal, too. She and Richie are the best sailors we have, pilots too if we ever need to fly something. Can add you to that list with your helicopter skills. None of us have that beyond basic survival in case we ever need to steal one."

"I'm just a civilian rotorcraft pilot, not military."

Carla shrugged, "More than the rest of us have. Kyle is also a good sailor, and anything the others do, Duane and Chad certainly have to try. Me? I grew up in Colorado. When it comes to boats, I'm smart enough to stay the hell out of their way."

There was a low roar as the engines rumbled to life. In moments, lines had been released. Smith swung open the doors to the boathouse and waved from the dock. They backed out beneath the stars and into the tropical night. There was a smooth assuredness to the action that made her suspect Richie and Melissa really did know what they were doing.

At barely a stroll, they eased through the sleeping harbor. Out the large side windows, Sofia watched the few lights on in the town glide by. She couldn't see any changes. No signs of anyone awake to witness their departure.

For twenty minutes they crawled, dodging among the anchored boats, slipping past buoys and channel markers. They reached the open sea with no sudden searchlights or chase boats.

Then Richie opened up the throttles and the boat roared to life. It was a very civilized roar, well muted on a luxury yacht, but the sense of power was undeniable.

Sofia did her best to shove aside the obvious parallels with Duane Jenkins.

The boat lifted its nose slightly and flew ahead.

"Let's explore," Carla tugged on her hand.

At the front of the expansive main cabin—"It's called a salon," Melissa informed them as she hustled by on some inscrutable task —were the pilot's seats. There was nothing to be seen out the sweeping window in front of Kyle and Richie except the darkness. However, the big display screens probably were telling them more than their eyes could, even in broad daylight. To the left, a door led outside. To the right, a stairway led down.

She and Carla started their down-below tour at the front of the boat. Two side-by-side cabins, each with twin-size bunk beds, obviously for the crew or kids.

Next was a galley kitchen done completely in brushed steel.

"Shit! I've never had a kitchen this nice," Carla began poking through the cupboards, which were filled with canned and dry goods. The refrigerator was empty, but the freezer was packed solid. "Mahi-mahi," she held up one package. "Chicken breasts," another. "Score! Wagyu beef tenderloins."

Sofia took it, dropped it in the sink, and turned on the warm water tap to trickle over it. "These will be thawed enough to cook in an hour."

"I've never had a fifty-dollar-a-pound steak before," Carla dug out some snacks and sodas, placed them on a silver serving tray, and carried them upstairs. She dusted her hands together when she returned, "There, that will keep them busy while we prowl some more." Carla popped the lid on a Pringles can, handed Sofia a couple inches of chips, and headed down the aisle scattering a trail of crumbs to follow.

There were three more suites—one king bed and two queen-size—before they hit the master suite.

"Oh, yes!" Carla said appreciatively when she peeked through a door of the main suite. "Sorry, Sofia. You can have the suite with the king-size bed. I saw this one first and I'm taking it. You gotta see this."

Sofia peeked into the master bath. It was worthy of her family's estate house. There was no tub, but the level of luxury was incredible. Toilet, bidet, and a shower big enough for an orgy. The bedroom itself had a comfortable desk, closet, dresser, and the inevitable large-screen television.

"Six bedrooms, five baths—this boat is bigger than anywhere I've ever lived." Propping up a couple pillows, Carla stretched out on the bed and continued working her way through the Pringles.

Sofia sat in the chair and took the steady hum of the engines as a good sign. The boat was well enough built that it wouldn't be hard to sleep even though the engines must be directly below them and running fast.

"So, are you going to tell me or do I need to go find a gold-plated crowbar?"

Sofia knew the question was inevitable, but she didn't know which answer she should give.

"I saw the news article—ever so carefully edited. I connected that to your helicopter 'breakdown,' though I doubt if anyone else did."

Oh, that answer. She'd been thinking about Duane.

"I did," Melissa came in, lay down on the bed, and accepted the short stack of Pringles that Carla offered her. "Did they really try to kill you?"

"Me and my grandmother. Duane would have just been collateral damage."

"Isn't family just fucking precious?" Carla sounded bitter.

Melissa started to shake her head in disagreement, but Carla cut her off before she could speak.

"Don't listen to her. Melissa's parents are far too normal and pleasant. You should have seen them at her and Richie's wedding. We ended on this little Bahamian island—where the concierge was terrified of you the entire time for reasons you still haven't explained, girlfriend," Carla's tone was accusatory, but she didn't slow down for an answer, "—and everyone wanted to adopt them before it was over. My mom died in the service and my dad is a worthless shit I haven't spoken to in years, but even I wanted to adopt them."

"Mine weren't like that," Sofia wondered what that would be like. Melissa seemed so...normal. White blonde, sleek, and pleasant. It took an effort every time to remember that she was also a Unit operator with a long list of "mission accomplished" entries in her file. She'd also been awarded several unadvertised medals for valor, including a Distinguished Flying Cross—a very unlikely award for a Unit operator. Richie also had one of those in his file. Neither had any explanation on this side of the need-to-know security wall.

"Okay, okay," Melissa snatched the Pringles can away from Carla. "My parents *are* totally sweet. Give me a freaking break!"

"Yep! Totally Canadian." Carla gave Sofia a wicked grin for having elicited such a reaction out of their soft-spoken teammate.

"So, Sofia, was Duane totally awesome?" Melissa handed her the Pringles can as if passing the baton of the conversation.

Sofia opened her mouth and closed it again. Instead she took out some more chips.

"Come on," Carla prompted. "It's obvious you've had sex. He

can't stop watching you and when he does, he gets all sorts of slack-brained. That's not like Duane at all. He's always on point, like a hunting dog or something. Please tell me it was amazing."

"Why should I tell you that?"

"Hey, we're married women. We have to get our thrills somewhere."

Melissa nodded in agreement.

Sofia wasn't buying it. "You are both married to warriors from the 1st Special Forces Operational Detachment-Delta."

"We are," they sighed happily in unison, making each other laugh.

"Doesn't let you off the hook," Carla continued while Melissa kept looking goofy happy. "Now give."

∽

"THERE'S GOOD. There's incredible. Then there's better than that. Somewhere past that there is Duane Jenkins."

Duane froze in the hallway outside the master suite. The heavy carpeting had masked his approach.

"Details. We want details." Carla and Melissa in chorus.

The question was, did he really want to hear details?

Go in?

Beat a hasty, and very silent, retreat?

"Okay already!" Sofia protested.

The silence was deep, just the muted thrum of the engines and the slap of the waves on the hull as it sliced through them.

"There's a lake I used to go to as a girl. It's actually on the backside of the neighbor's property. I'd go there whenever I needed to get away. Nana showed me how to get there. I never took anyone. No one. I don't think even my little sister knows about it. It's not easy to find and there's only one decent path."

"You took him there?"

"I took him there."

Duane waited along with the two other women.

"*Well?*" Unsurprisingly, Carla had the least patience.

"It was like letting him see something inside me that no one ever has."

Shit! Duane had completely missed that. It had been a pretty lake on a beautiful day in the company of a hot woman. He'd missed every goddamn clue. He wanted to smack himself.

"And…" Carla egging her on.

"I—"

"Hey, buddy!" Chad slapped him on the shoulder hard enough that the downward force was the only reason Duane didn't jump out of his boots. He'd come up from behind without Duane hearing.

There was a squawk of female surprise from the master suite.

"What you listening to so intently, bro?" Chad asked cheerfully before Duane could stop him. Chad, of course, knew exactly what he was doing—being a total ass.

Carla vaulted off the bed and came to the door. The sad shake of her head before she slammed the door in his face told him how much shit he'd just stepped in.

"We need to rustle up some grub," Chad yanked on Duane's arm hard enough to almost tumble him to the carpet.

"You're no help at all, you know that don't you?"

"Fuckin' A, Bubba. Don't want to see my main man going down 'cause of some cute chickie. Damn cute. I'll give you that much, bro. But you got it like a disease that seriously needs a cure."

Duane considered going back and knocking. To apologize for eavesdropping or something, but he didn't see any way that was going to go well with all three women together. Safer to follow Chad.

They found the thawing steaks. Duane put together a pasta sauce with jarred pesto, sundried tomatoes, and frozen vegetables.

Chad showed his culinary finesse by getting Tater Tots in the oven and finding some ketchup.

The women finally emerged as the meal was getting close to done. Whatever had transpired earned him a scowl from Melissa, an eye roll with a cheeky smile from Carla, and a deeply unhappy blush with averted eyes from Sofia. The steaks were too close to done and he didn't dare leave them in Chad's care to chase after her as she scooted up the stairs.

When he and Chad delivered the finished dishes upstairs, Sofia was nowhere to be seen.

Carla took pity on him and pointed him toward the ladder at the stern of the boat that led up to the flying bridge.

He grabbed two plates, a couple of sodas, took a deep breath, and headed up. With both hands filled, he nearly lost their dinners overboard several times as Richie kept them racing ahead over the Caribbean Sea out of Panamanian waters, through Colombian, and on toward Caracas.

Once he reached the upper deck, he ran into another problem, specifically the table. And he ran into it hard. There were no external lights on the boat. And the interior lighting below, which was too dim to show through the tinted windows, didn't help him either. He couldn't see a damned thing except the stars and the phosphorescent sea churned into a bright green strip by their wake. His hands were full, which didn't matter—his flashlight was down below anyway.

"Sofia?"

～

"I AM CONSIDERING NOT ANSWERING YOU," Sofia could just make Duane out as a silhouette blocking her view of the startling green light in their wake.

"Really? What have you decided? I have food." She could see him moving closer, bumping along the edge of the table in the direction of her voice. She'd used her flashlight to sit on the far side of the table, then shut it off to watch the night. Her inclination to assist Duane by turning it back on was minimal.

"I don't know yet. Are you worth the trouble?"

"That's a tough one," he stepped past the end of the table and right by her. "I know someone you could ask. Would that help?"

"I think I've had enough advice for one day." Carla and Melissa had certainly had plenty. She could no longer see Duane, which meant he could probably now see her, at least a little bit.

In moments, she heard two plates set on the table along with a rattle of silverware and then the solid thunk of a can of soda that must have been quite cold for him in his pockets. She reached a hand out and found it. Sure enough, the metal was cool on one side and cold on the other. A chair scraped back and she assumed that he was now sitting across from her.

"It's amazing how little breeze there is up here. We're running at about fifty knots. Almost sixty miles an hour." As if that was anything she wanted to hear about.

She'd already figured out that the boat was designed to divert the air over the passengers' heads. She'd confirmed that by raising her hand in the air while still standing. She'd been able to feel the edge of the world blowing past, so nearby.

It felt as if she was teetering on the edge and would soon be falling off.

But to where?

What lay beyond places on the chart marked "Here there be dragons"?

"It *was* quite peaceful up here."

"Ouch!" But he made no move to stand and depart—at least not that she heard.

"Duane?"

"Yes, ma'am?"

Unsure what to say next, she reached out until she found her fork and plate. But eating steak in the dark was ridiculous, and mostly impossible. She fished out her flashlight, flicked it to a red-lens night mode and turned it on at the dimmest setting. She set it down so that it lit their plates but little else. The meal looked delicious.

"Silent treatment, huh? Means I was right. I was going to suggest that you ask yourself, but then I thought that was a foolish answer fraught with unknown dangers."

"Because I might advise myself not to speak to you?"

"Exactly!" He pointed his knife at her for a moment to confirm her point before cutting into his steak.

She did the same. It was awfully good. A man who could cook. "I liked cooking with you back in Oregon."

"I enjoyed that too. A lot. I'm not nearly as good a cook as you, but it was fun."

And he was clearly enjoying himself in not telling her who she should be talking to, but she refused to fall into his trap and ask.

She could just make out his hands cutting another piece of steak and raising the fork into the darkness.

"Fine!" Sofia threw her own cutlery down on the plate and crossed her arms. "Who should I be asking for this ever-so impor-tant advice?"

His soda disappeared into the darkness for a moment, then returned to the light. "Me, of course!"

"You?" She couldn't help but laugh. "I'm supposed to ask you to advise me on whether or not I should be speaking with the likes of you?"

"Sure! Does the lady have any better suggestions?"

She didn't. "Okay, do your worst." She started eating again because the steak was too good to not keep eating as a demonstra-tion of pique.

"Personally, if I were you, I'd never speak to me again."

"Why not?" Not what she'd been expecting, but then Duane so rarely was.

"Well, setting aside the recent spate of rudeness and the fact that I'm a bit oblivious where you're concerned, I think you're just too damn good for a jerk like me. Trust me, Sofia, walk away while you still can."

"Okay," she agreed easily and kept eating.

"Good!" Duane didn't seem to be daunted for a moment by his own advice or her acceptance of it. "I'm glad we got that settled."

"I have a hypothetical question," she waved a Tater Tot in his general direction.

"Fire away!"

"If I *were* to speak to you, what would you be saying to me?"

"That you're the most incredible woman I've ever met and that the day you go back to The Activity will be the worst day of my life. Ever. Way worse than the day I told Dad to go fuck himself and joined the Army. If I was to actually say anything."

"Just that?"

"Just that."

Sofia was impressed that she'd been able to keep her tone as light as his, because she was having a terrible time breathing. All the air on the fly bridge had been sucked away by the racing air layer above them until she felt lightheaded, even faint.

"Sofia?" Duane's tone was completely different. Soft, serious for the first time since his arrival.

"Yes?" Her attempt to keep her own voice airy and unconcerned caught in her throat.

"I meant every word of it," his deep voice was barely louder that the boat's.

"Which? The part where you tried to make my bones melt into a happy puddle," *and completely succeeded.* "Or the part where you said I should never speak to you again?"

There was a long silence. Long enough for her to set down her silverware and push aside the mostly finished plate. She leaned forward, but still barely heard his reply when he spoke.

"Both." It was soft and filled with a pain that he wasn't explaining.

She turned off the flashlight, stepped carefully around the table. Her fingers found his shoulder, down his arm, to his hand. Tugging him lightly to his feet, she guided him to the plush sunbathing sofas that her earlier investigation had revealed. By the connection of their fingertips, she guided him onto the sofa with her.

He hesitated, but she pulled him down.

"Now I have some advice for you," she whispered in his ear once they were lying in each other's arms. "Show me more about the melting my bones into a happy puddle part."

And, without a single word, he did.

She was glad no one came looking for them, because Duane was very, very thorough in making love to her by the light of the warm, tropical stars.

CHAPTER 19

"Still don't have a plan," Duane knew he sounded grumpy, but he couldn't seem to fix that. He wasn't even sure why.

This morning, he'd woken at first light in a beautiful woman's arms. Beneath blankets scrounged from a locker, they'd watched the sunrise over the arid hills of Punta Gallinas, the northernmost tip of Colombia's Guajira Peninsula. By the time they came down for breakfast, the boat had cleared the broad peninsula and was racing into Venezuelan waters.

"We'll be in Caracas this afternoon, we should have a goddamn plan." Nobody was arguing. He ignored the strange looks he was getting.

Sofia was way too good for a man like him. She should be with someone who believed in relationships and all that shit. He sure as hell never had. Never expected to. Even if he did, his mental image was some bar babe who would scream and cheat, but fuck like a porn star. Sofia was all class. A guy like him didn't deserve that because he'd screw it up first chance he got.

He could feel himself screwing it up even now, but there was no stopping it.

"There is only one decent marina," Sofia studied her laptop, which was patched into the satellite uplink—now in her brilliant Activity-agent mode. "That is a starting place."

"That isn't a plan." Why did she get to be so damned cool and collected? It didn't matter. Why should he care? It wasn't like either of them wanted a relationship. Maybe she could rise above —she was Sofia Forteza, wine heiress; of course she could. He knew exactly what his past counted for—Mr. Rich Playboy turned Unit operator. Not a goddamn decent thing in his future. She might be the best screw he'd ever had, but that's all there was between them. He ignored the slice of pain at that last thought. He was Delta—he was used to pain. There was no way a guy like him could woo a woman like her. Keep sleeping with her as long as she let him, then wave the hell goodbye? "That isn't a plan."

"Duane," Kyle looked at him across the main dining table they'd all gathered around, except Melissa who was currently ten feet away at the helm to keep them at full speed toward Caracas.

"Yeah?"

"Shut the fuck up."

Duane clamped down hard on his tongue. Even in his current mood he wasn't dumb enough to argue with Kyle when he used that tone.

It was a ridiculous situation. Mission orders were supposed to be given to Delta, not created by them. The moment they had those orders, by standard protocols, the team went into isolation —full communication lockdown. It was up to the team how to carry out the assigned mission and the lockdown made sure that no one would know what they were actually up to. It cut down on leaks—unintentional or nefarious. It also cut down on regular Army command channels second guessing Delta methodologies. Yet another reason Colonel Gibson reported directly to the three-star general in charge of Joint Special Operations Command with no one else in the loop.

"You *were* the one who suggested we make this up as we go along," Sofia whispered to him.

He didn't need reminding of that. There were far too many things being "made up" at the moment. The problem was he'd "made up" a relationship that Sofia absolutely didn't deserve. He cared too much about her to saddle her with a guy like him. But the other thing he'd said last night was just as true. He'd die without her.

Chad cuffed him on the back of the head, harder than usual. Then spoke in a voice loud enough to be heard all the way to goddamn Atlanta. "Look, asshole. You gotta separate the mission from the woman. Get your fucking head in the game."

Duane had finally found the focus for his frustration.

His punch caught Chad hard enough on the chin to send him flying backward out of his chair. He did a head-over-heels somersault across the cushioned settee and landed on his feet.

On his feet as well, Duane dodged under Chad's grapple and rammed his shoulder into Chad's gut, lifting him clear of the deck.

He was too furious to scream when Chad pummeled a fist against his kidneys, but he lost his hold.

Chad had him back against the edge of the door for two crashing punches to Duane's gut and face. But he'd taken worse in hand-to-hand combat training. Didn't hurt nearly as much as being shot three times in the back by the Colombian FARC rebel barely old enough to have breasts.

Using the door frame for leverage, Duane launched at Chad. Hard grapple. Too close for blows. They both sought leverage to grab an arm, a leg, anything. They bumped against the railing.

Then something hit them.

Suddenly they were airborne.

For a single eye blink, he could see Carla standing at the aft rail of the upper deck, rubbing her shoulder after delivering a blow that would make a linebacker proud.

Then he heard Chad's, "Oh, fuck!"

They'd completely cleared the lower deck. They barely had time to fold their arms and twist to the correct positions for a high-speed bailout before they slammed into the water at fifty-seven miles an hour.

The sea hit him harder than any explosive he'd ever set.

~

"FIX THIS. AND FIX THIS NOW!"

Sofia could only cringe in front of Kyle's fury. It was a side of him she'd never seen, never even suspected to exist.

To have it suddenly aimed at her was too much. She got back up in his face.

"How in the name of all that's holy am I supposed to do that?"

"Hell if I know. Just do it!" And he stalked away, ending the conversation.

"Why is it up to me?" She yelled it at his back. But he didn't slow, instead going out the side door and up onto the foredeck. The problem was that, for reasons she didn't understand, somehow it really *was* up to her.

Melissa was circling the boat back to pick them up, but she too was watching Kyle's retreating back with wide eyes.

Just perfect! Looked like Melissa had never seen him that way either. That was *so* not a good sign.

Sofia stepped out of the cabin and went to stand beside Carla as Melissa eased the stern close enough for the two men to grab the swim ladder on the deck below.

"Any suggestions?"

Carla just shook her head. "Like you said, make something up."

"And if that doesn't work?"

Carla looked at her for a long moment. "Then try the truth." She squeezed a hand on Sofia's arm before turning to follow her husband.

Whatever that was. She certainly had no idea as she stood at the aft rail and watched them climb aboard, a deck below her.

"I can't believe you call that a right cross, bro. When did you become such a pansy?" Chad was checking on the flow of blood from his lip that a dip in the ocean had done nothing to staunch.

Duane was gingerly testing his ribs. "One of these days I'm going to have to teach your sorry ass how to throw a proper tackle."

"Excuse me for never being Mister College Football."

"I was track and field, asshole."

They gave each other the finger, then began ascending the stairs like two old frat buddies.

Chad looked up at her. "Uh-oh. Got some music waiting for you, bro. My advice: dive back in. The sharks looked less dangerous that she does." He walked by her with a lopsided smile, favoring the bleeding side. "Hey, Richie! Where the hell's the first aid kit on this junk heap?"

Melissa was returning them to their original course and cranking the engines back to running speed.

Duane still stood on the lowest step of the staircase looking at her.

She finally descended to meet him.

He backed up. There was a low bench built onto the outside of the closed garage door for storing the Zodiac and jet skis under the lip of the upper deck. He eased down onto the bench with great care.

She sat beside him, though not too close, and watched the wake racing away behind them.

"I was ordered to fix this. Any suggestions?"

Duane just shook his head, leaned back against the door with closed eyes, and groaned as he continued to probe his ribs.

"If you are looking for sympathy points, you are asking the wrong girl."

His halfhearted smile turned into a wince and had him probing his jaw. "Then what should I be asking you, ma'am?"

"You could try asking me what I think is wrong with you, but I have no ideas."

"You don't?" He opened one eye to look at her.

"Do you?"

"Actually, yes. But I thought you were the great analyst."

Sofia considered adding her own blow to all of Chad's. "Well, I don't. Does that make you ever so happy?"

"Yes, ma'am. Nice to be half a step ahead of you for once."

"Duane!"

"Okay. Okay," he held up his hands in surrender. "Just, well, try not to hate me for this one. Please?"

"I'll try, but I am making no promises." She folded her arms tightly to brace herself for whatever was coming.

He stared off the back of the speeding boat for a long moment. "I was right about there," he pointed off the stern just above the water, "when I figured a few things out."

"Such as?"

"Such as both of our families suck at relationships. Loyalty is right down the toilet, too."

Sofia looked down to inspect her toes. They did.

"But then I look at my teammates. Kyle and Carla. Melissa and Richie. These are good people. Ones that couldn't be closer."

"You and Chad."

"Nobody better."

"Even though you just beat the daylights out of one another."

"Even though," Duane agreed. "He's had my back through every horror show since the beginning and I've had his."

"Why am I suddenly in the way of your perfect bromance?"

"You aren't. You're just proving that I'm a total asshole."

Sofia finally looked at him. "There are many things that you are, Duane Jenkins. That is not one of them."

"Thanks. Too bad you're wrong on that, but thanks." He looked away, then after a long pause, thumped the back of his head against the door, hard enough to make them both flinch. "The thing is..."

"What is the thing?" She asked when he didn't continue.

"The thing is," he took a deep breath, then spoke fast. "I've been trying to treat you like just another good fuck."

Sofia felt her entire body go cold.

"That's all women have ever really been for me. But, goddamn it, Sofia, you aren't staying in that nice neat slot in my head. Shit, woman! You've changed everything. But the truth is all that'll be left standing when the world's afire, so what the hell. The day you walk away is gonna kill me—and that's not some *thousand percent* likelihood; it's goddamn fact. But looking at my past, at who I am, I meant the other part, too. You'd be better off with the goddamn sharks," he waved a hand toward the stern, "than you would with me. That's what's been ripping me up all morning." Then he folded his arms over his chest hard enough to make the muscles bulge, closed his eyes, and banged his head back against the door one more time. Hard. He was clearly done.

Sofia looked out at the realm of "the goddamn sharks" and tried to find some way to fit Duane's words into what she was feeling. Her family had tried to kill her, which wasn't exactly the most shining recommendation. *His* family had essentially disowned him, not that it sounded as if they'd particularly ever *owned* him in the first place. If she was to face the truth, she hadn't been the one to take Duane home to the estate in Oregon—her body had. She'd wanted him physically just as much as he'd wanted her.

So when had he become more than that?

From the first moment outside Aguado's compound. The way he'd accepted her as a woman in a combat role. Then the way he'd taught her what she didn't know and made her face the man she'd killed—which actually *had* cut down on the nightmares.

She slid a little closer to Duane and slipped her hand around his hard-clenched biceps just to see how it would feel. He didn't react, didn't look at her. He remained frozen like a coral statue.

Sofia liked the feel of Duane. Not just how his body made hers feel, but the surety of him as well. Actually, his surety of her. Since the first moment he had displayed an unwavering confidence in her capabilities. His belief that she was somehow better than she knew. His attitude was having the strange effect of making her believe it.

"Hey!"

She looked up to see Chad leaned out over the railing above them. His lip had stopped bleeding, but he held a bloody cloth that appeared to be wrapped around an ice cube.

"Are you and the asshole about done? Richie has an idea."

She looked at Duane, who was now facing her.

He wasn't going to speak first, but she still didn't know what to say.

Slowly, tentatively—an adjective that she'd never thought she'd use to describe him because Duane was always so sure of everything—he touched the fingers of his other hand to the backs of hers where they wrapped around his biceps.

She squeezed a little tighter. Then so did he.

"Jesus you two are glacial!" Chad groaned before disappearing from the railing.

"I think," Sofia had to swallow hard before she could continue. "I think I would be better off risking you than the sharks. I have already spent too much of my life among them."

He started to lean over to kiss her, but gasped and groaned again as he held his side.

"But for now I see that I will have to be taking a raincheck," she kissed him on the nose, rose to help him to his feet, and led him back up to the main cabin.

~

"I was messing with Sofia's laptop and—"

"What? How? It is very secure."

Duane could only grin at Sofia's protest. She clearly didn't know Richie's skills.

"Well," Richie actually blushed. "When Duane and Chad started fighting, you jumped to your feet without locking the screen. I ducked in and created myself as a second user. So when you remembered to lock it, I was already in."

"Very underhanded, Richie," Chad nodded. "Proud of you, *amigo*. You're finally learning."

Richie smiled, "Melissa is teaching me."

Duane joined in the others' laughter—only the still irritated Sofia holding back, though she eventually smiled. Even she had to understand that no one as wholesome as Melissa could be a corrupting influence on anyone except a man like Richie.

"Anyway, I looked at that marina outside Caracas that Sofia identified. It's the best one in the nation and reasonably secure. I made a reservation for a boat slip. Not a problem because tourism to Venezuela sucks right now." He pointed to the big-screen television as he'd also linked the laptop into the onboard systems.

It showed a satellite view of the marina, the surrounding park, and swimming pools.

"But we can't stay there. For one, the marina is too well guarded," Richie started listing watch rotations and the like until Kyle stopped him. Then he continued, "Heavy private security makes for a lousy launching point for operations. I did make a reservation at a nearby Marriott just in case. Security would still be a pain, but the hotel is just half a kilometer from the back corner of Simón Bolívar International Airport if we need access to a plane."

The team started razzing Richie about the Analie Sala mission. He'd been itching to get back at a plane's controls ever since—despite the fact that they'd almost all died from his piloting that time. If Duane was never again on a flight with Richie at the controls, that would be just fine, even if he had managed to save them in the end.

"What else did you learn?" Duane cut in to keep it moving. He'd certainly delayed the discussions long enough through his own rank idiocy. An idiocy that he still didn't understand how Sofia had forgiven him. Could they really just "make it up?" Was *that* how people made relationships?

"That marina and hotel are still ten miles to downtown—about an hour in typical traffic. Remember, at under forty cents a gallon, this is a car-crazy country. Of course, it's up from two cents a couple years ago, so the citizens are *not* happy. I made reservations at a rundown little *cama y desayuno* closer in. The beds are supposed to be sad and the breakfast worse." Richie paused.

He loved to be coaxed, so Duane did. "But…"

"But the B&B is less than a block from where the *barrio* meets El Helicoide." And he put a bird's-eye view of the building up on the screen. "It's the former headquarters and one of the two main buildings that SEBIN occupies in Caracas. It's also where most of their political prisoners are incarcerated."

They'd studied it back at the Yakima Research Station of course, but it was still an amazing thing to look at.

In the 1950s a visionary had designed El Helicoide—The Helix. A tall hill in the center of Caracas had been scalped into a helix-shaped architectural cone circling the hill nine times as it climbed to ever-smaller levels. At three-quarters of a million square feet laid out like a coiled serpent, it was to have been the largest and most modern shopping center in Venezuela's history. By following the nearly three-mile-long road as it looped upward, customers could park close in front of whatever store they chose. The ultimate in modern convenience.

Started but not finished, it ran out of capital in the '60s. To try to enliven interest, a Buckminster Fuller geodesic dome was even added to the flat uppermost layer—an area originally intended for the wealthiest people to arrive by helicopter. It hadn't worked.

The late '70s were defined by twelve thousand squatters moving in after the fast-encroaching *barrio* was leveled in a massive earthquake—the new residents eventually adding primitive water and power systems. The sewage system had still predominantly been dumping a bucket out over the edge and onto the next lower level.

"Shit rolls downhill," Chad remarked as Richie continued the review of something they'd all heard back at Yakima. But a review was always a good thing prior to an operation. Who knew what factoid could spark a strategy or save their asses if the mission went sideways.

Then in the 1980s, DISIP, the secret police forerunner to SEBIN, had moved in, ousted the squatters, and finished The Helix. Since then it had become a midtown icon of imprisonment and torture.

"The only thing worse than El Helicoide is La Tumba," Richie moved the image over to The Tomb. SEBIN's new headquarters lay just three miles away. "Sixteen stories above ground and five stories of prisons and torture chambers, that we know about, below ground. It was supposed to be a major station for their subway system at Plaza Venezuela, but that went away when the current administration seized power and needed somewhere to expand beyond El Helicoide."

"We need eyes on La Tumba as well." If Kyle was still pissed at them, he was doing a good job of hiding it. He was being as attentive as any of them.

"Which is exactly why I reserved a luxury suite in the Hotel King. It is directly across Olimpo Street from La Tumba. So, while you lot are languishing in your little B&B between El Helicoide and one of the city's worst slums, we'll be sipping a *cerveza* and watching the bad guys from our cushy armchairs."

"Why the hell do you guys get off so easy?" Chad growled.

"Simple," Richie was even more chipper than usual. "We thought it up."

"Damn it! Melissa *has* been teaching you too well." Chad raised his voice to Melissa's back even though the helm was so nearby, "Take it down a notch, will ya?"

She shot back a thumbs up that Duane would bet had nothing to do with toning it down and everything to do with staying in a luxury hotel rather than a ratty B&B.

It was one of Kyle's strange policies. Whoever had the idea got the most benefits from the idea—if everything else about the tactical situation was equal. Richie had earned his cushy night out with his wife—even if the night out would be in full reconnaissance mode.

"How much longer to landfall?" Duane didn't think he could take too much more of Richie's gloating. Or of anything.

"Seven hours from here to Caracas," Melissa reported from the helm.

"You've got six hours people," Kyle shifted to his feet. "I want you fed and rested by then. Last hour is full weapons check. We're finished here. Well done, Richie."

Richie's smile lit up. The look he traded with Melissa would melt steel.

Kyle must have caught it too. "I have the con. Get out of here, you two," he moved up to take Melissa's position.

Duane figured that was a good idea before he got assigned some shitty task.

"Things I want to say to you," he whispered to Sofia.

She nodded in response and led him downstairs.

There really were things he wanted to say to Sofia, but he wanted to say them in private. He wasn't sure what they were, but the feeling was there that he definitely had something on his mind. Talking to her seemed the only likely way he'd figure out what it was.

But when Sofia opened the door to one of the suites, all he saw was the big bed with its pristine comforter the color of her eyes.

He fell face forward into it… them… it. And didn't remember a thing for another six hours.

~

DUANE HAD SO OBVIOUSLY NEEDED his sleep that she'd let him have every minute of it and ten more.

Which had left her so frustrated at what he'd left unsaid that she hadn't slept a wink.

When Kyle had come down to locate his missing crew member, he'd taken one look at her eyes and said kindly, "It's time, Sofia. Roust him." Then he'd gone away with no other comment.

He'd yelled at her earlier for missing that Duane was upset, now he was being understanding about her sleeplessness.

What was it with *nice* men all of a sudden? She wasn't used to that and they were confusing the crap out of her. Not that the guys at the Activity were bad sorts, but there hadn't been one she'd have gone out with even if she was dumb enough to date someone from work.

Now she wasn't *dating* someone at work. She was…falling—

Tonto del culo!—Idiot of the ass! How was that even possible? But it was exactly what was going on. She was *falling* for Duane. And he wasn't someone at work. He was someone she was going into battle with. How insane was that?

It was her own fault. The Activity hadn't pushed her to get field experience, but all of the best agents had it and it showed. They didn't typically embed with the teams for more than a single mission. She'd never heard of one who got into it this deep.

While Duane was inventorying and checking the weapons and explosives he'd brought along, she'd spent some more time at her laptop. The first thing she did was find Richie's account on her computer and burn it out. Or she tried to. It wouldn't delete.

"Richie!"

He popped his head up out of a case of surveillance gear.

"Get your butt over here!"

He grinned at her, "Too busy." And he ducked his head back down. He knew *exactly* what she was upset about.

Well, she was no slacker. She went in and burned down the hidden system password file—overwrote it with the Department of Defense 7-pass 5220.22-M(ECE) standard of secure erasure and set up, only for her user exclusively, a new one. Let Richie get around that if he could. For good measure, she changed her user name to Duane so that he wouldn't guess it.

She stared at the screen. *Duane?* She'd completely lost it.

She changed it to MariaAliciaForteza for Nana and then went about her research.

Sofia suspected that, with the gas prices at forty cents, it would be easier to buy a pair of used SUVs than rent anything.

Once they were ashore, she'd been right. No one wanted such gas hogs anymore and American dollars had immense buying power on the street. It turned out far cheaper to buy the two vehicles than even a one-week rental from the airport car rental agency. The rental agencies honored the official exchange rate of ten Venezuelan bolívars to the US dollar rather than the black market rate of three thousand. Besides which, the SUVs they purchased were battered and dinged enough that no one would look at them twice, whereas even Venezuelan rentals were relatively new and clean.

The exchange rates—other than the official one—were so bad that even at forty cents per gallon it took a stack of bolívars almost a foot high to fill the tank of each SUV. The clerk at the station hadn't bothered to count the money, he'd weighed it. And grimaced until they'd added another inch.

Thankfully, Smith had anticipated this and equipped them with almost as many cases of money as ammunition. They paid the security guards a US fifty each to watch the boat, with the promise of another two hundred if it was untouched on their return. By the light in their eyes, there was a good chance it would be fine. If they had to exit the country another way, then they could sell the boat for all she cared.

The late afternoon trip into the city through the dragging rush hour had tested her nerves to the limit.

She sat in the back with Duane, but wasn't comfortable speaking. Kyle and Carla were up front and Chad was in the far back. Richie and Melissa were taking the other vehicle to their fancy hotel.

Kyle circled them about through the city to get the lay of the land. All she got was a little carsick.

That was cured when they finally pulled up to the Helicoide Cama y Desayuno. The only thing that the three-story, gray block B&B had to do with El Helicoide was that it was looking right at it. When she opened the car door, she went straight from carsick to nearly gagging. The smell of the *barrio*—something the SUV's air conditioning had at least mitigated—was brutal despite the mild fall temperatures. In the summer it must be unbearable. Frying onions, burnt meat, sewage, and...

Duane's arm was around her shoulders and he was escorting her inside.

"Was that..."

"Yes, don't think about it."

"This city has the highest murder rate outside a war zone," she knew the statistics. She couldn't block them. The *barrio* didn't reek of squalor—it reeked of death.

The B&B had a steel door. The man who opened it, after inspecting them carefully, wore a Makarov pistol and she'd wager there was a rifle or shotgun tucked somewhere close to hand. He was a lean man but addressed them kindly enough once they were inside and the door was locked again.

It was far nicer inside than out and Sofia managed to keep her dinner down.

"*Turistas locos.* Only craziest *turistas* come to here," he said in a heavily-accented mash of Spanglish—which he insisted on using as soon as he realized they were Americans despite the whole team being fluent in Spanish. "All come to see El Helicoide. Last year they come from England. Museum of...*arquitectura?*"

"Architecture."

"*Sí. Sí.* They want to take many pictures. *Policía* take cameras and smash! One man, he argue. They beat so bad he must go hospital. I warn them. But do they listen? *No!* You," he poked Duane in the chest as if he didn't tower a foot over him. "Do you listen?"

Duane smiled at him, "*No.*"

The man shook his head in disgust. But he gave them their keys and waved them toward the stairs. "*Arriba. Para arriba.* Up! Best view. It is at top floor. I give them to you." And he disappeared through a back door.

The three rooms took up the entire top floor. Once they were all up the stairs, Duane set a squealer infrared beam that would warn them if anyone else tried to climb higher than the second story.

In minutes, Sofia had her computer up and had opened a 3D map she'd downloaded of El Helicoide based on the original plans from the 1950s that they'd found in the archives of New York's Museum of Modern Art. Soon the team was standing far back from the windows, observing through their scopes, and calling out things for her to add.

"Level Three. At one-twenty degrees south. Gun emplacement. Nothing fancy. Probably a Kalashnikov RPK."

"Level Two. Directly above the Level One entrance. A pair of Vladimirovs. Mounted to aim down, not up."

She added the heavy machine guns to the diagram. They were more suited to anti-aircraft than building protection, but the half-inch rounds would punch easily through a car or truck.

Soon all four of them were calling out information so fast she could barely keep up. Chad was the sniper and was calling out the gunnery positions. Carla gave her structural changes, and seemed to have a real thing about wire fencing. Duane was defining weaknesses that could be exploited by the application of explosives. And Kyle was giving her patterns of movement, both of personnel and vehicles—reaction-time of gate guards and the like.

After two hours, Kyle called a break. Besides, the sun had set and there was little more to see. They kept bright lights facing out toward the *barrio,* which must be incredibly irritating to the residents, but only the uppermost layers of El Helicoide remained lit.

"Chad. First watch. Next door," Kyle pointed. "Keep the lights off—don't want them noticing us."

Chad slipped away carrying his rifle.

"Sofia, show us what we've got." He pulled the blinds down and they spent the next two hours crowded around her laptop breaking down what they'd learned.

∼

"WHO'S UP FOR A SIGHTSEEING TOUR?" Duane did his best to sound chipper over breakfast but it was hard.

He'd pulled third watch, right in the middle of the night. The only activity had been someone from the *barrio* snooping around even their sad SUV parked on the street. Not wanting to shoot anybody, he'd used his silenced rifle to shoot another car farther down the street. He didn't feel bad because it no longer had tires or seats, but the bullet's impact made a very satisfying—and highly recognizable—bang as it punched through the rusted hood and pinged off the engine block. The thugs on the street might as well have evaporated for how fast they were gone.

On top of that, Richie hadn't been kidding about the beds. They were miserable. Unable to stand it any longer, he'd gone for a morning run. The old man had been there to let him out and back in, just shaking his head at Duane's insanity.

Thankfully, the food wasn't as bad as Richie had predicted.

The old man pan-grilled *arepas*. He'd sliced the hand-sized circular maize-flour cakes in half, creating a *reina pepiada* sandwich filled with chicken, avocado, spring onions, and a wicked mayo-cilantro sauce. Duane could have eaten a tray full, if they weren't so filling. Just one did in everyone except Chad—even he couldn't finish the second one.

Breakfast, and completing his run to see Sofia's smile in the window above where she stood last watch, were the two highlights that said this was going to be a very good day.

"What are we seeing?"

He'd have answered anyone other than Sofia, but for her... "It's a surprise."

And it was. A quarter of a mile walk along the Calle Vuelta del Casquillo, they stepped out of the *barrio* and into another world. There were several tall buildings, the streets were wide and had sidewalks. In a nicely planted area stood a Metrocable station. It was a cross between a fortress on the lower stories—which the plantings did little to soften—and a fanciful forest of steel above.

"I present to you the Metrocable tramway. It provides a splendidly scenic view of the city."

Sofia was the first to trace the line of the aerial cables and then turn back to him with that radiant smile of hers. Once they were airborne, El Helicoide would be clearly visible from the tram car from a far different perspective than their B&B.

Inside, the station was again another world from the streets. It was a study in marble and bright steel. The squeezing pressure of the city was replaced by a vast expanse that could have handled a thousand people rather than the few dozen using it. There were signs for daycare, hotels, shopping...but they mostly pointed to chained-off stairwells and darkened storefronts.

But every thirty seconds a gondola rattled over the rails and into the station as another rattled out. State sponsored and controlled, the fares were just a few hundred bolívars, mere pennies on the black market.

With a little careful maneuvering—stepping into line after one large group and just before the arrival of another—the five of them got an eight-person car to themselves. As soon as they were locked in, Duane pulled out a sensor and ran it over the insides.

"We're clean. The microphone isn't engaged until we hit that 'in case of emergency' button."

"Then don't hit it, bro."

"I won't."

Sofia rolled her eyes rather than adding the last note to Chad's and his patter.

Then, as their car shot out of the building and began the steep climb toward the first pylon, they all turned to the windows.

Below lay the a single block of neat, multi-story brick houses, roofs of white or gray tin. The area was relatively flat and there were cars on the streets. At the end of the block, the terrain jolted upward. The housing changed completely from one side of the street to the other. A mixture of single-story, severely-marginal brick shacks were jumbled together worse than a pile of dumped-out jigsaw puzzle pieces. There were no roads, no straight passages. The walkways were often only a few feet wide, jogging this way and that around individual structures. The *barrio*, impossibly, looked even worse from above than it did on the ground. He'd done a little exploring this morning during his run.

And over it all loomed the towering edifice of El Helicoide, its upper heights quickly coming to eye level.

"What must it be like to live here?" Sofia was surreptitiously filming out the window. Her sunglasses had a built-in projection feed from the high-res camera peeking out through a hole in the purse over her shoulder. A hand tucked around the strap gave her access to the zoom controls. It was a slick piece of work that he'd enjoyed playing with while she was setting it up.

"I know," Duane felt the same thing. "To live in poverty and look up at that thing. At least it isn't a shopping mall anymore, that would be horrible."

"No, it is just the SEBIN who are oppressing them. I think maybe it would be like always seeing the Death Star no matter which way you turn."

"Aren't we in a bright mood this morning."

Sofia grimaced.

"Sorry." Duane wanted to brush a hand down her back, but didn't dare jar her camera work—*that* she'd never forgive. He missed their banter, but somehow it just didn't work looking down at the mess that was central Caracas.

Kyle pulled out his satellite phone. "Richie. Meet us at the Parque Central Metrocable station...That sounds better." And he snapped the phone closed.

The tram rattled into a station atop the hill in the center of the *barrio*. It was clear that buildings had simply been swept aside here to place the station. Unlike the lower San Agustín station, the El Manguito station made no qualms about being fortified. It was surrounded by high fences topped with razor wire.

Like the tourists they were, they got out and went to the viewing platform.

The two-hundred-foot geodesic dome atop El Helicoide was at eye-level less than two football fields away. A sign warned that photography was illegal and armed guards prowled the platform to ensure it was obeyed.

Sofia rested her purse on the railing.

"There, at the north end, you can just see the planned elevator."

Duane looked down. All he saw was a small, blocky building at the base.

"It was supposed to be a sloped elevator, six of them actually, in three separate shafts buried beneath the building into the hillside. They were never installed."

Now he could see the repeated structures up the face that would have been nine successive elevator lobbies. "Is that what the structure on the top is, beside the dome?"

Sofia made a show of looking at the skyline as she shifted her purse. "Yes. The bottom half. The top half appears to be a radio antenna. It's pointed slightly to the west from straight up."

Duane nodded. "Richie said that the Simon Bolívar spy satellite is in a slot at seventy-eight degrees west. Caracas is at sixty-six. So the antenna's angle makes sense."

She fussed with the purse's strap. "Cable housings running on the surface into the dome. If we could get in there, I'd wager we could get the codes."

"Oh, like that's gonna happen. You on drugs, lady?" Chad grumbled.

Duane wondered though. There had to be some way in. The trick would be to get in and out without drawing any attention to themselves.

Chad looked at him, waiting for something.

What? Oh. His second beat.

"If she's on any drugs, I hope I'm the drug." A lame response, but all he had at the moment.

~

IT WAS hard to believe they were in the same city. Sofia breathed in deeply and blessed the moment. Yes, she could still feel the oppressive city out there, but they were in a little bubble of normalcy.

The Metrocable whisked them over the eight lanes of the Autopista Francisco Fajardo—the freeway was an unmoving block of colorful buses, yellow taxis racking up huge fares while not moving, and cars packed so densely that even the motorcycles had trouble weaving through the gaps. They unloaded at the final Parque Central station and walked into the Parque Los Caobos. Suddenly they were crossing broad, grassy lawns beneath the shadows of ancient trees. The big-leaf mahogany trees—*caobo* in

Spanish—had somehow survived all the regime changes, revolutions, overpopulation, and avoided depredation since colonial times.

For five hundred years this park had survived in the heart of Caracas. It was surrounded by the national performance center for music and dance as well as museums of science and arts all around the periphery. But even that was lost beneath the trees. Here, quiet paths wandered through more shade than sunlight.

The trees were alive with other fauna as well. Green Amazonian parrots debated territorial rights with the brilliant scarlet macaws—especially when someone tossed out some leftover tortilla. Black squirrels countered the parrots' aerial strategies with racing ground strikes—down the tree, a dash to the prize, quick grab, and the fur infantry returned to the trees before the feathered air squadrons coordinated their forays.

Sofia wanted to purchase a whole stack of tortillas so that she could toss them about in little pieces and just watch.

Sculptures awaited them in surprising locations, but the best was the Fuente Venezuela—the Venezuela fountain. The quiet two-tiered pool with small water jets quietly splashing was peopled by large stone sculptures representing the different regions of the country. Beautiful, bare-breasted women and stunningly handsome loin-clothed men lounged for all to admire. The statues were self-contained, complete in themselves, needing no others.

She had thought that embodied her—alone, independent, and all fine with that. Now she had a sister—who had e-mailed her such a hilarious account of her efforts at the Dundee Wine Festival booth that Sofia would have laughed until she cried if others hadn't been in the room. For a moment she'd wished with all her heart that she'd been there beside Consuela.

And she had…a boyfriend? Sofia knew she had a lover, but that was physical. She strongly suspected that she now had both.

Among the couples admiring the fountain were Richie and

Melissa. They looked disgustingly well rested as they approached while holding hands.

Sofia had only slept fitfully last night, despite getting no sleep at all on the boat. After she'd spent a whole night on the boat wanting to know what Duane had been about to say to her, she'd now spent another wishing he hadn't said anything to begin with.

Then he'd jogged in the morning all bright and chipper as if life was perfect in Venezuela.

What the *hell* was she doing here?

She'd abandoned her family, abandoned Consuela to return to The Activity. Except was she with them? No. She was with Delta Force.

And if she bonded with Duane—if they had one more heart-to-heart talk—she'd want to leave her own team to join his.

Somewhere in the middle of the longest night in recent history she'd decided that *she* was the one who was screwed up. She'd left Nana, the Defense Intelligence Agency, Consuela, and now The Activity. How long before she left Duane? She was the woman who ran away from everything good. Not that she was *with* Duane...but she was and—

"I should go throw myself in the fountain."

"That dress. On you. Wet... Oh, yeah. Do you want me to help you in?"

She punched Duane on the center point of his sore ribs.

"Shit!" His gasp made her feel a little better.

She shouldn't have worn a dress. She'd thought the light, summery fabric would be the best way to blend in. How was she supposed to know that a woman's standard Caracas attire was faded jeans and a blouse or t-shirt that showed more cleavage than she typically did except at the swimming pool or an evening-gown fundraiser.

About the time she decided that she should apologize, Chad moved in to console his buddy.

Fine! Let their bromance blossom. They could invest in a rifle range together and live out their days teasing the customers with aplomb. Good for them.

Besides, Nana always said, *en boca cerrada no entran moscas* —flies don't enter a closed mouth. Yes, it was sometimes best to keep her mouth shut. She would do that from now on.

There were far more locals gathered around the fountain than anywhere else in the park. Several food vendors lined the edges of the surrounding square. She purchased a guava ice cream and selected a bench with easily observable approaches and relative privacy. Soon the others were seated about her on the low curb just a step away or on the lawn. They would look like a group of close friends to the dozens of passing observers.

By making a circle, they kept an eye out in every direction while looking casual. Somehow, she'd ended up being the focus of the whole circle.

Well, she was The Activity analyst, and it was nice that they respected that. She'd leave it to them to pay attention to all of the families passing by. With their training, they'd spot unwanted attention long before she would anyway.

Was she irritated, or pleased that Duane decided to stand close by rather than sit at her side?

Protective?

A wider area view and better response time from a standing position. She liked the feeling of that.

A few days ago, she'd have hoped that he was busy looking down the front of her dress. Her interests had been far more about sex just a week ago.

She wasn't comfortable that those feelings had shifted and she wanted something more. It meant that—

Focus!

Her tired brain was not cooperating.

Richie cured that particular ill by sitting next to her with a dangerously dark-red ice cream.

"Chili-pepper chocolate," he took a bite, then spoke around the mouthful. "I've never seen it before so I had to try. It's—" His voice squeaked off as his eyes crossed and began to water.

"Melissa?" Sofia asked when it was clear Richie wouldn't be recovering quickly. Her cone was sensibly vanilla-white.

"There's a reason La Tumba is called that. The security isn't merely good—it's alarming. Fresh guards on the entrance every hour, officer inspections at the half hour. Four-man squad on the roof armed with Dragunov SVU rifles good for close combat but effective past twelve hundred meters." She delivered in two breaths what it would have taken Richie a dozen to just get started on.

Maybe she should buy up a stock of the chili-chocolate flavor.

"No second entrance, at least not above ground. If there's ever a fire, they'll have to go out through the windows, which look to be thick enough to take a heavy round without breaking. It was originally supposed to be a major subway station before SEBIN took it over, so I would assume there are underground connections, quite possibly reaching in both directions: west to El Helicoide for prisoner transportation and east to Generalissimo Francisco de Miranda Air Base, commonly called La Carlota, for potential escape."

Sofia hadn't thought to look that direction. A new factor to integrate, though she didn't see how it might affect the current operation. Caracas had grown until La Carlota was in the heart of the city. Multiple administrations had promised to turn it into a park, a music venue, a water theme park complete with surfing, even new housing to relieve the urban core crushing in from the sides. Despite promises, it was still the Air Force's primary base in the country. For now, she dismissed it.

"What about the roof?"

"Why do you think we got the luxury suite?" Richie had managed to recover. He was continuing to eat the ice cream, in very small bites. His eyes were still watering from the chili's heat, but apparently he thought he looked less foolish than tossing it away and admitting defeat. "Helipad and some point-to-point microwave, nothing aimed up at the satellite."

"What would it take to tap their microwave feed?" Duane was the first one to speak from the rest of the team.

Well, at least Duane had been paying attention to what was going on.

∼

DUANE WISHED that Sofia would stop breathing so that he could concentrate. Each breath drew his attention sharply downward— his top-down view of her chest revealed the most wonderful things when she breathed. He'd always been a lucky shit when it came to women. Maybe not as lucky as Chad, but damned fortunate. But never even close to her.

Sofia in a dress... *Goddamn amazing!* Yet another side to the woman: from jungle fatigues on up. About the only thing he was missing now was seeing her in an evening gown. That thought actually sent a shiver up his spine. She'd look *beyond* amazing in a gown. It was enough to get him to jump back into that social set just to see her dressed up.

Never in his life had a woman as beautiful and smart as Sofia even given him a second glance. Keeping up with her was a challenge that really pushed him to stay on his toes and he was coming to particularly enjoy that part of being around her.

He forced his scan from the enticing view of her cleavage out to the wider world. Couples with kids. A group of teens. A dad with a squealing toddler on his shoulders as he galloped toward a swing set. A group of children in awe watching a juggler. No loners except for a beautiful teen girl reading a book and nodding her head to the music on her earphones.

He'd always been blown away by the beauty of Venezuelan women, always rated in the top five on hottest country lists. Somehow, on this trip, he hadn't even noticed the other women. There was a disproportionate ratio of pretty women in the park: tall, strong-shouldered, with good figures, perfect natural tans, and flowing long hair. He hadn't noticed one of them except to track them.

The pretty teen paused, then began absently nodding her head to a different rhythm with a song change. It was a shift that she wouldn't have made if she was somehow listening to them rather than her soundtrack. He tagged her as "likely harmless" and let his attention drift mostly back to their own circle.

"Tap their microwave?" Richie accidentally took a bigger bite of his ice cream while he was busy thinking. With a gasp and a choke, he looked around for somewhere to spit it back out. Melissa held out a napkin that he spit the soggy glob of ice cream into it without taking it from her hand first.

She grimaced, placed her half-finished vanilla in one of his hands, plucked the chili-chocolate one free, and dumped the glob and cone into a nearby trash can. Several fresh napkins and a good rinse from a water bottle washed the worst of it off her hand —all the while Richie was absentmindedly eating her vanilla cone. He looked surprised when she took back what little was left.

Duane shared a smile with Chad, but one glance at Kyle showed he wasn't in the mood for any goofing around at the moment. That, and Duane didn't want to break Sofia's train of questioning. He could feel her building a picture in some kind of intel-geek layers.

"Tapping into the system isn't the problem," no longer distracted by the ice cream, Richie finally started speaking. "The problem is getting onto the roof. We could shoot a line over easily enough from the King Hotel—angle's not bad for a decent zip line. But you'd have to take down the rooftop guards first. Too far to dart them. You'd have to lob over three or four canisters of sleepy gas to get them all; they always stay spread out to the corners. Their radio check-ins are very frequent. SEBIN didn't get to be SEBIN by being sloppy."

"Other end of the feed?" Duane guessed at Sofia's next question.

"El Helicoide as far as I can tell. Angle is right."

Sofia didn't respond. She was fiddling with the strap of her handbag. Oh. Reviewing her recordings of El Helicoide, searching for the microwave receiver. Now that he thought about it, he was pretty sure that she hadn't mentioned her camera and viewing sunglasses trick to anyone else.

Cover, dude. Cover quick!

"Does anyone see a point in pursuing the La Tumba angle any further?"

A particularly loud burst of laughter had several of them turning their heads. Duane missed the natural beat for the turn, so he didn't. Kyle's and Carla's eyes tracked back quickly and the look on Chad's face said hot women rather than potential threat. So Duane ignored it. The head-bobbing beauty looked up brightly as an equally stunning girl plopped down beside her and gave her a big kiss. So much for appearances.

Melissa shook her head no on the La Tumba question even as Richie continued. "I wanted to get underground, check out their defenses inside the subway tunnels, but Melissa didn't think that was such a hot idea."

Duane was inclined to agree. If they were that compulsive above ground, they'd be just as paranoid below ground.

"So, we're not to touch the regime, we're just supposed to mess with SEBIN?" Duane voiced it for discussion.

"Uh-huh."

He waited.

Had to nudge Chad to get his attention back—which earned

him a friendly punch. "Damn but I love some things about this country."

No one else had anything to add.

"There *is* a microwave receiver close beside El Helicoide's satellite dish. That should be our target," Sofia's voice was soft. But no one seemed inclined to question it.

CHAPTER 20

*S*ofia didn't have a chance to catch her breath again.
They'd left the Parque Los Caobos by midmorning.
Dispersing widely through Caracas.

Kyle and Chad *had* gone down into the subway system but found nothing interesting at the La Tumba end. They were now probing in the other direction toward El Helicoide.

Richie and Duane were off to see exactly what was going on at La Carlota—the Air Force base across town—in case they needed a contingency exfiltration plan. It would be much harder to get out after they stirred up the hornet's nest than it had been to slip into the city while everything was quiet.

Carla and Melissa had swept her under their wing and the three of them had armed up and gone deep into the San Agustín *barrio.*

They'd talked to a lot of people through the afternoon: sharing *parrilla* barbeque with a couple of drug runners, squatting over a cup of fresh ground coffee with a circle of women as their children played around them, scouting the layout of paths and alleyways. Then, at the hottest point of the afternoon when the *barrio* was particularly fragrant from the beating of the tropical sun, a lone boy had come up to them with an invitation to meet the leader of San Agustín's *colectivo*.

The *colectivos* had replaced the police in many of the most dangerous neighborhoods. Ex-military, some were pro-government and some not. But they were the law. They cared less about the government's policies and more about *La Policía's* failures and corruptions.

"I kill a crooked cop as fast as I kill the druggies you speak with at lunch," word of their presence in the *barrio* had spread fast ahead of them.

Sofia would have been freaking out except Carla and Melissa appeared to have some form of a plan. It would have helped her nerves immensely if they'd told her that beforehand. Perhaps they hadn't known it themselves and were still making it up as they went. That did *not* increase her comfort level.

"I catch the drug runners selling anything to people here, I shoot them." The former Army major held up a well-worn Browning Hi-Power 9mm pistol. "The police do not care about San Agustín. So, I take care of it. You hurt my people, you dead. No matter how fine you look. You don't hurt them? You're not my problem."

His cell phone had rung while they sat in his bunker.

He'd listened, then snapped the phone closed without responding past a grunt of acknowledgement.

"You have ten minutes. Someone else is on your trail. *Mis amigos* will lead them sideways for a little time. Now, why do I listen to you?"

"We only need two minutes," Carla said without even blinking.

He waved his Hi-Power for them to continue.

Sofia didn't doubt that, if he felt it was necessary, he wouldn't hesitate to put down all three of them despite his curiosity.

"How do you feel about SEBIN coming into your neighborhood?" Carla jumped in with both feet.

Sofia held her breath.

"An attack?"

"Running."

"From you?"

Carla's smile sent a chill up Sofia's spine.

The *colectivo* leader's smile was even chillier. "I could get to like you, *señorita.*"

"*Señora.* You would not like to meet my husband."

"He's more dangerous than you?"

She simply nodded, which earned her a deep laugh.

Then he'd turned very serious and abruptly shifted his pistol to aim at the center of Carla's forehead.

Carla didn't even blink.

"Not *el presidente?* Only SEBIN?" So, this *colectivo's* leader still believed in the government.

"Only SEBIN." Carla had to be the coolest-nerved person Sofia had ever met.

"When?"

Carla had merely looked at her watch as if she was counting minutes, then back at him, ignoring his unwavering Hi-Power.

Tonight? Sofia couldn't believe it. Or maybe she could. Once ready, they hadn't hesitated to blast their way into General Aguado's compound. That meant that, one way or another, this would be over tonight.

With a sharp jerk, he shifted his aim up and away from Carla's face. Then he holstered the weapon with a slap of metal into leather and held out his empty hand.

Carla shook it once, hard.

"Your husband. He must be very brave."

"Yes. Unless I do something stupid, then he gets very angry."

"Like when three beautiful women walk into my *barrio.*"

"No, this wouldn't surprise him...much."

Again he laughed as if he meant it. "Tonight, *señora,* we will be keeping watch at the gates."

~

DUANE HAD TRIED PACING, ordering room service, and glaring out at La Tumba from the window of the King Hotel, but still the minute hand refused to move any faster. It certainly couldn't have moved any slower.

Richie had locked himself in one of the suites with a whole array of strange gear, leaving Duane with even less to do than usual. A thorough check of his own gear had lasted him under half an hour before he was back to pacing.

The sound of the key in the door hit him like an electrical charge triggering a detonator. He had one hand on the door knob —and the other on his weapon, of course—before it had time to open.

Sofia stepped in.

He didn't hesitate.

Didn't think.

He simply slammed her into a hug and hauled her against his chest so hard that she squeaked in surprise as her duffel tumbled to the floor.

Melissa stepped over it, with a bag of her own gear, and smiled at him. He nodded toward the closed door at the other end of the suite's living room. Her smile and hip-loose walk told him that Richie had better be done with whatever he'd been working on.

Duane kicked the door shut and looked down at Sofia.

"Hi," he held her tighter. "That seems to be the best I've got at the moment." He breathed her in. She smelled...awful. He barely resisted coughing the air back out. She smelled like...the *barrio* on a hot fall afternoon.

"It is plenty good enough for me," she planted her face firmly against his chest and didn't complain about how tightly he was holding her. It felt like heaven—

"Uh, please don't take this wrong, honey. But you *really* need a shower."

"Am I that bad?"

"You're always good to me, but yeah."

She pushed back enough to look up at him, her smile teasing. "I think you are just trying to get me out of this dress."

"Only wanted to do that since the first moment I saw you in it."

She turned her back, "Unzip me then, you low brute."

"Yes, ma'am," he ran the zipper down and popped loose the bra strap while he was at it.

She kicked off her shoes, a long dark line of skin showing between draping sides of light floral dress. Just before the bedroom door, she shrugged. Dress and bra slithered down to the floor and she stepped out of them without breaking stride.

He wasn't going to get caught again. He raced forward and managed to get his hand in the door jamb before she could close and lock it. Thankfully, she hadn't swung it too hard. He flexed his fingers and shook them out—*use your boot next time, doofus.*

Duane closed the bedroom door just in time to hear the bathroom door snap shut. Thankfully it was a pocket door with no lock. He followed her in. By the time he was stripped down, she was in the shower.

No dancing. No hot Spanish mama waiting for her man. Instead, she had her forehead planted against the shower's plastic wall and the hot water was pouring onto her unmoving back.

He managed to crank down what she did to his libido and considered that maybe he should think about what *she* needed. Grabbing a bar of soap, he began working over her. Shoulders first, digging into tight muscles. She groaned as they loosened, but didn't move. He slowly went over her body, soaping, massaging, soothing. Fingers, palms, wrists, arms. Toes, feet, calves, thighs. If he spent extra time on her butt and up her front, who could blame him?

He had switched over to shampoo and was working on her luxurious fall of hair before she spoke the first time.

"This is what you do all the time?"

"No. Because I've never had you in the shower with me."

"That is not what I am meaning," she twisted around so that her back was leaning against the shower wall.

He smoothed her hair back to keep the soap away from them.

"I mean what Delta does."

"Rub down beautiful women in showers? Oh, yeah, all the time."

"Duane," he heard the growl in her voice.

"Yes, ma'am. Doing impossible shit in dangerous damned places is about the size of it. Before Iraq and Afghanistan, those early operators were stuck with doing much more training and rarely doing shit. Modern Delta op tempo is so high that it's a challenge getting back to Fort Bragg for new skills training. We were supposed to get another South American team and be rolled back Stateside already. But the reengagement in Libya, Syria, and the fuckin' Caliphate in the Dustbowl has left us pretty much on our own. Now close your eyes." He stepped her under the water and rinsed out the soap, only burning his hands in the scorching water a little to make sure it was well rinsed.

He pulled her back out of the water, sniffed her wet hair, then kissed her on top of the head. "All clean; now move aside, woman." He nudged the temperature down a little with his elbow. Kinda too far, but a cold shower at the moment might be a good idea. Sofia looked amazing, but not up for much.

She leaned on the wall at the end of the tub and just watched him.

He was soaped and half rinsed before she spoke again.

"I could get used to this."

Duane eyed her carefully, which earned him a stinging drip of shampoo. He rinsed and tried the other eye. "This, as in showering with an incredibly handsome Unit operator or this, as in..." he waved a hand toward the madness that was Caracas.

"I meant Caracas."

Yep! Cold shower had definitely been the right choice.

"But I could also get used to this," she stepped forward and yelped. "But not if you are going to be freezing me like a chili-chocolate ice cream." She reached past him and turned the water back up to scald.

Then she moved the rest of the way into his arms and turned her face up for a kiss, her lovely length pressed tightly against him.

"Worth putting up with a little heat to draw the fire."

"Absolutely," Sofia agreed.

∾

SOFIA LET GO. Let Duane do whatever he wanted to her, she would just lean in and enjoy it.

What he did was hold her close and start a slow dance in the shower. Nothing much, just a slow shuffle step that matched his heartbeat when she laid her ear on his chest. An easy sway of their hips in perfect harmony, his hands just holding her close. This she could *definitely* become very used to.

"What are you thinking, Mr. Jenkins?"

"Do you ever have those fancy dress receptions at that winery of yours?"

"Sometimes. Why?"

"With dancing?"

She nodded against his chest.

"I'm picturing you in a slinky, revealing evening gown."

"One with cleavage down to my belly button and no back, I am guessing." That was an easy guess with Duane.

"Yes, ma'am," he rubbed his hand slowly up and down her spine to make his point. "Exactly like that."

"Well, it just so happens that I have a dress exactly like that."

"The color of your hair?"

"Yes."

"Good. What do I have to do to arrange a private preview of that?"

"You must be very, very nice to me. Nicer than you ever are to anyone ever before."

"I'll have to work on that." He slapped off the water, reached out, and took one of the big towels off the rack.

Starting at the top of her head, he rubbed her down until she was warm all over from the attention. He even grabbed the hair dryer and a brush and attempted to dry her hair. He was clumsy, awkward, and sometimes pulled the brush too hard through a snarl, but she was too charmed to complain. Instead, she just held onto the sink with both hands and watched him in the mirror—he was concentrating so hard that it was cute.

Then Sofia watched herself. She'd always thought that happy equaled smiling. But she was fast mapping a new terrain beyond that. Duane was teaching her that there was a quiet place where her eyes lidded half shut on their own. When the feeling was too good, too strong to do more than breathe. Her hair began to fill and billow. At the rate he was going, he might soon turn it into a teased disaster.

"Duane?"

He turned off the dryer. "Yes, Sofia?"

"Now."

"Now?"

"Right now."

No one could ever accuse a Unit operator of being slow on the uptake. The dryer and brush clattered onto the shelf. He bent out of sight of the mirror for a moment over his pants, then she heard the tearing of foil.

"Sofia?" Duane looked at her in the mirror, restraining himself long enough to be sure.

"Yes," she was absolutely sure.

She continued holding on to the sink as he eased his hands on her hips and pulled her back against him in a single, soul-filling slide. His palms cradled her breasts as he leaned over her to kiss her between the shoulder blades. Even in this position, his hand traveled to make sure that she would be satisfied as well.

She watched Duane, watched his face as the smile faded but the joy rose. Saw how he saw her as special beyond words. Watched his eyes as they slowly lidded closed. How had she ever thought their blue was icy? How had that been possible when they were really so clear that they saw her in ways she'd never seen herself?

Unable to watch the sensations crossing her own face anymore, she let her eyes slide shut.

He wrapped his hands around her as he carried her aloft to places she'd never even known in her dreams.

Because her dreams had been merely dreams of the flesh. With Duane they were turning out to be so much more.

CHAPTER 21

$\mathcal{T}$his time when they reached the San Agustín Metrocable terminus, Chad led them at an easy saunter to one of the closed-off stairwells. In rapid succession they stepped over the chain and descended the stairs. No hurrying. No rush. Hurry drew attention—walking as if you belonged hid the actions in plain view.

Chad and Kyle had been here this afternoon and led the way. Carla was, typically, moving ahead of them as if she was the one who'd found the access. He and Richie brought up the rear. Richie had brought so much gear that he had to split it up among everyone except Duane, who had his own fifty-pound pack to tote around.

Melissa and Sofia were off on some other assignment that he knew nothing about.

Sofia.

Damn but that woman had crawled up inside him somewhere and taken residence there—a very comfortable residence. Time had been so precious. He'd held her tight as they lay together on the bed and watched the day fade over La Tumba and Caracas.

Neither of them had spoken because there simply wasn't room for words in the last hours they might have together. Maybe he'd have to ask her if The Activity ever recruited from Delta. He'd hate to leave the team but—

"Head in the game, bro?"

"Head in the game," he assured Chad. They donned night-vision gear and flicked on infrared flashlights. They'd moved down past an uninstalled movie theater and through the lobby of a nonexistent hotel. A door hung loose on its hinges there, its lock neatly blown in a style he recognized—because he was the one who'd taught Chad how to do it.

"Good. Don't want you getting all weird over a woman."

"You mean like that time you almost stepped into the middle of Lake Maracaibo over a woman while wearing forty pounds of gear." They trotted down the stairs after the others, entering a vast unfinished subway station.

"Looks unfinished, but the third rail is hot," Kyle called out. That meant that trains moved down here, even if the line was listed as planned but not built. Good sign.

One after another they jumped down onto the tracks and picked up that special rhythm for trotting on railroad ties without bunging up an ankle.

"Tanya Zimmer," Chad sighed wistfully. "Be worth going under for a woman like that."

"Actually, why haven't we run into her again? She was working Venezuela for the Israelis. Seems like we'd have had a job in common again. Why didn't you keep track of her?"

"Tried to, bro. Me! I actually tried to keep track of a woman. Slipped away."

Duane thumped him on the shoulder in sympathy. He couldn't imagine how he'd feel if Sofia Forteza "slipped away." Actually he could—it would suck beyond imagining.

He almost stumbled sideways into the third rail. Not just beyond imagining, no way in hell was he going to let it happen.

Not to him. Not to her.

It might not work out. Hell, he'd screwed up enough relationships in the past to know that he was good at *that*. Too good.

Head in the game.

But the game had been changed by a slip of a Spanish whirlwind who barely came up to his nose. Whirlwind? Woman was a goddamn summer breeze, enticing, tempting, then slipping away when you weren't paying attention.

Well, he was paying attention now.

Bring it on.

∿

SOFIA SAT on the roof of the King Hotel and tried to look for the stars above Caracas, but she wasn't having much luck. There was a rolling blackout that covered most of the neighborhoods to their south, from the university to Bello Monte. But the area around the Plaza Venezuela and La Tumba still blazed brightly. She suspected that they had very few blackouts in this neighborhood —SEBIN wouldn't like it.

"I miss the stars of home."

"You thinking of leaving the service?" Melissa sat in the dark beside her. They were both dressed in Venezuelan military camos and black t-shirts. They'd dumped most of their personal gear, though Sofia had carefully folded and tucked away the dress that Duane had so liked. Their duffels weren't light, but there wasn't room for anything as extraneous as clothes tonight.

"No. I..." It wasn't the stars of *home* that she was thinking of. It was the stars above the speeding boat where Duane had made such perfect love to her. "I miss Duane. But that's crazy. We've been apart for under two hours. That doesn't make sense."

"Of course it does."

"How?"

"It makes sense because you love him."

Sofia sighed. "I was afraid that's what it was. Do you know of any cures?"

"You mean other than marrying him?"

"Yes, other than that."

"Nope!" Melissa was being entirely too glib about it all.

She must have felt it, because she reached out and rested a hand on Sofia's arm.

"Richie is the best man I've ever met. I'd have been an idiot to let that slip away…and I'm not an idiot."

"Neither am I."

"That's my point," Melissa squeezed her arm.

"You're not helping."

But Melissa actually was. Assuming they got out of this mess alive—it was one of the craziest plans she'd ever thought up—but she wasn't going to stop until she figured out how to make this work.

"What do we do in the meantime?"

"We wait for their signal." At least for the operation.

Was she going to wait for Duane's signal about them? She'd give him a chance, then she'd light the fuse.

"So we sit around and wait for the men. Where have I heard that before?"

Sofia sighed.

"Don't worry," Melissa nudged their shoulders together. "Carla's with them. She'll keep them in line."

～

THEY'D BEEN underground for almost half a mile when Kyle led them down a side tunnel.

Duane could see a lit platform ahead.

Kyle clenched his fist for a hold. He peeked up over the edge, watched for a long thirty seconds, then held up two fingers. He pointed at Carla and signaled her ahead.

Duane nodded to himself. She was the most lightly burdened of them but she was also the stealthiest, at least if they weren't in sniper mode—that was his and Chad's forte. But in everyday situations he'd seen her walk into the middle of a firefight with no one else even realizing she was there until she put an abrupt end to it. And if a distraction was ever needed, Carla's figure in a tight t-shirt definitely counted.

The other thing Duane noticed was the stone resolve that that made Kyle such an amazing leader. His best asset in this situation was Carla, so he hadn't hesitated about sending his wife into harm's way. Man had balls of steel—his would be totally shriveled if that was Sofia out there.

Carla vaulted up onto the lit platform and strode toward the guards. She was dressed in Venezuelan Army camo and black t-shirt. She had a Kalashnikov AK-103 rifle over her shoulder, the most ubiquitous in the infantry.

He translated the Spanish automatically as she strode up to them.

"Hi! Have either of you seen the colonel yet tonight? He's supposed to be here by now. I gotta give him this message," she waved what he was fairly sure was the B&B's room bill at them. "No chap off my ass if I gotta sit here and wait for him, but the general is gonna have his ass if there's no answer fast, and I mean super-fast. You know what I mean, don't you?"

She so overwhelmed them that they didn't even speak until she was close between them. Not even bothering with her silenced sidearm, she used her knife to make quick and silent work of them.

He and Chad had their sniper rifles ready to fire, but there was no need.

They dragged the bodies into the office and out of sight after Carla had wiped her blade on their SEBIN uniforms. They were definitely in the right place.

Kyle locked the door and doused the station's lights as if no one had been there.

They all switched back to NVGs.

"They use ground transport from here for prisoner transport up the road. But Chad and I found the access to the old unfinished elevator system this way."

Still no need to rush, they maintained a light trot down a long hall, through a door—picked lock this time—and up a flight of stairs into a room that smelled of raw earth and old concrete. The construction was rough, unfinished: a lobby area to the unfinished shopping mall. The outer doors were sealed. Duane hustled over and threw some quick-weld on the seams. He triggered it off and the thermite filled the room with a bright red glow for twenty seconds. No one would be opening those doors now without a good supply of high explosive or a tank.

They entered the forty-five degree shaft together.

At the first level, Chad veered aside. "This is where I get off. Catch a beer with you later, bro."

Duane slapped a high-five and continued up the shaft after the others.

At Level Six it was Duane's turn to exit the shaft and go out onto El Helicoide.

"Brought you something cool," Richie fished into the pack that Kyle had been carrying. It took him under twenty seconds to assemble it. "Cool, huh?"

"Cool," Duane agreed. "What the hell is it, Richie?"

He looked crestfallen. "It's a street luge. The road that wraps around El Helicoide is two point five miles of non-stop descent. Too bad you can't take it from the top, but you're missing less than a half mile. These handles are your brakes."

"Uh…"

"If you get caught out, it's your best bet. Just pretend that you're one of those extreme sports guys," Richie must have sensed his hesitation and rushed on. "You can top a hundred miles an hour on this—be sure you lean *into* the curves." He held up a hand and it took Duane a moment to realize he wanted a high-five himself.

Duane gave it to him. Then he was left staring at the "street luge" as the other three continued up the shaft headed for the topmost level.

The luge was a flat board to lie back on for the length of his body from butt to head. A T-bar extended forward, where he was obviously supposed to put his feet. The brakes were a pair of side bars that would dig into the pavement. The wheels were six sets of skateboard trucks.

"Great, I'm gonna be a twelve-wheeler." No. Richie had doubled the last three axles—eighteen-wheeler it was.

Duane exited the shaft, crossed the disused lobby, and peeked out into the night.

He was at the northern narrow end of the egg-shaped Helix. Level Six was approximately five hundred by eight hundred feet. The portion that he could see was made up of fifty-foot-deep storefronts turned into offices, a nose-in parking strip, and another forty feet of roadway for the up and down traffic. A low barricade marked the edge of the level before the fifty-foot drop to the next level below.

There were four rapid clicks on his radio. The top team of Kyle, Carla, and Richie, designated Team Four, was now in position.

Chad answered with three clicks from below.

Melissa and Sofia back at the King Hotel answered with two for their own team number.

He held the most strategic position, so he was Team One. No need to click, they were waiting for him.

Taking a deep breath, Duane looked east and wished he could see the hotel, but the sightlines wouldn't be right except at the very top of El Helicoide.

Duane keyed his mic and whispered, *"Grupo dos.*

Ándele!"—Team Two. Go!

Then he moved off into the shadows of Level Six.

CHAPTER 22

"Ready?" Melissa asked.

"Absolutely not. But that doesn't seem to be stopping me. Let's do it."

Melissa fired the launcher three times over the hotel roof's low parapet.

Sofia had rigged a small camera on the edge of the parapet looking across at the roof of La Tumba—one of her expensive night-vision ones; one thing that Duane's store-boughts couldn't do was see in the dark.

In her glasses she watched Melissa's three projectiles thunk down on the three corners of the roof and explode in puffs of gas. The snipers of the roving roof patrol barely had time to jump to their feet before the gas caught them and they collapsed where they stood.

"Nice shooting."

"Thanks," Melissa patted her launcher. "That will keep them down for an hour."

Sofia checked her watch. "They'll be missing their next radio check in less than a minute."

"How's your throwing arm?"

"Five-three win-loss record on the inter-winery softball team when I was playing first base. I could hit third every time— without a pitcher relay." Well, after the first year where she'd embarrassingly missed a double-play at third three times in the same inning. She'd made sure she was much better practiced by the second season.

"Batter up," Melissa tossed her a percussion grenade.

Sofia popped up over the parapet, sighted down eighteen stories and across a quiet boulevard, pulled the pin, and threw it. Then dropped back out of sight.

"Here's another."

Sofia caught it and was shifting to kneel high enough to see again when Melissa grabbed her shoulder and yanked her back down on the roof.

"No! Never pop up in the same spot twice."

Sofia could see in her glasses that the rooftop snipers were all still asleep, but she could feel the hot path that a bullet might have made right through her chest for such a beginner's mistake.

She began crawling as the first grenade went off far below with a thump followed by the sound of shattering glass. They weren't fragmentation grenades because they didn't want to risk killing passing civilians. But they would definitely shake up the door guards and do some property damage.

She tapped the control on her glasses to the second camera's feed, and earned herself a disorienting bout of vertigo as she was suddenly looking eighteen stories straight down.

The third-story windows of La Tumba had been blown in. The guards down on the street were staring upward in surprise.

Right! She'd arced the grenade high to get the distance across the boulevard, forgetting that there would be plenty of time for the grenade to cover the distance as it fell eighteen stories.

She winged the second one out and down and then ducked down to crawl back to Melissa.

This time the guards went down, though they should only be

dazed. The first floor windows were undamaged, but several cars had lost their windows.

Sofia flipped back to the first camera just as a second sniper team burst onto the roof. She signaled Melissa, who sent over three more gas canisters. One bounced off the far side of the roof, but it didn't matter. The other two landed at the second team's feet and they dropped where they stood.

La Tumba would be well convinced that they were the target of an attack.

Sofia triggered her radio, "*Grupo tres. Ándele!*"

"Let's get out of here," Melissa was staying low and hustling toward the roof door.

Sofia crouched and followed.

∾

DUANE DIDN'T HAVE to wait long for the next stage of the attack.

Delta was transmitting in the clear, because opposition rebels —of which Caracas had more every day—wouldn't have high-tech encrypted radios. They'd be lucky if they had walkie-talkies. So, for whoever was listening in on The Unit's transmissions, they'd hear about team after team—even if Chad was the entirety of Team Three—all reporting in Spanish.

He didn't bother answering over the radio, of course. Instead he answered with a South African M32 MGL—Multi-shot Grenade Launcher. It looked like an oversized revolver, right down to the six-slot rotating cylinder—big enough to launch fist-sized explosives over four hundred meters. He began lobbing rounds high into the air so that they'd drop from the sky, completely masking what direction they were coming from.

The first two 40mm grenades destroyed the security check-point that crossed the road at the very base of El Helicoide. The next four landed on Levels One and Two.

Duane waited for Chad to reload the cylinder. This time he

dropped two rounds on Level Two, three on Level Three, and one on Level Four. The attack would appear to be moving up the hill fast enough to scare the shit out of any SEBIN agents who had pulled the night shift. Most importantly, it would be seen as *moving up,* drawing attention away from the real action on Level Nine.

"Team One is a go," he called his own intentions over the radio. "Team Four. Go." That would tell Kyle, Carla, and Richie that they were now on their own.

Duane hit the first remote trigger. He'd wired three Mercedes Benzes, four BMWs and a Toyota SUV on Level Six while waiting for Team Four to get into position.

They blew with a very satisfying roar. Window glass for the entire southeast quarter of the level was blown into the offices. He'd spiked his charges into the gas tanks, so the explosions had been particularly violent and impressive. They roiled upward lighting the nearby *barrio* in an evil red glow and blowing flaming gasoline into the deserted offices. For a moment he was afraid he'd done too much, which would spoil their game—but sprinklers came on and the flames were already quieting.

While he'd been waiting on Team Two of Sofia and Melissa, he'd ridden Richie's street luge down to Level Five, managing not to kill himself in the process. Damn, the thing was fast. Lying back with his feet on the T-bar and his hands white-knuckled on the brake handles, he'd practically flown down to the next level.

Now he understood why Richie had also given him knee and elbow pads. The pavement flashed by mere inches below his elbows. He'd bitten his tongue almost hard enough to make it bleed out of near panic before he got the feel of it. His first parachute jump hadn't felt this fast—of course, then he'd only been falling through air. Here the ground was a very immediate reminder of just how fast he was going. When he pulled the brake handles up, all they did was pivot the other end of the bar into the ground. The concrete had screamed as sparks shot behind him in a great twin rooster tail.

However, Richie had clearly forgotten to account for the fact that he had a large backpack of explosives, which forced him to sit partly up into the wind and did nasty things to his balance in corners. Still, it was the most fun he'd had since the time he and Veronica—a very limber airline stewardess—had jumped at New Zealand's Nevis Bungy, the world's third highest bungee. If he ever lived in a place like the Dundee Hills, instead of the ass-flat landscape of Atlanta or Fort Bragg, he was definitely going to get himself one of these luges.

The quality of cars had shifted with his descent—fewer Benzes, more Toyotas here on Level Five.

Now he scooted far enough around the road to be safe and hit his second trigger. In moments the southeast quadrant of Level Five was engulfed in flame.

The top levels of El Helicoide should be mostly empty already —top ranked SEBIN officials apparently were given the highest level offices and they weren't the sort of people who pulled night shifts. Any techs who were working late would be Team Four's problem.

The real challenge now was to buy enough time for Richie to get in, figure out their passwords, and hopefully find a way to intercept their microwave transmissions from La Tumba as well.

A peek over the side barricade revealed a line of explosions: the east park, a truck parked to the southeast, and four more on the front security gate. There were also a number of gaps blown in the fence to either side. Chad looked like he was a whole goddamn Army.

Duane lay down on the luge, picked up his feet, released the brakes, and raced down to wire some cars on Level Four.

"No! No! No! No!"

"Shh!"

"Don't shh me!" Though Sofia did drop her voice to a whisper —a fierce whisper. At least that's what she hoped it sounded like, rather than the stark terror she was feeling.

They had raced the old SUV the seven kilometers to La Carlota Air Base. *No problem!* This late at night the roads were empty. Besides, all emergency equipment was racing in the other direction toward the "attack."

They'd parked exactly where Duane and Richie's diagram had said to park. *Great!*

They'd crawled through the precut hole in the perimeter fence. *Perfect!* Though how Duane had gotten his broad shoulders through the narrow gap she had no idea.

Then she and Melissa had scanned the field. Dozens of helicopters were parked close by the hangar. And the one right in front of them, the one marked with a big X on the diagram, wasn't some nice little five-seat Bell JetRanger.

"Tell me I'm not losing my mind."

Melissa giggled.

"I'm going to kill Duane."

"Actually…" Melissa seemed to be having trouble controlling her laugh.

"If you weren't a girl, I'd hit *you*," she growled.

"Girls can hit girls, it's boys who can't hit girls."

"Fine," Sofia wanted to bury her face in the dirt. "I can't hit you because *I'm* a girl. Happy?"

"Immensely," but Melissa did get some control of her laugh. "This looks more like something Richie would do. Remind me to tell you about the time he stole a Gulfstream jet when he'd never flown anything faster than a Twin Otter seaplane before. I'll bet he chose this just *because* he wants to know how it flies."

"How about you? Do you fly?"

Melissa raised her hands palm out, "Only little planes. The

Twin Otter is the biggest thing I've ever had to fly and that's plenty. When it comes to rotorcraft, you're the only one on this team with that skill."

"I'm not on the team."

"Yeah, right," Melissa didn't sound convinced.

"But…" Sofia could only wave her hand helplessly.

The helicopter was one of several dozen sitting on the tarmac. There were plenty of smaller ones. But *no-o*. None of those were marked on the diagram. The aircraft those idiots had selected was a Mil Mi-26—the largest production helicopter made anywhere in the world. It could pick up a twin-rotor Chinook or even a Marine Corps Sea Stallion—with the Marines still in it. It could carry a Boeing 737 in its harness sling. She wanted to scream. The little JetRanger had one engine and a two-blade rotor all of thirty-three feet long. It weighed one ton, not *sixty*. The Mi-26 had twin eleven-thousand-horse-power engines to drive its hundred-foot-across, eight-blade rotor.

"I can't do this. I just can't."

"Duane said you'd say that."

"I'm going to kill him," this time she did bury her face in the dirt.

"He said to say he knows that he can count on you."

"Dead man!" She told any passing earthworms, though they probably spoke Spanish here in Venezuela. "*Hombre muerto!*"

Melissa tugged on her arm.

"He said that?"

She looked up to see Melissa's nod.

"Bastard! Next time he helps save my life, to hell with him. I'm just going to die to prove him wrong."

"That's the spirit."

After scanning the field—everything here was still quiet—they raced to the helicopter at a professional-looking stroll. They entered the helicopter through one of the passenger doors on the side of the cargo bay. Inside was a cavern ten feet high and wide that stretched forty feet long.

"What are these?" Melissa shown a light on the mounded crates that filled most of the massive space. Stenciled clearly on the side in Russian: Igla SA-18.

"*Mierda!*" They swore in unison.

Sofia swallowed hard. "I saw a report that Venezuela had recently purchased five thousand surface-to-air missiles from the Russians."

Melissa patted the side of the a box, "I'd say this is most of them right here. No wonder the boys chose this helicopter. I don't want these in Venezuela either. How paranoid *are* these people?"

"Very," Sofia began working her way forward along a narrow gap between the crate rows. "After you tell me about Richie and the jet, remind me to tell you about—" Her words dried up in her throat.

"What?" Melissa came up and looked over her shoulder. "Wow!"

There were five command seats spread comfortably in a cockpit bigger than an entire JetRanger. Each position was surrounded with more controls and readouts than the smaller helo had—total.

"I can't wait to see how you pull this one off."

Sofia decided she was out of options, so she punched Melissa.

But not very hard because she was going to need all the help she could get.

~

LEVEL FOUR OF EL HELICOIDE had also blown spectacularly, but on Level Three, most of the cars were gone. Duane barely had enough vehicles to make an impressive show, which was just as well, he was running out of explosives.

He'd also been spiking the vehicle closest to each machine gun emplacement that showed up on the map projected inside his shooting glasses—the map Sofia had assembled from all of their observations last night and this morning. With Chad taking out the lower emplacements, they hadn't been much of an issue. That and the shooters wouldn't be able to find any identifiable targets. They were looking for an attacking army pouring out of the *barrio*, not for him and Chad with backpacks.

He paused to lean on the barricade a while to watch the mayhem at the front gate.

Chad had pounded enough grenades onto the roof over the security checkpoint to collapse it onto the roadway. All it had taken was three cars abandoned in the exit lanes and that had put an end to anyone else driving off the complex. The clutter of vehicles behind them was a fast-growing snarl of dinged vehicles and men yelling at each other over the hoods.

Duane had counted up to seventy trapped vehicles when Chad dropped a single grenade at the back of the packed traffic jam.

The panicked exodus was instantaneous. Everyone was running out the gate, across the road, and into the *barrio*. He wondered how many of the fleeing SEBIN would survive the waiting *colectivo*. Sofia told him how she, Carla, and Melissa had spent their afternoon—damn but she just kept getting more amazing. No way was she getting away from him.

Duane spotted a man in rags coming across the Level Three roadway. His hands were empty, so Duane waited him out.

"Disculpame, por favor."—Excuse me, please. The man's voice was hoarse as if from lack of use. He was so thin that he didn't even decently fill out the rags he wore. One of the hundreds of political prisoners incarcerated in El Helicoide.

"Sí?" Duane could see others in the distance watching them curiously.

"Is it safe?" The man continued in Spanish.

"To run?" Though Duane was surprised he could even walk in his present condition.

"Yes."

"If you go quickly, yes. Free as many as you can and go."

"*Gracias! Gracias!*" The man hobbled back to the group and in moments they were on the move. He heard glass shattering and more people joining them as they were freed. The lower levels of the massive shopping mall had been turned into a prison. He'd blown open doors where he could, but there'd been too much else to do to pay attention to the results.

Duane watched them a while longer. He wondered if any of these prisoners had lost their wives to General Aguado's jungle compound. He hoped so, he liked the idea of the two separate missions reuniting families. Liked it a lot.

Once they were out of sight down the road, he blew the shit out of the three vehicles left on Level Three.

He supposed that was good. It would look as if the attack was failing and leaving the top levels of El Helicoide untouched. Which was exactly what they were supposed to think.

He hopped on the luge, popped the brakes, and swooped down toward Level Two. He was getting good at flying.

~

MELISSA WAS READING THE CHECKLIST, which was thankfully in the same language as the labels on the helicopter—Spanish. That was a good thing because her technical Russian sucked.

"You look scared," Melissa commented while they waited for the engine temperature to stabilize. "You're white as a sheet."

"*Más blanco que poto de monja.* Whiter than a nun's butt," one of Nana's favorite expressions after she'd chewed out one of Sofia's brothers. "And I'm not scared, I'm terrified."

She was about to risk easing up on the collective to take off when the radio squawked to life, scaring the daylights out of her.

"Mil 7432, this is Carlota tower. You don't have clearance. What are you doing?"

Melissa shrugged when Sofia looked at her.

"Some help you are." Sofia keyed the mic, "Tower, this is 7432. I have a request for immediate evac from El Helicoide. They're under attack."

"Whose orders?"

She didn't have a good answer to that. "General Aguado," then she cringed. What if they knew he supposedly had been killed during the fire at his jungle compound?

"7432, cleared to Helicoide. Tower out."

Melissa merely raised her eyebrows before reading off the next item on the list.

Sofia eased up on the collective and the Mi-26 wallowed aloft.

Smooth, small motions. That's what her flight instructor had told her. She just hoped that the Mi-26 knew about that rule.

Collective up, cyclic forward, and they eased aloft without too much amateur wobble.

"Which way?"

"Which way to what?"

"El Helicoide, Melissa! Which way?"

"Uh, try a bit more to the left. I wasn't on the airport team so I didn't pay attention to exactly where it is."

"I'll get you for this. Right after I put down the rabid dogs Duane and Richie."

"As long as someone else doesn't do it first," Melissa sounded worried.

And Sofia shut up. She was merely trying to fly the hugest helicopter on the planet.

She'd climbed high enough that she could see El Helicoide less than ten miles away. It was easy to spot because of the leaping flames.

Even as she watched, another explosion roared skyward.

∾

"Have a good ride, bro?"

"I was…" Duane growled at Chad, "really flying along until I planted my board in one of the holes you punched in the pavement on Level Two. Must have tumbled a couple hundred feet before I stopped. Hurts like hell."

"Aww, poor little Duane. Has he got him some owies?"

"Shithead."

"Proud to be, bro."

They had met at the south end of Level One and were leaning out to inspect their handiwork. The fire brigade couldn't get in because of all of the cars abandoned inside the gate. Finally someone began using the heaviest engine like a battering ram, shoving luxury sedans, crumpling late-model SUVs, and battering light trucks aside.

"We should invest in a Caracas body shop, quick."

Duane nodded. "But it's only a short term investment. Besides. It's SEBIN. They'd pay you only at the official exchange rate."

"Man, you sure know how to take the joy out of a young boy's dreams."

They turned away from the mayhem at the gate and rounded the south end headed west, which quickly hid the flaming southeast corner of the structure except as an on-going reflection off the facing *barrio.*

The west side was dark and quiet. No traffic. No lights. No people.

Duane shone a light in a couple of the storefronts. The doors were each smashed open. Every cell door inside was standing open. The prisoners were gone, filtering out through any number of gaps Chad had blown in the perimeter fence. They'd disappear into the *barrio* and find a very different welcome than the SEBIN who'd made the mistake of going in there.

Maybe it was time to dream a few dreams himself.

They arrived at the very west side of the lowest roadway, just as a length of black 9mm tactical line snaked down from the level above. In moments Carla, Richie, and finally Kyle slid down to join them. With a yank Kyle recovered the doubled-over line. They'd rappelled down from Level Nine—a much faster and more discreet descent than following the miles of road, pieces of which were probably still on fire.

"Is it done?"

Kyle nodded, but Richie jumped in with both feet.

"Sure. The techs were all out at the railing watching the fireworks. The hardest part was I couldn't decrypt their password. But they hadn't locked their screens, so I did the same thing I did to Sofia: I created a new user. Only this time I hid it so that they won't know it's there to delete it."

"What about the microwave feed?"

"Well, they put an awful lot of comm channels aloft in that bird for such a small country. So, I picked an empty one and routed everything from the La Tumba feed over to an empty satellite channel."

"Will that work?" Duane thought he understood that, sending the intelligence signal traffic from La Tumba up to SEBIN's own satellite so that Yakima could hear it when it was echoed back down.

"Sure! I called Yakima, they're fully online already."

"My bro," Chad crashed a fist down on Duane's shoulder, "kicked a whole rack of political prisoners down the ramp. Gone now," he nodded toward the *barrio*. "At least those poor bastards won't get trafficked, or worse."

"While I was in the system," Richie waved skyward, "I found a tracking list of trafficked families. Carla suggested I send it to the underground newspaper."

"*What?*" Duane couldn't believe what he was hearing. "So much for hiding the fact that we were ever in their system. Well done, assholes!"

Carla simply gave him one of those looks that said maybe he was the one being an idiot.

"Okay," might as well eat the bullet. "What am I missing?"

"Carla had me send it from the SEBIN commander's e-mail account, with a copy to his assistant and his boss."

Carla's smile dared him to say it wasn't slick as all hell. But it was, so he shut up.

"Whether they read it as a betrayal or a mistake, it's not going to turn out well for him. Then we got out before the techs were back at their desks. Classic Delta, no one knows we were ever here."

"Yeah," Chad chimed in. "Except we *are* still here. Where's your honey, bro?"

"She'll make it. Sofia can do anything," Duane knew that for a fact.

As if in answer, the heavy beat of a very large helicopter sounded overhead. That's why they'd left the west side untouched and met here—it was where the designer had moved El Helicoide's helipad to when they'd originally built the geodesic dome on the top.

∿

"I CANNOT FLY this helicopter to a friendly country."

"Why not?" Duane had sat in the copilot's seat. He might not know anything about helicopters, but still Sofia found it comforting to have him there. Richie and Melissa were getting a handle on the engineering and navigation stations behind them. Outside the big windows, Caracas was petering out. She didn't know how to read the radar and couldn't spare time to find charts or the altimeter—to clear the mountains between the city and the coast. Instead, she flew above the highway. She just hoped that it was the one leading out to sea and not off into central Venezuela somewhere.

"Two reasons. Three. One, it's everything I can do to fly it a few miles." She was amazed that she hadn't blown a blood vessel—

or crashed. The landing next to El Helicoide had been ugly but not lethal, so she supposed it was okay. "Two, even if I *could* land us in some country, the Venezuelan government is bound to find out and know it was stolen, where and when. That is the end of your great plan to be invisible."

"Yeah, that is a problem," Duane didn't sound worried.

"So glad you see that. Three—"

"There isn't enough fuel," Richie piped up from the engineer's console. "We have about twenty minutes of air time. I can't believe they don't keep their helos fully fueled. I'm sorry. I should have thought to check that."

"That wasn't my Number Three. That makes mine Number Four," Sofia sighed. "At some point they're going to miss their helicopter and send a fighter jet out to turn us into much littler pieces of ourselves. So you had better think up something brilliant, Mr. Unit Operator."

"Humph!"

She waited, but he didn't say anything more. Neither did anyone else. "That's it? That's all you've got? *Humph?*"

"It's better than 'Oh, god! Oh, god! We're all gonna die!' isn't it?"

"Not by enough to count." She looked ahead, but there were no more lights. Was she about to run into something like an unlit mountainside? Oh. "Well, there's the ocean."

The gods or somebody were definitely laughing. She'd ridden out of the jungle on a stealth helicopter with Duane, jumped out of another into a cruise ship's swimming pool beside him, filmed her brother busy at sabotaging yet a third one at the vineyard, and now she was flying the largest helicopter built—once more over the night-shrouded ocean.

"That's it. Take her down," Duane practically shouted.

"Down where?"

∿

"RIGHT OVER THE MARINA," Duane jumped out of his seat. "Everyone get ready to jump. We're going to dump you in the marina. You swim to the boat. We'll take the helo out to sea, ditch it, and you come fetch us."

"But—" Richie protested.

"No time!" Duane yanked him from the engineer's console and hauled him toward the door.

"Where—" Kyle started to ask.

"You'll have to figure it out."

"What about—" Melissa looked toward Sofia in the pilot's seat.

"I'm staying with her. All the way."

At that, Carla grabbed him by the shirt—hauling him down to her level—and kissed him hard, then moved away to stand by the door.

"On the flip side, bro," Chad gave him a high-five.

"Now!" Sofia cried out. "I can't hover this beast for long."

Kyle opened the door and his five teammates streamed out, plunging down into the water as fast as bullets.

"Good to go!" he shouted and leaned out to make sure everyone surfaced as Sofia eased them away. Five heads, already striking out toward the moored *GoldenEye*.

He returned to the copilot's seat.

"They're all safe."

"That's nice. Any ideas how to do the same for us?"

"Got me. How do you ditch a helicopter?"

"No idea. They didn't cover that in let's-go-for-a-scenic-flight-over-the-vineyards school. All I remember on the topic is: *don't do it.*"

Duane looked out the windshield. They were out over the Caribbean Sea by now. A couple miles farther and they could safely ditch it where it wasn't likely to be noticed.

No help out there.

He began looking around inside the cockpit. Something caught his attention. It took him a moment to figure out what, but then he pinned it down again and he pointed at it so that it couldn't slip away again.

"*Piloto automático*," Duane read out.

"Do you know how to run an autopilot?"

"No idea. You?"

"No."

"Wait! Melissa had a book of checklists somewhere. Let me see."

"Hurry."

"Okay."

"No, really hurry!"

Duane turned to look where Sofia was focused. There was a red light blinking brightly in the darkened cockpit.

He could just make out the label: *motor #1 combustible.*

Fuel.

Then a second light blinked red: *motor #2 combustible.*

"How many engines do we have?" He'd bet that he wasn't going to like the answer.

"Two."

"Helo-2, Delta-0, sports fans." Nope. He didn't like that answer one bit.

~

Sofia had told Duane he was crazy too many times. Some balance had tipped and now she was just going to trust him blindly and hope for the best.

He read fast, tapping at the autopilot's keypad.

"Get us down near the water."

"I can't."

"Why not?" Duane didn't pause in his programming.

"Because I don't know where it is. And no, the altimeter isn't calibrated, so it won't help much. And if you can find a radar altimeter in all this, more power to you." She had found the compass—holding northeast away from the coast—and the airspeed—slow so that they didn't leave that coast too far behind for the *GoldenEye* to rescue them. She also didn't like the idea of hitting the water at a hundred or so kilometers an hour. Everything else was a blur of dials and switches except for the two fuel indicators now blinking at a truly alarming rate.

"Uh, how about this?" Duane flicked a switch and she was blinded by the landing lights reflecting off the waves.

The ocean was so close she could almost touch it.

She jerked upward on the collective, and earned the harsh buzz of a stall warning for her troubles.

Sofia managed to ease back on the controls, but her arms were trembling with adrenaline and the effort.

A pilot holds the controls lightly. She added the flight instructor to her personal better-off-dead list. How was she supposed to ease her grip when she knew it was the only thing keeping her and the man she loved alive?

"There!" Duane declared as he punched a button and it began blinking green. "If I did it right, when I hit that, the helicopter will fly away without us."

"And if you're wrong?"

"Remember that 'Oh, god! Oh, god! We're all gonna die!' part?"

"Oh, is that all. When do we do this?"

One of the fuel gauges shifted from blinking red to solid red and a loud buzzer sounded. There was a sudden change in the sound of the engines—as if one was out of fuel and winding down.

"I think now would be a good time," Duane reached over and released her seatbelt. "Are you ready, Sofia Forteza?"

"Always."

"I love you so much, lady."

"Tell me later," though if that was the last thing she was going to hear before she died, it was a good way to go.

Duane punched the button. It turned solid green, and she could feel the controls move in her hands without her.

Before she could even fully unclench her fingers, Duane yanked her from the seat and dragged her to the side door. He grabbed a rubber raft and tossed it out.

"Get into the raft as fast as you can!" he yelled over the turbine noise flooding in through the open door. He kissed her on the forehead and shoved her out the door.

She fell ten feet.

Twenty.

Th—

The water slammed into her like a hammer.

She surfaced and looked up through the battering spray generated by the huge rotor's punishing downdraft.

Duane was still standing in the door, fumbling with something as the helicopter moved away.

She screamed his name, but knew he couldn't hear her.

Her next scream had her swallowing a faceful of seawater, which sent her into choking spasms.

Just before she could recover enough to scream his name again, he finally jumped, plunging into the waves a hundred feet from her.

She began swimming toward him and plowed into something large.

The uninflated raft.

Sofia clung to it and kept kicking.

Duane came up to her, shouting, "No time! No time! Get in!"

He yanked the ripcord and the raft practically exploded open, dunking her underneath it.

A hand reached down, grabbed her, and dragged her to the surface. Continuing the motion, he bodily threw her into the raft as if she was weightless.

Then he joined her with a hard landing that knocked away

what little air she'd managed to recover when his shoulder slammed into her gut.

"Look!" He pointed out into the night.

As she watched, the helicopter nosed down sharply and plunged into the waves just a few hundred yards away. The huge rotor beat the sea and shattered. She heard parts of it winging by to splash around them, but they weren't hit.

It began sinking. "I'm not sorry to see it go. Don't you ever do something like that to me again or I'll—"

"Hang on!" Then Duane wrapped his arms around her, pinning her to the bottom of the raft. It reminded her of the moment in the Venezuelan jungle when he wrapped his breathtakingly powerful arm around her waist the moment just before—

~

DUANE FELT the explosion slam into them. The massive compression-wave pulse through the water that would have killed them if they'd still been in the water. A towering fountain bloomed up in the night, lit from within by the last of his explosives that he'd set on a timer and thrown deep into the cargo bay.

The helicopter was fully underwater when the second pulse hit them. A new fountain was borne aloft as several thousand surface-to-air missiles created a cascading series of explosions. He'd worried about the debris, or the explosion drawing attention from shore, but programming the autopilot to descend rapidly after just two hundred yards had the water masking the worst of it.

The surface waves hit next, almost flipping them out of the raft, but he managed to keep them both in it.

Soon there was no evidence on the surface but a vast patch of phosphorescent green stirred up by the air still bubbling upward from the sinking helo.

"Well," Duane couldn't quite catch his breath. "That. Was fun," he helped Sofia sit up. "You okay?"

"Sure," her voice sounded just like her, but he wished he could see to find out. The life raft didn't have even a basic survival kit and his flashlight had been in his pack.

"Does anything hurt?"

"Only where you put shoulder into my belly."

"I'll try not to do that again."

"Please don't." After a long pause, she spoke softly. "We're alive."

"We are. Which is a little surprising given the circumstances." He'd had plenty of close calls, but this was a new level of extreme even by his standards.

"I think there were things that needed to be said later," Sofia prompted him.

"I love when you get that haughty tone with me."

"Haughty?" Which she said even more archly.

"Actually I have a serious question. Maybe a couple of them." He really wished that he could see her, but some things couldn't be helped.

"So ask," said the queen from her watery life raft throne.

Unable to stop, he pulled her against him until she was straddling his lap. No woman could ever feel better.

"I am waiting."

"Does The Activity ever take Delta operators?"

$\approx$

SOFIA WAS SO happy to be alive. So happy to be with Duane that the unexpected question stopped her for a long moment as she tried to make sense of it.

"They do," she said it carefully.

"What do I have to do to apply?"

She put her hand on his chest, on his cheek. He felt...serious. As if he really meant it.

But it wasn't right.

"No."

"What do I have to know?"

"No, I mean N-O no, not the other kind of know. English is such a crazy language." Even if it was her native tongue.

"What do you mean 'no'?"

Sofia patted her hand against his chest again, unable to believe what was happening.

"Sofia, lovely lady, what do you mean 'no'?" Duane said it as softly as a caress.

"You would leave your team for me?"

"I'd leave the military for you."

She couldn't imagine him doing that any more than she would. At least not for a long while. "There is something you should know."

"What? Already married? I'll kill the bastard. Secret baby hidden away somewhere? Fine, I'll adopt it. As long as we get to make one or two of our own along the way."

Sofia slapped a hand over his mouth to stop him. "How can a man who everyone says never talks, talk so much?"

She could feel his smile against her palm as he shrugged.

"Well, be quiet for a minute."

He nodded, then she could feel one of his hands brush along her cheek.

She moved her hand, kissed him briefly, and then quickly recovered his mouth before he could speak.

"No, no, and yes. I am not a married-type person, yet. I have no secret baby. Yes I very much want to have a child with you—as long as," she tapped the index finger of her free hand against the tip of his nose. "She is a rational person like me and not a crazy person like her father."

His smile grew bigger. She wished she could see his lovely blue eyes.

"But there is one big no. Huge!"

His smile faded against her palm.

Over his shoulder she could see the light of the fast-approaching *GoldenEye*.

Duane reached up to pull her hand aside, "What's the huge no?"

"No. You may not leave your team. They are your family."

"But—"

She covered his mouth again. "But I do not have a team that ties me so tightly to The Activity. Maybe, with some more training, Delta can become my family too."

"More training? You mean than this?" He waved his hand back toward the mainland. His laugh of joy hit her square in the heart. "I know Carla and Melissa would induct you today. Hell, they all would. You're completely incredible. We could train you in the field. It's been done plenty of times before."

She kissed him to shut him up.

By the time Richie pulled the boat alongside the raft, Duane Jenkins had made his own vote very clear in other ways as well.

They were all gathered on the swim deck to greet her. No, to welcome her.

But she hesitated halfway up the ladder with Duane close behind her. She leaned down to whisper in his ear.

"Remember—our child. She will be like her mother."

"Yes, ma'am." Then he muttered softly, but she could just hear it over everyone's greetings and it warmed her heart. "*Two* Forteza women. I'm gonna be in *so* much trouble."

AFTERWORD

Operation Prime Cause, my anti-sex trafficking team, was inspired by the very real Operation Underground Railroad. These ex-military heroes put themselves at great risk to battle child sex-trafficking around the world, saving the children one at a time if they have to. I will be donating a significant portion of this title's gross income to support their cause. I beg you to supplement that with your own contributions to fight this horrific scourge:

https://ourrescue.org/

If you note that this title inspired your donation, it would be appreciated.

ABOUT THE AUTHOR

M.L. Buchman started the first of, what is now over 50 novels and as many short stories, while flying from South Korea to ride his bicycle across the Australian Outback. Part of a solo around the world trip that ultimately launched his writing career.

All three of his military romantic suspense series—The Night Stalkers, Firehawks, and Delta Force—have had a title named "Top 10 Romance of the Year" by the American Library Association's *Booklist*. NPR and Barnes & Noble have named other titles "Top 5 Romance of the Year." In 2016 he was a finalist for Romance Writers of America prestigious RITA award. He also writes: contemporary romance, thrillers, and fantasy.

Past lives include: years as a project manager, rebuilding and single-handing a fifty-foot sailboat, both flying and jumping out of airplanes, and he has designed and built two houses. He is now making his living as a full-time writer on the Oregon Coast with his beloved wife and is constantly amazed at what you can do with a degree in Geophysics. You may keep up with his writing and receive a free starter e-library by subscribing to his newsletter at: www.mlbuchman.com

Join the conversation:
www.mlbuchman.com

IF YOU ENJOYED THIS, YOU MIGHT
ALSO ENJOY:

TARGET OF THE HEART (EXCERPT)

THE NIGHT STALKERS 5E #1

*M*ajor Pete Napier hovered his MH-47G Chinook helicopter ten kilometers outside of Lhasa, Tibet and a mere two inches off the tundra. A mixed action team of Delta Force and The Activity—the slipperiest intel group on the planet—flung themselves aboard.

The additional load sent an infinitesimal shift in the cyclic control in his right hand. The hydraulics to close the rear loading ramp hummed through the entire frame of the massive helicopter. By the time his crew chief could reach forward to slap an "all secure" signal against his shoulder, they were already ten feet up and fifty out. That was enough altitude. He kept the nose down as he clawed for speed in the thin air at eleven thousand feet.

"Totally worth it," one of the D-boys announced as soon as he was on the Chinook's internal intercom.

He'd have to remember to tell that to the two Black Hawks flying guard for him...when they were in a friendly country and could risk a radio transmission. This deep inside China—or rather Chinese-held territory as the CIA's mission-briefing spook had insisted on calling it—radios attracted attention and were only used to avoid imminent death and destruction.

"Great, now I just need to get us out of this alive."

"Do that, Pete. We'd appreciate it."

He wished to hell he had a stealth bird like the one that had gone into bin Laden's compound. But the one that had crashed during that raid had been blown up. Where there was one, there were always two, but the second had gone back into hiding as thoroughly as if it had never existed. He hadn't heard a word about it since.

The Tibetan terrain was amazing, even if all he could see of it was the monochromatic green of night vision. And blackness. The largest city in Tibet lay a mere ten kilometers away and they were flying over barren wilderness. He could crash out here and no one would know for decades unless some yak herder stumbled upon them. Or were yaks in Mongolia? He was a corn-fed, white boy from Colorado, what did he know about Tibet? Most of the countries he'd flown into on black ops missions he'd only seen at night anyway.

While moving very, very fast.

Like now.

The inside of his visor was painted with overlapping readouts. A pre-defined terrain map, the best that modern satellite imaging could build made the first layer. This wasn't some crappy, on-line, look-at-a-picture-of-your-house display. Someone had a pile of dung outside their goat pen? He could see it, tell you how high it was, and probably say if they were pygmy goats or full-size LaManchas by the size of their shit-pellets if he zoomed in.

On top of that were projected the forward-looking infrared camera images. The FLIR imaging gave him a real-time overlay, in case someone had put an addition onto their goat shed since the last satellite pass, or parked their tractor across his intended flight path.

His nervous system was paying autonomic attention to that combined landscape. He also compensated for the thin air at altitude as he instinctively chose when to start his climb over said goat shed or his swerve around it.

It was the third layer, the tactical display that had most of his attention. At least he and the two Black Hawks flying escort on him were finally on the move.

To insert this deep into Tibet, without passing over Bhutan or Nepal, they'd had to add wingtanks on the Black Hawks' hardpoints where he'd much rather have a couple banks of Hellfire missiles. Still, they had 20mm chain guns and the crew chiefs had miniguns which was some comfort.

While the action team was busy infiltrating the capital city and gathering intelligence on the particularly brutal Chinese assistant administrator, he and his crews had been squatting out in the wilderness under a camouflage net designed to make his helo look like just another god-forsaken Himalayan lump of granite.

Command had determined that it was better for the helos to wait on site through the day than risk flying out and back in. He and his crew had stood shifts on guard duty, but none of them had slept. They'd been flying together too long to have any new jokes, so they'd played a lot of cribbage. He'd long ago ruled no gambling on a mission, after a fistfight had broken out about a bluff hand that cost a Marine three hundred and forty-seven dollars. Marines hated losing to Army no matter how many times it happened. They'd had to sit on him for a long time before he calmed down.

Tonight's mission was part of an on-going campaign to discredit the Chinese "presence" in Tibet on the international stage—as if occupying the country the last sixty years didn't count toward ruling, whether invited or not. As usual, there was a crucial vote coming up at the U.N.—that, as usual, the Chinese could be guaranteed to ignore. However, the ever-hopeful CIA was in a hurry to make sure that any damaging information that they could validate was disseminated as thoroughly as possible prior to the vote.

Not his concern.

His concern was, were they going to pass over some Chinese sentry post at their top speed of a hundred and ninety-six miles an hour? The sentries would then call down a couple Shenyang J-16 jet fighters that could hustle along at Mach 2 to fry his sorry ass. He knew there was a pair of them parked at Lhasa along with some older gear that would be just as effective against his three helos.

"Don't suppose you could get a move on, Pete?"

"Eat shit, Nicolai!" He was a good man to have as a copilot. Pete knew he was holding on too tight, and Nicolai knew that a joke was the right way to ease the moment.

He, Nicolai, and the four pilots in the two Black Hawks had a long way to go tonight and he'd never make it if he stayed so tight on the controls that he could barely maneuver. Pete eased off and felt his fingers tingle with the rush of returning blood. They dove down into gorges and followed them as long as they dared. They hugged cliff walls at every opportunity to decrease their radar profile. And they climbed.

That was the true danger—they would be up near the helos' limits when they crossed over the backbone of the Himalayas in their rush for India. The air was so rarefied that they burned fuel at a prodigious rate. Their reserve didn't allow for any extended battles while crossing the border...not for any battle at all really.

~

IT WAS pitch dark outside her helicopter when Captain Danielle Delacroix stamped on the left rudder pedal while giving the big Chinook right-directed control on the cyclic. It tipped her most of the way onto her side, but let her continue in a straight line. A Chinook's rotors were sixty feet across—front to back they overlapped to make the spread a hundred feet long. By cross-controlling her bird to tip it, she managed to execute a straight line between two mock pylons only thirty feet apart. They were made of thin cloth so they wouldn't down the helo if you sliced one— she was the only trainee to not have cut one yet.

At her current angle of attack, she took up less than a half-rotor of width, just twenty-four feet. That left her nearly three feet to either side, sufficient as she was moving at under a hundred knots.

The training instructor sitting beside her in the copilot's seat didn't react as she swooped through the training course at Fort Campbell, Kentucky. Only child of a single mother, she was used to providing her own feedback loops, so she didn't expect anything else. Those who expected outside validation rarely survived the SOAR induction testing, never mind the two years of training that followed.

As a loner kid, Danielle had learned that self-motivated congratulations and fun were much easier to come by than external ones. She'd spent innumerable hours deep in her mind as a pre-teen superheroine. At twenty-nine she was well on her way to becoming a real life one, though Helo-girl had never been a character she'd thought of in her youth.

External validation or not, after two years of training with the U.S. Army's 160th Special Operations Aviation Regiment she was ready for some action. At least *she* was convinced that she was. But the trainers of Fort Campbell, Kentucky had not signed off on anyone in her trainee class yet. Nor had they given any hint of when they might.

She ducked ten tons of racing Chinook under a bridge and bounced into a near vertical climb to clear the power line on the far side. Like a ride on the toboggan at Terrassee Dufferin during *Le Carnaval de Québec,* only with five thousand horsepower at her fingertips. Using her Army signing bonus—the first money in her life that was truly hers—to attend *Le Carnaval* had been her one trip back after her birthplace since her mother took them to America when she was ten.

To even apply to SOAR required five years of prior military rotorcraft experience. She had applied after seven years because of a chance encounter—or rather what she'd thought was a chance encounter at the time.

Captain Justin Roberts had been a top Chinook pilot, the one who had convinced her to switch from her beloved Black Hawk and try out the massive twin-rotor craft. One flight and she'd been a goner, begging her commander until he gave in and let her cross over to the new platform. Justin had made the jump from the 10th Mountain Division to the 160th SOAR not long after that.

Then one night she'd been having pizza in Watertown, New York a couple miles off the 10th's base at Fort Drum.

"Danielle?" Justin had greeted her with the surprise of finding a good friend in an unexpected place. Danielle had liked Justin— even if he was a too-tall, too-handsome cowboy and completely knew it. But "good friend" was unusual for Danielle, with anyone, and Justin came close.

"Captain Roberts," as a dry greeting over the top edge of her Suzanne Brockmann novel didn't faze him in the slightest.

"Mind if I join ya?" A question he then answered for himself by sliding into the opposite seat and taking a slice of her pizza. She been thinking of taking the leftovers back to base, but that was now an idle thought.

"Are you enjoying life in SOAR?" she did her best to appear a normal, social human, a skill she'd learned by rote. *Greeting someone you knew after a time apart? Ask a question about them.* "They treating you well?"

"Whoo-ee, you have no idea, Danielle," his voice was smooth as...well, always...so she wouldn't think about it also sounding like a pickup line. He was beautiful, but didn't interest her; the outgoing ones never did.

"Tell me." *Men love to talk about themselves, so let them.*

And he did. But she'd soon forgotten about her novel, and would have forgotten the pizza if he hadn't reminded her to eat. His stories shifted from intriguing to fascinating. There was a world out there that she'd been only peripherally aware of. The Night Stalkers of the 160th SOAR weren't simply better helicopter pilots, they were the most highly-trained and best-equipped ones on the planet. Their missions were pure razor's edge and black-op dark.

He'd left her with a hundred questions and enough interest to fill out an application to the 160th. Being a decent guy, Justin even paid for the pizza after eating half.

The speed at which she was rushed into testing told her that her meeting with Justin hadn't been by chance and that she owed him more than half a pizza next time they met. She'd asked after him a couple of times since she'd made it past the qualification exams—and the examiners' brutal interviews that had left her questioning her sanity, never mind her ability.

"Justin Roberts is presently deployed, ma'am," was the only response she'd ever gotten.

Now that she was through training—almost, had to be soon, didn't it?—Danielle realized that was probably less of an evasion and more likely to do with the brutal op tempo the Night Stalkers maintained. The SOAR 1st Battalion had just won the coveted Lt. General Ellis D. Parker awards for Outstanding Combat Aviation Battalion *and* Aviation Battalion of the Year. They'd been on deployment every single day of the last year, actually of the last decade-plus since 9/11.

The very first Special Forces boots on the ground in Afghanistan were delivered that October by the Night Stalkers and nothing had slacked off since. Justin might be in the 5th battalion D company, but they were just as heavily assigned as the 1st.

Part of their training had included tours in Afghanistan. But unlike their prior deployments, these were brief, intense, and then they'd be back in the States pushing to integrate their new skills.

SOAR needed her training to end and so did she.

Danielle was ready for the job, in her own, inestimable opinion. But she wasn't going to get there until the trainers signed off that she'd reached fully mission-qualified proficiency.

The Fort Campbell training course was never set up the same from one flight to the next, but it always had a time limit. The time would be short and they didn't tell you what it was. So she drove the Chinook for all it was worth like Regina Jaquess water-skiing her way to U.S. Ski Team Female Athlete of the Year.

The Night Stalkers were a damned secretive lot, and after two years of training, she understood why. With seven years flying for the 10th, she'd thought she was good.

She'd been repeatedly lauded as one of the top pilots at Fort Drum.

The Night Stalkers had offered an education in what it really meant to fly. In the two years of training, she'd flown more hours than in the seven years prior, despite two deployments to Iraq. And spent more time in the classroom than her life-to-date accumulated flight hours.

But she was ready now. It was *très viscérale,* right down in her bones she could feel it. The Chinook was as much a part of her nervous system as breathing.

Too bad they didn't build men they way they built the big Chinooks—especially the MH-47G which were built specifically to SOAR's requirements. The aircraft were steady, trustworthy, and the most immensely powerful helicopters deployed in the U.S. Army—what more could a girl ask for? But finding a super-hero man to go with her superhero helicopter was just a fantasy for a lonely teenage girl.

She dove down into a canyon and slid to a hover mere inches over the reservoir inside the thirty-second window laid out on the flight plan.

Danielle resisted a sigh. She was ready for something to happen and to happen soon.

～

PETE'S CHINOOK and his two escort Black Hawks crossed into the mountainous province of Sikkim, India ten feet over the glaciers and still moving fast. It was an hour before dawn, they'd made it out of China while it was still dark.

"Twenty minutes of fuel remaining," Nicolai said it like a personal challenge when they hit the border.

"Thanks, I never would have noticed."

It had been a nail-biting tradeoff: the more fuel he burned, the more easily he climbed due to the lighter load. The more he climbed, the faster he burned what little fuel remained.

Safe in Indian airspace he climbed hard as Nicolai counted down the minutes remaining, burning fuel even faster than he had been while crossing the mountains of southern Tibet. They caught up with the U.S. Air Force HC-130P Combat King refueling tanker with only ten minutes of fuel left.

"Ram that bitch," Nicolai called out.

Pete extended the refueling probe which reached only a few feet beyond the forward edge of the rotor blade and drove at the basket trailing behind the tanker on its long hose.

He nailed it on the first try despite the fluky winds. Striking the valve in the basket with over four hundred pounds of pressure, a clamp snapped over the refueling probe and Jet A fuel shot into his tanks.

His helo had the least fuel due to having the most men aboard, so he was first in line. His Number Two picked up the second refueling basket trailing off the other wing of the Combat King. Thirty seconds and three hundred gallons later and he was breathing much more easily.

"Ah," Nicolai sighed. "It is better than the sex," his thick

Russian accent only ever surfaced in this moment or in a bar while picking up women.

"Hey, Nicolai," Nicky the Greek called over the intercom from his crew chief position seated behind Pete. "Do you make love in Russian?"

A question Pete had always been careful to avoid.

"For you, I make special exception." That got a laugh over the system.

Which explained why Pete always kept his mouth shut at this moment.

"The ladies, Nicolai? What about the ladies?" Alfie the portside gunner asked.

"Ah," he sighed happily as he signaled that the other choppers had finished their refueling and formed up to either side, "the ladies love the Russian. They don't need to know I grew up in Maryland and I learn my great-great-grandfather's native tongue at the University called Virginia."

He sounded so pleased that Pete wished he'd done the same rather than study Japanese and Mandarin.

Another two hours of—thank god—straight-and-level flight at altitude through the breaking dawn and they landed on the aircraft carrier awaiting them in the Bay of Bengal. India had agreed to turn a blind eye as long as the Americans never actually touched their soil.

Once standing on the deck—and the worst of the kinks worked out—he pulled his team together: six pilots and seven crew chiefs.

"Honor to serve!" He saluted them sharply.

"Hell yeah!" They shouted in response and saluted in turn. It was their version of spiking the football in the end zone.

A petty officer in a bright green vest appeared at his elbow, "Follow me please, sir." He pointed toward the Navy-gray command structure that towered above the carrier's deck. The Commodore of the entire carrier group was waiting for him just outside the entrance. Not a good idea to keep a One-Star waiting, so he waved at the team.

"See you in the mess for dinner," he shouted to the crew over the noise of an F-18 Hornet fighter jet trapping on the #2 wire. After two days of surviving on MREs while squatting on the Tibetan tundra, he was ready for a steak, a burger, a mountain of pasta, whatever. Or maybe all three.

The green escorted him across the hazards of the busy flight deck. Pete had kept his helmet on to buffer the noise, but even at that he winced as another Hornet fired up and was flung aloft by the catapult.

"Orders, Major Napier," the Commodore handed him a folded sheet the moment he arrived. "Hate to lose you."

The Commodore saluted, which Pete automatically returned before looking down at the sheet of paper in his hands. The man was gone before the import of Pete's orders slammed in.

A different green-clad deckhand showed up with Pete's duffle bag and began guiding him toward a loading C-2 Greyhound twin-prop airplane. It was parked number two for the launch catapult, close behind the raised jet-blast deflector.

His crew, being led across in the opposite direction to return to the berthing decks below, looked at him aghast.

"Stateside," was all he managed to gasp out as they passed.

A stream of foul cursing followed him from behind. Their crew was tight. Why the hell was Command breaking it up?

And what in the name of fuck-all had he done to deserve this?

He glanced at the orders again as he stumbled up the Greyhound's rear ramp and crash landed into a seat.

Training rookies?

It was worse than a demotion.

This was punishment.

Available at fine retailers everywhere

Other works by M. L. Buchman:

SIGN UP FOR M. L. BUCHMAN'S NEWSLETTER TODAY

and receive:
Release News
Free Short Stories
a Free Starter Library

Do it today. Do it now.
www.mlbuchman.com/newsletter